C000091426

"This is your last chance!" The commissioner shouted to Huey. "We don't have to do this. Innocent blood can be spared today. If you continue this path, you know that there is only one way that this can end!" Huey stared back at him for a moment and then laughed. It wasn't something that Commissioner Greenfield imagined it to be. It was cold and dark. It was a laugh that one would make as if they heard a really funny joke, and if he was being honest with himself, that made Huey look even more menacing.

"No." Huey corrected as he raised his hand in the air. Every officer in the line took out their weapons, and at the same time, The Panthers drew theirs. In the next few seconds, Commissioner Greenfield will thank God that they were able to get everyone out of the city.

"There is only one way that this will end."

RISE

OF THE

PANTHERS

R.D. CARTWRIGHT

"Tell them we are rising."

-Richard R. Wright Sr.

Chapter

1

Inglewood, CA; 10:25 PM

"Are you ready?"

"Hold on! Give me a second." The woman shouted through the door. Turning back to the mirror she checked herself one last time, smoothing out her blazer after putting her braids in a bun. She made one more adjustment with her eyeliner, making sure everything was perfect.

"Jasmine the crew is ready. I see the other stations coming and if we want the best spot, we need to move now."

"Alright! Alright! Stop rushing a girl!" As Jasmine stepped out of the van and walked with her crew towards the site, it was plain the see the scenario that was presented to her. Through the darkness of night, the park lights illuminated the area enough to catch the yellow taped sectioning of the basketball court that sits on the edge of the park. Police and emergency responders surrounded the area.

Walking closer to the court, Jasmine suddenly stopped. She caught a scent; one that she was more than familiar with. Every location she has had to go to, dealing with the same situation as this, always has the same scent...blood. That sick copper fragrance penetrated her senses, making her shiver. Moving closer, Jasmine noticed the paramedics covering the body that laid motionless on the ground.

"Good they haven't taken the body yet; this will be a perfect shot. Jasmine let's hurry and set up before they take him away." Her cameraman said. She paused. Was he serious? She somehow knew he would say something like this. But still, she couldn't help being astonished.

"No, not yet."

"But-" Jasmine turned and stared at her cameraman. The glare alone was all the warning he needed to shut up. She couldn't believe that was where his priorities were right now. It's true that in this business, it's imperative to be where all the action is and to get the best shots. Good shots get ratings, but not this time!

She stood as the paramedics passed by with the body covered by the blanket. Staring at the body before it was carried into the ambulance, she saw an arm hanging from the stretcher, a child's arm. From the information that her team was given, the poor kid was only thirteen. In all her years in this field of work, she has seen many dead bodies, but it was always difficult when the bodies were children.

They barely had a start in life and to have their future taken away from them was devastating. She waited until the ambulance drove out of sight before looking back at her crew. She gave a nod and they immediately started setting up. She looked at the basketball court gate and could see dark red stains. There was blood all over the basketball court and one could see a trail that ended at the gate. Whatever happened, that poor kid must have desperately tried everything to cling to life. It must have been agonizing. She couldn't even imagine the pain and fear he went through.

"Jasmine we're ready." She looked back at her crew. Everything was set and it was time to start. She nodded her head one last time as the signal to begin. Her cameraman raised his hand and started the countdown. 3...2...1.

"This is Jasmine Jones. I'm standing outside of Roger's Park in Inglewood. The scene behind me can only be described as a tragedy. As stated by a witness, thirteen-year-old Jerome Washington was walking through the park heading home. A witness reported that he stopped at the basketball court to play with two other youths that were there. It is not an odd thing to see young people around this basketball court playing during late hours.

It is reported that Jerome was at the court past sunset until LAPD Officer Alex Smith arrived. It is unknown what words were exchanged between Officer Smith and Jerome, but witnesses reported that shouting could be heard. Their conversation soon escalated into a deadly confrontation as witnesses claimed to have heard gunshots being fired off from the area.

As at this time, it is unknown what truly transpired as the two youths that were with Jerome Washington disappeared from the scene and Officer Smith was taken into police custody. Unfortunately, Jerome was unable to escape this confrontation as his life was taken from him. Reports described that there were about six gunshots fired from the basketball court.

The reports following the incident are putting the actions of Officer Smith into question. There are be more information that is being put together that will decide if Officer Smith's supposed actions are indeed justifiable. No further answers have been given from the LAPD. Officer Smith will be held in trial for manslaughter on Tuesday. Tonight, a family has lost a son and California has lost another youth due to confrontations with the police. This has marked the fifth incident that a life has been lost from the actions of the police this past year. Our hearts and prayers go to the family of Jerome Washington."

South Los Angeles, CA; 11:00 PM

Travis Miller shut the TV off as the reporter finished giving her reports. He stayed on the couch and took a deep breath. He got up and went to the kitchen taking out a half-emptied water bottle chugging its content down. He reached into his pocket, picked up his phone to read Janaye's, his best friend, text. He looked at the message asking if he saw the news about the kid being shot by the police.

He honestly didn't want to think about it right now. Another soul lost due to police inadequacy. Watching the news brought back feelings of uncertainty of where this country is heading to if something like this is a norm of some sort. Of course, the kid probably shouldn't have been out that late at night, but for it to escalate to him being shot by the police is something that never should have happened. What's worse is that the cop will somehow walk away with this by saying his life was in "danger". What complete bullshit!

Marcus Martin, Linda Scott, Nichole Waters, and Trevon Stone; all four lost their lives due to incidents that involved the police. Each police officer justified their actions on why they had to use deadly force to kill and were able to walk away free. He sometimes wonders how he could live in a country where the law protects those who kill innocent black people.

They weren't murderers or drug dealers or rapists or anything! They were honest citizens!!! People that just wanted to live and survive in a world that, for some reason, finds any excuse to demean their very existence. They were Americans! They lived in this country too, though it seems that only the minority thinks so. It infuriated him how worthless the lives of African Americans, well minorities in general, are seen by this country.

Musing in his thoughts, something that Travis didn't think about before suddenly popped up. He hasn't gotten any notifications in his timeline. This would have defiantly shown up on social media by now.

When the others died, their confrontation with the police officers, of course, went viral and it was all over Facebook and Instagram. He searched through his phone to see if anything popped up.

There was no surprise when he found nothing. Well, if Travis was being honest, it was to be expected, it had just happened. Wait...What about the two kids that were with Jerome? Kids always record stuff, so if they were there, they definitely would have posted it.

Engrossed in his research he had forgotten to reply to Janaye. He looked back at his messages to see that she had texted something else, saying that she needs to talk to him after class tomorrow. Travis pondered on that for a second. There was something in her message that made him remember that there was something he has to do, but what?

Travis looked over the message again and found the word that was sticking out to him. Class, but what about it? It took him a minute to finally figure out what it was that he had forgotten. The term paper, which he barely even started on, that was due at the end of the semester. He turned his laptop on and opened the file containing his term essay, praying that at least he had some of it done.

Damnit! He cursed. *Barely a page done. I need to stop being lazy or I'm screwed.* The topic his professor, Dr. Lanika Jones, had assigned to them was to choose an incident that had a major impact on America. Looking at the paper, he remembered what topic he was going to write when he saw the name "Hector Garcia". Hector was an illegal immigrant that turned out to be a serial killer.

He killed twelve people within three years, and it put the whole nation on high alert. Travis was sure the only reason it sparked so much outrage was that Hector didn't kill any minorities.

All the victims were white, and the strange thing about it was that they were not random people; two doctors, four lawyers, three politicians, two CEOs, and a judge.

It was obvious that they were targeted, but no one knew why they were Hector's targets as he did not reveal anything when he was captured. Well, the news said he was captured, but the man literally showed up at the police station and turned himself in. The fact that he turned himself in shocked people more than the murders he committed. Most people assumed that he was a hitman, but nothing was confirmed.

Travis looked at his paper again thinking about whether to change his topic or not. He had all semester to finish but he knew he would just wait till the last minute and haul ass on writing something up. He looked at his phone, re-reading the message that Janaye sent him and it made him remember that the trial of that police officer that shot Jerome Washington would be on Tuesday.

That's two days from now and it would be great material for a topic to write on. He erased all his work about Hector and started again, labeling his paper, "Justice for Jerome Washington". He gave a bitter laugh at the title. The irony wasn't lost to him that most likely; Jerome's killer would never pay for his actions. Looking at the clock, he gave a yawn seeing that it's midnight and decided to get some rest. He had a feeling that today is going to be a long day, especially since Janaye already texted him about Jerome Washington; that's all he was going to hear about at school.

It seemed that his instincts were right; walking through the halls of the Political Science Building, he could hear the whispers of students passing and the only topic he could hear was about Jerome Washington. Knowing his professor this would definitely be the main topic of discussion. Dr. Jones takes current events very seriously. Her pride as a Doctor in African American Studies implores her to teach black culture and history to its fullest even if, unfortunately for the students, it means a longer class time.

She takes her time to be up to date on current events and makes sure to present them to the class for discussion. When she's not teaching, she is out in the community as one of Los Angeles' well known African American Civil Rights Activists. She's the head of many organizations that defend and support the black community. The University's administration and Dr. Jones are not on the best of terms because of some organizations she is affiliated with, mainly those that dealt with political issues, but since she has tenure, she makes a point of not giving a damn.

Walking into the classroom, Travis took a seat in the middle row. He made sure to save a seat for Janaye, otherwise, he would never hear the end of it for the rest of the day. Time passed as the rest of the students came in and took their seats. Janaye still hadn't shown up. He looked at his watch to see that the class would start soon.

Dr. Jones is a bit of a hard ass when it comes to attendance. Thankfully for the students, she doesn't outrightly dismiss them if they are late, but she has a habit of embarrassing those who in her words, "have the audacity to show up late to her class". Tavis checked the time again to see that there's two minutes left, Janaye is as hell cutting it close. He turned to the door one last time to see Janaye rushing in, panting heavily. He motioned to her where he was and showed her the empty seat next to him which he had reserved for her.

"Hey, thanks for the save. Did you see the news last night? Crazy right?" Well, of course, he saw it and didn't understand why she asked him that when she was the one that texted him about it literally thirty minutes after he saw it. However, looking at her disheveled state, Travis decided to keep his mouth shut and just nodded his head.

"Yeah, crazy."

"And what pisses me off about it is that that cop is going to make some bullshit excuse and people are just going to eat it up like idiots." In Travis's opinion, she wasn't wrong; he had the same thought. It's painfully obvious that this is going to turn out just how the others did;

why would this one be any different? A black kid gets shot by a cop and said cop gets away. Classic! He shook his head at the stupidity of it.

"That poor kid! I can't even imagine what his mom is going through right now. To make it worse, his family will never have any closure knowing the system will let his killer go free."

"Well, you never know, Janaye. The trial hasn't started yet." Even though Travis knew better, somewhere in his heart he still had a flicker of hope that people would do the right thing.

"Always the optimist, aren't you?" Janaye lightly scoffed. Travis never thought of himself as one, but he genuinely believed in the good of the people, even when his mind and experiences tell him otherwise. Travis and Janaye continued their discussion until Dr. Jones entered the classroom. Travis immediately noticed that something was off.

Dr. Jones is an animated individual, and if anyone asked Travis, she has a somewhat overbearing bright personality. You know it's her every time she enters a room. Right now, though, there is something different about her. Travis, being a natural introvert, takes pride in his observation skills: seeing and taking note of every little detail in his surroundings, especially details of people he interacts within his environment.

"Good morning my beautiful students!" Though this is her usual greeting, Travis noticed that there was something in her tone that threw him off. It didn't sound entirely natural, almost as if she's forcing it out. He paid closer attention as Dr. Jones walked down the steps to the front of the classroom.

Her posture was stiffer. When she walks, she usually has a light and bubbly demeanor that looks like she's skipping, but this time her walk is so smooth that it seems like she's gliding down the steps. He looks around to see if anyone else has noticed, but it seems that everyone is more concerned about themselves as they continue their own conversations.

Travis felt a hand on his shoulder and turned around to see Janaye with a concerned look on her face. He gave her a small smile and told her it was nothing. Janaye raised an eyebrow, obviously not believing him, but, thankfully for Travis, decided not to push further. His facial expression was all the answers she needed to know that something was up, and it was about Dr. Jones. Everyone started to quiet down and take out materials for the class as Dr. Jones approached the center.

"Everyone, I'm sorry to say that class will be canceled today." That was a shock. Dr. Jones has never canceled class and always says that teachers who cancel their classes shouldn't be teachers at all. The woman would even teach when she's sick and looks like she's on her deathbed. There was only one time that Travis can remember when class was canceled and that was when Dr. Jones was so sick that the woman passed out in the middle of a lecture. That was one hell of a class session.

Everyone started whispering amongst themselves and giving each other side glances. Guess now they can see the red flag that a few moments ago only Travis noticed. Dr. Jones didn't even give anyone a chance to ask questions because as soon as she was done with her announcement, she walked back up the stairs and left the classroom. It took a minute for the rest of the students to process what just happened before they started leaving too. Travis looked at Janaye to see that she was already at the door giving him an expecting look.

"Well, are you just going to sit there looking stupid or get up?" Travis looked back at the front of the classroom. Something is definitely wrong. When Dr. Jones made her announcement, he noticed that her eyes didn't have its lively expression. They looked tired, not physically but emotionally. Whatever made Dr. Jones cancel class must be serious. Travis couldn't help but think that this may be about what happened to that kid, but what could the relation be for Dr. Jones to have this bad of a reaction?

He followed Janaye out of the classroom and into the hallway. Exiting the Political Science building, they continued until Janaye spotted a less crowded bench. They sat down and for the next few minutes not a word had been exchanged between them and for Travis, the increasingly awkward silence was starting to get to him.

"So, what's this thing you need to talk to me about that's so important to drag me out here?" She didn't give him an immediate answer. Janaye had a contemplated look on her face as if debating what she needed to say.

"Sorry. I just want to talk where people aren't around. I assume you already know what about." Travis nodded his head. He knew whatever she wanted to talk about was about Jerome Washington. However, the main thing that Travis is confused about is what about Jerome that Janaye needs to talk to him face to face out here for. Usually, if she just wanted to rant about something, she would just text or FaceTime him.

First, it was Dr. Jones and now Janaye is acting weird and all because of the Jerome Washington incident. That same feeling Travis had in the classroom about Dr. Jones came back. Something is going on and that deep-rooted instinct is telling him that he's about to get involved in whatever storm is about to brew. When Janaye turned to face him, Travis was startled to see tears falling down her face. Red flag!!! This is an immediate red flag! Janaye isn't the type of person to cry...at all. Whatever this is, it must be personal, extremely personal.

"My brother was there." Silence. Time seemed to have stopped to Travis. *What?* He didn't fully comprehend what Janaye had said at first. It took a few seconds of silently staring at her that he was able to piece the words together. He wanted to ask but could not force the words to come out of his mouth. *She said her brother was there? At the park that night?!*

Suddenly, realization slapped him in the face. That's why she's acting this way, but there's still a piece to the puzzle missing. After a few quiet minutes, Travis finally had his thoughts together to speak.

"Where is he?" The moment he asked that Janaye's face scrunched. She closed her eyes and wrapped her arms around herself as if she was in horrible pain.

"I don't know." Travis blinked a few times. *Wait...What?!* He took a moment to think everything over. If she doesn't know where he is, that means he never came home that night. So how in the hell does Janaye know that her brother was at the park that night? The look Travis was giving Janaye portrayed his exact thoughts, it was demanding her to tell him what is going on.

"He came back home that night. In fact, it was before I texted you last night. He told me everything that happened." Tears continue to fall down her face. Janaye took a few seconds to get a grip on herself.

"This morning, I went to check on him before I left, and he was gone. He was nowhere in the house. I looked all over for him this morning, that was why I came late to class. You saw how Dr. Jones canceled class today right?" Travis nodded his head. He wondered why Janaye brought her up, but he has a feeling that both are connected.

"Last night the news said there were two others with Jerome when he died. One of them is my brother and the other one is Dr. Jones' son." Her answer only left more questions. This was too much for Travis to process. Things are happening way too fast. If he understands it correctly, the only two witnesses that had seen what happened at the park are missing. Not only that but right before the trial. This can't be a coincidence! Lost in his thoughts, Travis didn't realize when Janaye got up from the bench.

"Wait," He called out to her. "Where are you going? You said your brother told you what happened. Janaye, what's going on?" Travis' heart was racing over the flood of information that was presented to him. Nothing was making any sense.

"I'm sorry Travis. I knew that if I didn't say something to you, you would have gotten off on your own. You have a bad habit of not minding your own business when it comes to people you know. You're smarter than most people and would have eventually figured out something wasn't right. Things are going to be complicated for a while, so please take care of yourself, and don't worry about me." He stood speechless. Take care of himself? Don't worry about her? What does she mean by that? Janaye took his silence as her cue to leave.

"Wait!" Travis yelled. Janaye stopped but didn't turn around to face him. "What did your brother say to you?" Travis stressed each word. It's starting to dawn on him that this isn't really about her brother missing but it's truly about what he told her. Whatever her brother said started this and Travis' instincts are saying that what her brother told her will also be the reason why things will be complicated. Janaye stood for a few seconds before giving a heavy sigh.

"1301 Woodland Drive. There's a meeting at 8:30. When you get there tell them I sent you. I'm sorry Travis that's all I can say. I'll see you later." She said before she ran away from him. Travis was too shocked to chase after her. That red flag from before just transformed into a huge red neon flashing light.

Travis couldn't make sense of what just happened and what Janaye had just said or, more accurately, what she didn't say. It was something that she couldn't text to him probably because she was afraid of someone somehow getting a hold of either of their phones and seeing the message. It's also something that she couldn't say to his face because she didn't want to involve him in whatever is coming. Travis has a feeling that this storm is going to quickly turn into a hurricane. First thing though, he needed answers. 1310 Woodland Drive.

"What the hell is happening here?"

Chapter

2

Central Los Angeles, CA; 8:15 AM

Jasmine stared at the folder that was dropped at her desk. She got ready to cuss out whoever lost their mind thinking they can just toss stuff at her like she's a dog until she looked up to see the company's chief editor, Peter. Peter usually doesn't bother her with any kind of work unless it's involved with places that the network calls "urban areas" or in other words too ghetto and dangerous for the other featherweights. She decided to ignore Peter and looked back at the folder lying on top of her work. She was about to go through with whatever material they decided to dump on her if it wasn't for the fact that Peter was still standing next to her desk.

"Can I help you, Peter?" She said annoyed. Jasmine never had a high opinion of Peter, who everyone knew only got his position because of his family. If you asked anyone, they would say he's an arrogant son of a bitch who looks down on others and their work just because his family has money.

He acts like the world should bow to his feet only for breathing. Unfortunately, his uncle is the network's director, and since nobody wants to get fired, everyone has no choice than to tolerate him. It seems

Jasmine has no problem telling Peter exactly how she feels about him, in a professional manner of course. His very presence irritates Jasmine to her soul, but she tries to be somewhat civil towards the man.

"The director wants to see you." Peter said with a smug face. *Shit!* Jasmine cursed with a groan.

Being called to see the director is never good. She doesn't remember doing anything that will cause her to see the director unless he heard about what happened last week. It was an already busy week, and Peter was not making it any better by being a constant annoyance. Finally, one day Jasmine couldn't take it anymore and lashed out at him.

It was the first time anyone yelled at Peter at the office, and to be honest, it was well long overdue. Perhaps she shouldn't have called him a baby dick Pillsbury doughboy or threaten to rip his tongue out, but hey there's only much ignorance a person can handle in one day. She tried to remember why exactly she lashed out at him.

"I tried to help you and warned you about how your attitude affects people." Jasmine resisted rolling her eyes. Now she remembers. That day was particularly stressful, and she was in a more irritable mood than usual, and Peter, in all his wisdom, decided to try to talk to her about her attitude. Taking a deep breath, she calmed herself down.

"Peter, unless you have something worth contributing to say, shut up and mind your own business. Now move!" She emphasized by moving him out of the way. She could still feel him staring at her with that smug face of his. For some reason that she cannot fathom, Peter has some sort of satisfaction riling her up. She doesn't usually take into his childishness, but at the same time, she refuses to let anyone talk to her in that kind of manner. She walked into the director's office, and she was met with both the director and the assistant director.

"Ah, Miss Jones! Come in and sit." Jasmine relaxed a bit seeing that the director didn't look to be as stern as she thought. The man was always a friendly person, but he was all about business, so if this is anything like a reprimand, he would have a more severe expression.

"I'm sure you're wondering why the director called you here." The assistant director stated. Jasmine gave herself a moment to collect herself, still thinking that this is about the altercation between her and Peter. If she was about to fight a losing battle, then she wasn't going to go down without a fight.

"I know, and I apologize for lashing out like that and letting my emotions get the better of- "

"You can stop right there," The director interrupted. "Yes, I know what happened between you and my nephew. I don't care about that; in fact, I'm glad you did yell at that idiot. But that's not why I called you here today." Though she was relieved to hear that, the question of why she's in his office still eludes her.

"Then why am I here?" She asked.

"We got a call from a family whose son is missing, and they wish to have an interview with us." Jasmine rose her eyebrow at that. Usually, they had Sarah take care of interviews, and Jasmine is still invested in the Jerome Washington story.

"Sir, why me? I'm still busy with the Jerome Washington case with the court hearing being tomorrow."

"Yes, I know that, and the fact that you're leading that story is why I want you to do this interview. The family is claiming that their son was with Jerome Washington at the time of his death." Before Jasmine could leap out of her chair in excitement, she had to assess what the director just said to her. Jasmine was not able to get much information on her story, especially from the police.

It was strange to her that though the officers are supposed to wear body cameras, somehow, Officer Smith's camera was damaged beyond repair, so not even the LAPD could use it. Besides the trial, she had nothing else as a lead for her story. Perhaps this interview could be the big break that she needs, but at the same time, they could just be trying to get their time in the limelight.

"Director, how do we know that this is even true? What facts are we basing their statement on?" Although this could be what she needed for her story, she wasn't about to go on a never-ending story kind of chase. A missing person, especially someone's child, is tragic, but at the same time, most missing children's cases don't lead to an interview, so something about this whole situation didn't sit well with her.

"I understand your concerns, but I believe that this is genuine. The other day, there was another missing child reported. Two children were missing right after Jerome was killed. I do not believe that this is a mere coincidence." Jasmine could not help but agree with that. While thinking about the upcoming interview, something clicked. Two children reported missing right after Jerome's death, but only one of the families had requested an interview. Why not both? Something didn't seem right about this to Jasmine.

However, if she can get an interview with both the families, she would have more to the Jerome Washington story. As soon as that thought left her, another one popped in. If those kids were there at the time, then they're key witnesses and could turn around the entire court hearing tomorrow. It's possible that someone does not want them around. This could be even bigger than she initially thought. The director took notice of Jasmine's expression and nodded, confirming her theory.

"Now you know the importance of this. Hopefully, their son could see this and decide to return home to be a witness."

"Director, what about the other missing child? Do we have anything on him or his family?"

"We couldn't get the name of the child, but we do have the mother's name, she made the missing report. She's popular around the area, and you might already recognize who she is."

"What's the mother's name?"

"Dr. Lanika Jones. A professor in African American Studies at the University of California. She's well-known in the African American community, and you might be able to convince her to do an interview since..." Jasmine immediately felt sick. She couldn't focus on anything else around her. Her breathing was picking up at an alarming rate, and her hands were shaking so badly that she couldn't control them. The only thought that crossed her mind was to leave. She needed to go now. Jasmine abruptly got up and quickly left the office. She ignored all the callouts to her; the only thing that mattered was that she had to get out.

Jasmine grabbed her phone and instantly searched her contacts. She found the name she was looking for and made the call praying the person would pick up. However, no one answered. She tried again and again, but the result was the same.

Damn it! Jasmine cursed. She continued to call the number back, but it kept going to the voicemail. *Pick up, damnit!* she kept calling; Jasmine refused to give up. *Please! Please pick up!* Jasmine chanted the mantra- like a madman praying to God that they would answer her call. After the umpteenth attempt, Jasmine realized that they would not answer her. The only thing she could do now was to leave a message.

"Lanika! I know what happened. Please call me; I can help you! I know you have every reason not to trust me, but please give me this chance. You don't have to do this by yourself. He's not just your son; he's my nephew too. Let me help you, sis."

South Los Angeles; 9:45 AM.

Travis entered his apartment dragging his feet. The only thing that was on his mind was the conversation he had with Janaye. His head was swimming with questions, and it seemed that one answer only leads to more questions. Why couldn't she have just told him what's going on? He put on some music to hopefully calm his nerves. He sat down on the couch and closed his eyes, allowing the mellow beats to soothe him. He sat still for a few minutes until he felt a vibration in his pocket. He pulled his phone out to see a text message from an unknown number saying to turn on his TV to Channel 4. *Channel 4?*

Putting aside the fact that he's about to follow the orders of an unidentified person, he turned on the TV to the channel to see the same reporter that he saw last night, he recalled that her name was Jasmine Jones. She was sitting on a couch in the room that looked oddly familiar to him. The confusion was written all over his face as to why someone wanted him to watch this.

At first, he thought it was Janaye that texted him but quickly squashed that idea. Why would she try to hide herself contacting him? It wasn't until he saw who the reporter was talking to that he realized why he needed to watch it and that he seriously needs to stop questioning his instincts. It was Janaye's mother. He sat motionlessly watching the exchange between the two.

"Thank you, Ms. Freed. I know that this is a hard time for you."

"Yes, I appreciate your concerns, but I will be ok. Just trying to keep it together."

"Can you share what happened that night?" Travis watched as Janaye's mother had a pained look on her face.

"I was working the night shift and didn't come home till around eleven-thirty. I didn't know my son was out that late. By the time I came home, he was already in his room. My daughter, Janaye, was still up. She had this panic look on her face and told me that when he came home, he was so pale and didn't say a word to her. This morning I was planning on staying home so I could talk to him, but he disappeared. The only thing he left was a note for my daughter."

"Do you have it with you right now or know what your son wrote?" Jasmine asked.

"No. Janaye has it and didn't tell me anything. and now she's gone too."

"Do you believe that letter has something to do with Jerome Washington?"

"I'm not too sure, but they were close friends. He will bring that boy over here practically every single day. When I found out he died, I knew it would devastate my son. I did not think he would just run off to God knows where! First, my husband, then my son and now my daughter has left me. I'm losing everything!" Travis watched as Janaye's mother broke down, crying during the interview. The rest of the session quickly wrapped up.

Travis figured that Janaye didn't return home based on their last conversation and the fact that he did not see her with her mom. Why was it that someone wanted him to watch this? It's not entertaining watching a mother breaking down on live television. There's something else that Travis is missing. He sat in deep concentration. What was it that he needed to hear? Travis had a feeling that it was something that Janaye's mom had said. He then remembered that she mentioned a note that Janaye's brother wrote.

A note? He questioned. Janaye said that her brother told her what happened between Jerome and the officer, so what's the point of writing a letter about it? Unless it's not about that. Was he supposed to figure that out? For what purpose? Travis grabbed his keys and left his apartment. He drove down the road to see the familiar Washington street sign. Parking by the street across Janaye's house, praying that he'll be able to make some sense of this situation.

He walked up to the door, knocking on it, hoping someone would answer. His request met with silence. He tried knocking on the door three more times, and again, no one answered. He stood for a couple of minutes and when no one came out he concluded that no one was home. He turned around, ready to leave when he heard the creaking of the door open and saw the face of Ms. Freed.

"Oh, Travis. Come in." She said, opening the door for him. The way that Ms. Freed greeted him sounded like she was expecting him to visit her. He followed her into the living room, and Ms. Freed gestured him to sit on the couch. The deafening silence between them was beginning to be extremely awkward. Even though shitting there not saying anything was getting more than uncomfortable, he didn't know where to start, let alone look at her in the eyes. He was probably the last person to see Janaye and here he was, too scared to talk. Travis gave a deep breath and mustered up his courage.

"Ms.- "

"I know why you are here, Travis." She interrupted. Travis quickly looked up at her with a puzzled face. Does she know he's here because of the letter? How could she if Janaye left, and he was the last person to see her? Ms. Freed went into the kitchen to grab a coffee mug and a folded piece of paper. When she entered back into the living room, she handed the paper to Travis before sitting on the sofa chair across from him.

"My daughter told me to hand this to you if you showed up today before eight o'clock."

"Hold on Ms. Freed. Janaye was here?" Ms. Freed sighed and took a sip of coffee.

"Yes, but only for a moment. It seems my daughter is going to be involved in something that she doesn't want either of us to get caught in too, but apparently, she's giving you a choice." A choice? What could she possibly mean by that? He thought back to the events that happened today. Janaye's last words to him, the interview, and now this. Looking back, the only thing that stuck out was when Janaye said for him to take care of himself.

He soon realized that Janaye's last words to him was a warning. She was right when she said that he has a hard time staying out of other's business. If she would have just disappeared, he would have done everything and searched everywhere to find her, and possibly landed himself in trouble that he wouldn't have been able to get out easily. Now, it seems she's offering to direct him where the problem is but is giving him the option of backing off.

"Before you ask, she didn't say where she was going or what she wrote to you, and I didn't bother looking. Knowing wouldn't have changed anything. She's a grown woman, and I can't stop her even if I wanted too. All I know is whatever this is all about. I don't want to be around here when it starts." Ms. Freed said.

"What about Jason? He's still missing, isn't he?" Travis figured she wouldn't just abandon searching for her son when he's still out there, somewhere. What he saw that night between Jerome and Officer Smith could very well change everything for tomorrow.

"He's alive. That's all I need to know. I suggest you figure out what it is that you want to do. I'm leaving and you're more than welcome to join me, or you can stay and take whatever chance my daughter is offering you. You decide." She finished as she got up and left. Travis sat staring at the folded note on his lap. What should he do? He still has no idea what is happening, and the fact that everyone is all cryptic is starting to piss him off.

The most confusing thing about this is that Janaye is not the type to beat around the bush. She's direct and straightforward on what she wants. If she's going this far to hide what she's doing and what she knows, then he must accept this and all the risks that it contains. Right now, he shouldn't worry about whatever Pandora's Box he's about to open and just dive in and think about the consequences later. With his decision made, he opened the note which turned out to be an invitation.

For the voices that cannot be heard. For the justice that is never seen. For the truth that is not spoken. We are here. We will rise.

1301 Woodland Drive @ 8:30.

Travis recognized the address as the same one Janaye told him. Would she be there? What kind of meeting is this, anyway? Question after question flooded his head. To be honest, this invitation sounds like some propaganda from the Civil Rights era. Travis hopes that this isn't something like "we'll riot if the police get away with murder again" kind of thing. Protesting, Travis can support, but straight rioting is the last thing he wants to be involved in. Rereading the invitation, he looked at the end and noticed something peculiar at the bottom right corner. *A golden paw print?*

Chapter

3

Beverly Hills, CA; 8:25 PM

Travis wasn't expecting much when he arrived at 1301 Howard Drive. He had honestly thought he would drive to some abandoned warehouse or basement. A huge house in a gated neighborhood in Beverly Hills was not in the realm of what Travis imagined. If there's a moment to feel out of place, he will put this at the top of his list. He's never been in a neighborhood like this and was surprised at how easy it was for him to get in. The security guard seemed to know why he was there since he asked for the invitation Ms. Freed gave him.

When Travis arrived at the address, he marveled at the size of the place. It looked like the mansions you see on TV. Parking on the street, he carefully walked up to the front door. He could hear soft music playing in the house. More confused than ever, he was hesitant to knock on the door. He concluded that he probably got the wrong address. From the noise, it sounded like an elite social event was going on. *This can't be the right place,* he doubted. He looked at the door and sure enough saw the number 1301. *Well damn, this is definitely the place then,* He signed.

Travis stood at the door, going over the options he could take. Should he go inside or leave? This could be his only clue to finding out what Janaye is hiding, but at the same time, his uneasiness is propelling him to leave. His decision, however, was made for him as the door opened and Travis was greeted by someone that looked like a bouncer. The guy was at least half a foot taller and was built like a tank that could easily crush him.

He was wearing a black suit with a golden paw print embroidered on the right pouch of the jacket. He held his hand out which startled Travis. The man gave him an unimpressed look and gestured to him, looking at his hand that still stretched out. Travis was confused at first on what the man could want from him. Money? Did he have to pay to get in? That, sure as hell, wasn't in the invitation. Then it dawned on him what the man in front of him wanted. Travis took the invitation in his pocket and handed it to the guard. The guard then took out a clipboard and compared it to the invitation before looking back at Travis.

"Name?" Travis was startled again at the gruff voice of the man.

"Travis Miller." He was able to spit out. The guard looked over the clipboard before facing Travis again.

"I don't see you on the list." The guard said. Travis cursed his luck. Of course, there was an actual list. Was his name supposed to be on the invitation, or did he have to RSVP? Janaye didn't say anything to Travis about this. What is he supposed to do now? It's a little too late to turn back since the guard had the invitation already. If he tries to run off now, that would be highly suspicious, and the guy would most likely call the cops on him. Looking back, Travis remembered what Janaye said to him before she disappeared. She said to mention her name. Oh well, it's not like he had any other ideas.

"Janaye Freed sent me." Travis answered back. Hopefully, it's enough for the man to let him in. The guard raised his eyebrow at Travis.

"Sister Freed sent you here, huh?" He asked, holding the invitation Travis gave him. It's not like Travis is lying, but he wondered why the guard sounded surprised that he said that Janaye sent him. Also, why did he referred to her as 'Sister Freed'?

"Yes. We're close friends, and I hope to find her here."

"Unfortunately, I doubt she will make an attendance tonight," He said. His answer crushed Travis' hope of thinking he would find Janaye here. "But if she sent you here, then I have no right to argue. Welcome, brother." *Brother?* Travis felt weird being addressed like that. It reminded him of when he was a kid going to church, and everyone would call each other "sister" or "brother."

Well, as long as he's able to go inside, he'll just put it aside. Travis walked past the guard and entered the house. If the outside wasn't grand enough, then it paled in comparison to what it looks like on the inside. Travis felt like he was in a celebrity's home with all the expensive-looking art and decor. He followed the guard to the living room and was greeted with a sight that can only be described as elegant.

There were people everywhere and all of them were in suits and dresses. If Travis felt out of place before, then this really sealed the deal. What kind of high-class function is this? Why didn't anyone tell him there was a dress code? No wonder the guard looked at him weirdly.

Everyone here looks ready for the red carpet while he just rolled up in jeans and a hoodie. *Maybe it's not too late to retreat.* With all these rich people here, he was positive that they probably didn't want him around. Travis slowed down his pace and tried to turn around and leave, but the guard grabbed his hoodie.

"Where are you going?" The guard asked. Travis gave a nervous look at the crowd, and the man immediately knew what the problem was.

"Trust me; no one is going to care. The fact that you have an invitation means you belong here." That little speech didn't give Travis much comfort. Still, he had a point, and he made it this far, so there's no sense of backing down now. Travis walked into the living room, and just as he expected, he became the center of attention. Everyone was staring at him. Travis immediately regretted coming, and if he ever found Janaye, he was going to let her have it for playing him like this.

"Hello, young brother, it's good to see you here." Travis turned around to see who was talking to him. Behind him was a middle-aged man in a khaki suit and on his coat pocket, he also had the same golden paw imprint that the guard had. The man had his hand out in front of him, but Travis was hesitant to shake it.

After getting over his nervousness, he shook the man's hand, and after that, it became a chain reaction, as the rest of the occupants began introducing themselves to him. It seemed many were shocked about how young he was. Looking around, Travis noticed that he was probably the youngest person here, which would explain why everyone was staring at him when he entered, besides his attire.

Everyone started going back to their conversations, ignoring Travis once their initial shock was over and that was fine by him. Time passed and Travis found himself on the couch, watching everyone converse with themselves, wondering what the point of this meeting is. If this turns out to just be some meet and greet, then he is going to let Janaye have it for wasting his time like this when he finds her. Deciding that he had had enough, he got up and was about to leave until he saw the same guard that greeted him at the entrance of the room.

"Thank you, everyone, for your patience as we will now begin." *About time,* Travis sighed in relief of boredom. Finally, he's going to find out what this is all about.

Travis looked around and saw that everyone was gazing up at the stairs. He turned his head and saw three women walking down the steps. Two of them had on the same outfit as the guard while the one in the middle had a long black gown that glided down as she walked.

Travis noticed that all of them had the golden paw badge on their clothes as well. When they reached down the stairs, the other two stood aside as the woman in the dress came up to address everyone.

"Good evening and welcome. I'm so pleased that all of you are here tonight. For those who do not know me, I am Hope Carter, Co-founder and one of the CEOs of the Black Diamond Industry." Upon hearing that name, Travis' eyes widened in surprise. Black Diamond Industry is a company that is familiar to everyone.

It is a multi-billion-dollar transportation company that was founded by a black man named Lucas Turner in Brooklyn, New York. Travis watched a documentary on the company and was amazed at how Lucas turned something as simple as a small cargo shipping company into one of the world's largest shipping industries in the world. Though it's rare to have a company like that being founded by a black man, it's not the reason why their reputation is notorious.

It was a secret that they were trying to keep, but eventually, everyone found out how Black Diamond Industry makes its money. They're arms dealers. Thanks to social media, one of their employees revealed a warehouse that the company owned at the time was filled with weapons. Not just ordinary pistols and ammo, it contained high-tech weapons.

There were tanks, missiles and even drones in there. It was a huge scandal and of course as soon as that was posted, the FBI was all over the company. They raided every property owned by Black Diamond Industry and brought every employee into question but couldn't find anything. All of their warehouses were emptied, and no one talked. The authorities tried to charge Lucas Turner for possession of illegal firearms, but in the end, they had no defensive proof and no credible witnesses, since the employee that made the post disappeared as well.

Since then, Lucas left the country and moved Black Diamond's headquarters from Brooklyn to the United Kingdom. If Travis remembered correctly, they have recently been doing deals with certain countries of interest such as Iran, North Korea, Russia, and China. Knowing that, what is one of their CEOs doing here in Los Angeles? Or a better question is, how was she able to even enter the country with her company's reputation like that? His musing was cut off as Hope spoke again.

"These recent years of our self-imposed banishment has been hard. We were only able to help on the sidelines. Thank you to everyone here for your loyalty and support during those troubling times." Travis wondered what she was talking about considering the setting here; he guess that everyone is some sort of investor, but to what? Black Diamond? It can't be that the company has been doing well, more than well ever since it left America and went international.

"Yesterday, an innocent boy was mercilessly killed by the very person whose duty is to protect the people! Young Jerome wasn't the only victim. For decades, countless people of color have died due to the incompetence and prejudice of the police. We had to sit and suffer, watching our brothers and sisters be treated as if our very lives don't matter to this country. We will not let Jerome and all the others die in vain. This city, no, this country will hear us! Tomorrow, we will march to the courthouse and fight this injustice!"

The sound of clapping could be heard throughout the house, but Travis highly doubted these people would be taking any part in anything like a protest. He turned back to see Hope and found her staring right at him. She whispered something to one of her attendants as they walked off, leaving her alone in front of the audience.

"Thank you again for coming. Please enjoy yourselves. Let's continue to be the voice that isn't heard, the justice not seen, and the truth not spoken. We are here. We shall rise." She finished her speech by placing her fist in front of her chest.

"We will rise!" Everyone chanted back while copying her stance.

Travis could not stop wondering what kind of cult crap he got into. Hope went back upstairs while everyone else immersed back to their conversations. Travis was lost on what to do. He showed up, and the only thing he got out of this was that whatever this meeting was for, they're planning on doing a protest.

That didn't give Travis any of the answers that he was looking for. Believing to be at a dead-end, Travis felt no further need to stay, so he turned towards the door and was about to leave when he felt a hand on his shoulder. He turned around to find that the person who tapped him was one of Hope's assistants.

"Ms. Carter would like to have a few words with you in private, follow me please." Travis smirked; this is what he wanted. After seeing her make her grand speech his instincts were screaming at him that somehow Hope is involved with all of this, and if he's lucky, she might even be the ringleader in this craziness.

Whatever the case may be, Hope Carter is the only clue Travis has on finding Janaye and what she is hiding from him. Travis followed the attendant up the stairs and into a study room. Greeting him as he opened the door was Hope in her desk looking over some papers that were in a black folder. Walking closer, he looked over the desk, curious to see what she was reading.

Travis was too far away to read any of it but was able to see a familiar picture. It was a mug shot. The person in that photo wasn't some common criminal either, it was Benjamin Jackson. The entire west coast knows that man as the 'Blue King', the leader of one of the most notorious gangs in the country, The Crips. Three years ago, the LAPD was able to bust down one of the biggest drug smuggling deals in the state.

During their investigation, they were able to trace it all back to Benjamin and was able to arrest him. Travis thought, at the time, how the LAPD didn't even know who Ben was when he was arrested. The only thing that was disclosed throughout the media was his name and the drug bust. Capturing the leader of the West Coast Crips would have made the headlines big time.

He figured that they weren't that idiotic not to know and must be covering up his involvement with the Crips for some reason. Either way, what interest would a CEO of a multi-billion weapons shipping company would have in the leader of a gang? Maybe they have a history between them? Whatever it is, Travis is fairly sure that's not what Hope wants to talk to him about. After a few more seconds of flipping through more papers, Hope finally noticed Travis standing in front of her.

"Hello, Travis. Please take a seat." Not surprised that she knew his name, Travis casually sat down.

"Coffee?" She offered.

"No thanks." He shot down. He can understand if she thinks that he's nervous given the situation, but right now, the only thing he feels is anticipation.

"How did you enjoy our little get-together?"

"A bit too bougie for me. It would have been nice if the invitation mentioned that there was a dress code." Hope chuckled at his complaint.

"Yes, well I'm sure Janaye had her reasons for not telling you." Travis sat up straighter when Hope mentioned Janaye. This is it. The fact that she mentioned Janaye's name means she knows why he's here as well. At this stage, there was no point beating around the bush, but before he spoke, he was cut off.

"Before you start your little interrogation, let me say this first. I'm under no obligation to tell you anything. Though I am curious about you, I'm not as desperate as you seem to be for information. Besides, I don't like being bombarded with questions, so let's do it this way, I'll ask a question and then you do. If there's something that you don't want to answer, just say I can't say, and I'll do the same.

You may have questions that I can't answer, but I'll try all the same. Sounds fair?" Travis could only nod his head at her proposal. He is in her house and it's not like he can just bust the door down and force her to answer him, considering that her attendants are here, as well, basically acting as her bodyguards. To be honest, even without her bodyguards, he doubted he could force the woman to do anything.

"Good. Then I'll start. How old are you?" Travis was taken back by that question. Why does she care about that?

"Why do you want to know my age?"

"Just humor me."

"22. My turn, how do you know Janaye?"

"Her father was an employee of ours during the early phase of Black Diamond. When Janaye was a small child, he would take her to the shipyard that we owned, before the whole incident. Even after we moved our headquarters, Janaye and I still kept in contact." Travis questioned that last statement.

There is no way in hell Janaye would have been able to form any kind of communication with one of the CEOs of a company like Black Diamond without the government getting involved. Several ideas were swarming in Travis' head but decided to put it off for another time.

"So, Travis, were you born in Los Angeles?" *What's with her?* Travis questioned. He didn't know how to answer that, and in fact, he didn't want to because he honestly doesn't know himself. He was found on the streets as an infant and was dropped off in an orphanage. No records about his birth or his parents were found. The people at the orphanage made his birth certificate say he was born in L.A., but no one knew where he came from for sure.

He was later put into the foster care system when the orphanage ran out of the room to support him. He grew up in the system until he became an adult and went to college and after all those years, Travis stopped caring about it as there was no point trying to find answers to his past if no one had any clue of it. For all he knows, he could have been born in a different country, but then he would have needed a passport or visa, so that theory was out unless he was smuggled in the country, and he doesn't want to entertain that idea.

"Yes." Technically, he's not lying. However, by the unbelieving look that Hope was giving him, it seemed she wanted another answer.

"Hmm." That was the only reply she gave to his answer.

"Who do you really work for?" Hope raised her eyebrow at the question.

"What do you mean by that?" She asked back. Travis readied himself. There was something off about this conversation he's having with her. In fact, there's something wrong with all of this. Sitting here face to face Hope is not giving off evil leader vibes, but right now, this is the whole reason why he even bothered to show up at this thing and he's not going to get anything by dancing in a circle. It's time to be direct.

"I know this gathering of yours isn't just for Black Diamond. Why would a shipping company be organizing a protest here in L.A. when you've been gone from the country for years? Now all of a sudden, you're back? No, you're working for someone and it shows because of that paw print you're wearing!" Hope sat in silence. Suddenly, Travis felt a dangerous aura coming from her. Crap, he might have jumped the ball too quickly on this one. He turned to the assistant behind him and saw that they had stiffened up. Travis tensed when Hope got up from the chair.

"Well, well, well. We're finally getting to the subject at hand. Took you long enough." Hope commented as she walked around her desk and stood right in front of Travis.

"You want to know who I work for? As I said earlier, I am the co-founder and the CEO of Black Diamond, so I don't work for anybody. However, there is an organization that my company supports. A group of likeminded people that are seeking changes in this country."

"And what exactly is this group called?" Travis asked cautiously.

"We call ourselves 'The Panthers'." Travis blinked for a few seconds. There was something oddly familiar in that name. His eyes widen when he realized what it was.

"The Panthers? As in the Black Panthers? Are you serious?"

"In a way, but not exactly. When the party was shut down, numerous people tried to bring it back but were never fully recognized. This organization is different. The Panthers are in a league of their own and we have the resources that others could only dream of." It was no hidden secret on how the original Black Panthers was forcibly disbanded, mainly due to fighting within the organization that was later revealed to be caused by interference with the FBI.

Many tried to imitate them, but none of the original members officially recognized them. So how are they any different from the others? Is it because a company like Black Diamond supports them? Even if that was the case, why hasn't he heard anything about them until now? Something like this would have caught some attention. Hope saw the skeptic look on Travis's face.

"I know it's hard to believe just from word of mouth. Unlike the failed imitations, we stayed away from the public eye and supported smaller organizations within the communities across the nation. But make no mistake, this is the real deal. We have been in the shadows, slowly gaining influence and followers. If we want to survive when we go open, then we need resources and supporters. It wasn't until a few weeks ago that we received everything that we need to begin."

"And that's why you're organizing this march tomorrow?"

"Yes. That will be our introduction. As we speak, there are countless other gatherings like this all over the city being overseen by The Panthers. Last time I checked; we will have about three thousand people who will be at the courthouse tomorrow." Travis will give them this if anything else, they work fast to be able to gather that many people in such a little time.

Travis wondered why they needed to work underground in the first place but realized if they have representatives like Hope, then they are probably individuals who are in professions that aren't what you would call "white picket fence". Still, why wait till now? Hope mentioned they needed resources, and he wondered what kind of resources they needed to have a company like Black Diamond to support them? What is their real goal?

"Let's just say I go along with this, what are The Panthers after?"

"I believe it was supposed to be my turn, but I'll answer anyway. What The Panthers want is simple, true equality. There's something wrong with this country, with how African Americans are treated like third-world citizens. We are hoping to put an end to that. Now, why did you come here?"

"I'm surprised you're asking that considering you know who Janaye is. Obviously, I'm here to find her and I have a feeling you know where she is." Hope rose an eyebrow at his accusation.

"Is that so? Well, that was pretty much given, What I meant to say was why did you come, knowing that she wouldn't be here and that you wouldn't get any information on her whereabouts. An even if I know where she is right now, it's hardly my place to say so." Travis clicked his teeth in frustration.

Of course, he knew that there was little to no chance that he would find anything on where Janaye was. Though deep down, that wasn't the true reason why he came; it was what he just told himself. More than anything, he was curious about what Janaye got herself involved in.

She's tough as hell and can take care of herself, so her safety wasn't the main issue to him. Whatever Janaye is hiding has something to do with this new Panther Party. She never mentioned anything about this in all the years they've known each other. It's that big of a secret that she has kept it from him for years, and he's more than sure that she hasn't told anyone about these people. Travis looked over to the stack of folders on the desk that contained the mug shot of Ben and that got him curious.

"One last question before I go."

"Aww, and I was enjoying our conversation." Travis ignored her attempted to sound hurt.

"What interest do The Panthers have in Benjamin Jackson?" Hope turned around to see the file that she was looking over that contained Benjamin's picture. She looked back to face Travis with a smirk.

"Can't say," Well, Travis figured she would say something like that. "Why do you think The Panthers have any interest in him at all? It could just be for my own curiosity" She asked playfully, but Travis knew better. He entertained this woman for long enough.

"Can't say." Her smirk turned into a wide grin at his response.

"Well, this has been a fun game." Travis took that as his cue to leave. He stood up and walked to the door.

"Oh, and Travis," He stopped to turn around. "You should come tomorrow. The trial will be at ten, and we'll begin around nine. It'll be a great opportunity for you to see how we operate." Travis nodded his head and left the room. The party was still going on as he quickly left the house. There were many things on his mind when he reached his apartment. At least he has some answers, even if they weren't the ones he wanted. The Panthers. He has to know more about them. He looked at the clock to see it saying 11:30 PM. Tomorrow at the courthouse should be interesting.

That morning, Travis sat on his bed in anticipation. He barely had any sleep. He looked at his phone, telling him that it's 7:30 AM. He has an hour and a half to make his way to the courthouse. Travis almost forgot that he had a class this morning, oh well, missing one class won't kill him. Getting himself ready, he ordered an Uber just in case things turn out messier than he envisaged, he rather not have his car anywhere near there if things turn for the worse. For some reason, when people riot, it's always the cars that get messed up first, and he still has payments to make on his.

Luckily, the drive was a quiet one. Some Uber drivers tend to be more talkative than Travis would want them to be. They would ask all kinds of questions just to be nosy. He got it, they want to be friendly and it can be awkward driving someone without speaking to them, but he is not the social type. Approaching his destination, he could see a gathering of people all over the street. The crowd increased as they drove further into the area. Eventually, the driver had to stop as the street was filled with people.

"I'm afraid this is as far as I can take you, my friend." The driver apologized.

"Don't worry about it; this is the street I need to be on anyways." Travis reassured him. He got out of the car and was surprised by the number of people that were there. Hope wasn't kidding when she said they had about three thousand people; this is crazy!

He could see many of them carrying placards and wearing paraphernalia about black power, black injustice, black lives matter, police brutality, and all sorts of things. He tried to get out of the street, but the growing crowd wouldn't allow him. He figured it would be best to follow the flow of traffic instead of trying to fight it. Walking closer to the courthouse, he noticed specific individuals blending in with the crowd. He spotted them wearing an all-black uniform, and while he usually wouldn't give much thought about it, he couldn't ignore the golden paw that they were spotting.

He didn't have to make an educated guess on whom they belonged but made sense since The Panthers are organizing this. But what's with the all-black though? Is that supposed to be a thing? Travis can get with it if it was a night operation kind of thing, but out here with the sun out; he can only imagine them burning up in those.

Closer and closer, he reached the courthouse as the traffic of people stopped. The anticipation that he felt before he left his house came back in full force. He prayed that this would end as it began, only a protest. However, with the number of people here, his instincts are telling him otherwise and so far, they have been on point. In front of the courthouse, he could see the figure of Hope Carter holding a microphone.

Beside her was a lineup of police officers guarding the path to the entrance. The courthouse must have expected something like this to show up at their doorstep and decided to call in some backup. Hopefully, nobody does anything stupid. He could hear Hope speaking to the crowd as he got closer.

"Brothers and sisters, we gather here over the injustice that took place in Inglewood. We will not let this monster that killed an innocent child go unpunished! They will hear our cry!" The deafening roar of the crowd made it almost impossible for Travis to hear anything. He tried to push his way to get closer, but the journey was proving difficult. Once he reached close enough, he saw a line of police cars arriving.

The car in the middle opened to reveal Officer Smith still in his uniform with no cuffs on being escorted. The crowd exploded in fury. Travis could hear the people shouting out, calling the officer "child killer," "pig," and every other insult under the sun. The police officers that formed the line to the courthouse did their best to control everyone so they couldn't harm Officer Smith. There was another man with Officer Smith in a suit that Travis assumed to be his lawyer.

Four hours later, Travis stood amongst the crowd, waiting for the outcome of the trial. During that time, numerous news stations showed up. Some of them talked to the people, while others waited for the outcome as well. Travis even saw the reporter that interviewed Ms. Freed. Seeing her made him he remember that Ms. Freed was the only one that had an interview.

What about Dr. Jones? Her son is missing too, so why didn't they do one with her? Maybe Dr. Jones declined to do one, or it could be something else. He tried to get closer to where the reporter was to ask her, but the door to the courthouse suddenly opened. Travis held his breath to see who would be coming out. Everyone stood in silence, waiting for the person to emerge.

Travis' heart danced in his chest. Whoever comes out and why will determine the actions of this huge gathering. Travis has no doubt that if the outcome is not to everyone's satisfaction, things will turn dangerous fast. As if being mocked by some kind of foreign entity, the person that came out was Officer Smith, but there was something wrong with this picture.

Travis dreaded when he inspected Officer Smith to find out that he's not in handcuffs with his lawyer beside them and both of them giving the biggest grins. That could only mean one thing; the court found him not guilty. The following reaction was imminent as the crowd erupted in rage. The people came rushing at Officer Smith and his lawyer as the police line did their best to restrain the crowd.

The lawyer quickly rushed Officer Smith into the car and drove off. Travis stood as the scene intensified and the protesters were swiftly becoming a mob. He turned his head to the sound of sirens as more police came out and even three SWAT trucks appeared.

More police and the SWAT team came out to control the raging mob. Their efforts only brought more chaos as the people refused to back down. The police gathered in a formation with the SWAT carrying shields to barricade everyone into a corner. Initially, their plan was beginning to work until they heard the sound of a gunshot. Travis looked around him to see where it came from and saw a protester fall to the ground. What happened next, Travis could only describe as pure anarchy. Floods of screams and furious roars could be heard as the people fought back.

Travis watched in horror as the people fought the police with their placards and anything else, they had on them. Some of them took the police's shields and started bashing them with it. The SWAT team that was with them began to use tear gas on the populous. The gas made things worse because Travis couldn't see anywhere around him. The only thing he could do was hear the sounds of shouting, screams, and the footsteps of running people.

Travis had to get the hell out of there. Doing the best that he could, he tried to maneuver through the smoke as people ran into him. His efforts not be trampled stopped as soon as he heard the sound of gunshots. Not being able to see was dangerous enough, and now suddenly people started shooting and he can't even see where! Forgetting his fear of being trampled on, he ducked to the ground. Frantically looking around, he was able to see a light through the screams and gunshots piercing through the smoke. Getting up, he ran as fast as he could to get away from this madness.

Ignoring all the people that passed by him, he reached his destination, but his salvation was cut short when he heard the click of a gun. He turned his head slowly to face a police officer with his gun pointing at him. Frozen like a deer in a headlight, he could only move his eyes as he followed the movement of the officer's fingers tightly clutching his weapon. Time stopped as Travis tried to move, but his body wouldn't obey him. *Move damnit! Move!* He screamed at his body to cooperate. He could see the look of pure fear on the officer's face. He must think Travis is part of this mob and that he's going to attack him.

The officer's twitching finger on the trigger made Travis more aware of his mortality…He's going to die. His mind went blank as he heard the firing of the gun. A few seconds passed and Travis found himself in a surprising position that he was still standing. Coming back to reality, Travis felt a strange sensation. It wasn't pain, in fact, he doesn't feel anything at all. One would think being shot would follow up with immediate agony.

He looked over to where the officer stood to find him on the ground dead. A pool of blood was flowing from him. He looked up to see one of the guys that wore all black with the golden paw print that was in the crowd before this all started. Travis couldn't get a good look at them as they were wearing a half-face mask, the only thing he could see were hazel eyes, but by their posture and the fact that they were holding a gun, it wasn't hard to figure out who fired that shot.

The person looked back at Travis while raising their hand holding the gun in the air and fired off multiple shots. The person emptied the entire clip before they tossed the weapon on the ground near the dead officer and ran off. Travis was too shocked about what just happened to move at first but was soon able to move his legs. However, before he could run, he was surrounded by the SWAT.

"You little shit!" One of the members yelled. Looking at the dead body in front of him and back at the SWAT team. Travis tried to say something, anything to have them see that this is a misunderstanding and that he didn't do this. He opened his mouth to speak, but the only sound that came out was an anguished cry as he was shot in the leg. Falling to the ground, Travis could feel his consciousness fading. The last thing he saw was the SWAT Team surrounding him before everything turned black.

Chapter

4

Harvard Heights, Los Angeles, CA; 4:25 PM

Jasmine dragged herself up the stairs of her apartment building. She couldn't believe the nightmare she just survived. It was only supposed to have been a peaceful protest and she only meant to stay until the verdict of the trial came. Well obviously, a peaceful protest went to straight hell as soon as she and everyone there saw Officer Smith coming out of the courthouse as innocent. She knew she should have left that moment, but her boss wanted her to stay to get the protester's reaction. Confrontation brings in ratings, but this was more than just a simple altercation because it turned into a battle zone as soon as the SWAT team came in and decided to use tear gas.

Speaking of which, they came in pretty fast as if knowing that a riot was going to happen. She didn't want to describe what she witnessed as one, but she would only be lying to herself. The people attacked first, and the police responded to their assault. It didn't make anything better when they started using tear gas as she had gotten separated from her team. The situation got more dangerous once she heard gunshots through the gas.

She was able to stay safe by finding a path through the chaos to the sidewalk and hiding on the side of a building. She later reunited with her crew. However, her cameraman got shot in the process. It wasn't anything life-threatening and, the dumbass tried to catch everything on camera, risking his life to do so. Luckily, their van wasn't damaged, and they quickly made their escape to the hospital. After dropping him in the hospital, they went back to their office, where the director had them play the video that her cameraman was able to take. Everyone that was in that room could only watch in shock.

The footage captured everything clearly until the moment that the tear gas was used. At that point, most of the recording was covered in smoke, but you could see people running for their lives. The main thing that was most disturbing was the screams of the protesters being attacked by the SWAT and the gunshots. Towards the end of the video, Jasmine caught a glimpse of a person in all black that had some kind of emblem on them that was oddly familiar to her.

When the video was over, she made a copy of it and replayed it back on her desk. She fast-forwarded to the part of the individual in all black and paused it. Looking closer to the emblem that she saw; she saw that it was the form of a paw print. A golden paw print. She knew she recognized it from somewhere. It was the same symbol that was in an invitation that she had received two days ago.

She didn't bother showing up to whatever that the invitation was for, but it had some curious words. The phrase 'we will rise' spoke to her.

She has seen that same phrase graffitied in local neighborhoods along with a golden paw. She remembered only hearing a name in passing. The Panthers. Originally, she thought it was some kind of gang, and decided to do some research on them. Over time she realized that they were an organization that hid from the limelight, and even though they help to better the communities there's something ominous about them that she couldn't shake off. Are they somehow involved in this?

When they took her cameraman to the hospital, there were already many people there from the riot. After talking to the staff, she estimated that there were about 150 people here, with 25 being in critical conditions though, they obviously didn't give her any names. She was able to learn that there was one death and it shocked Jasmine when she found out that it was a police officer.

The staff told her that it seemed that they already had a suspect who was shot in the leg in the hospital, but they refused to let her know who it was. The one thing that she did remember was the face of a young man who was frozen solid when this whole mess began, and she hoped that he made it out safely.

Reaching her apartment, she opened the door and tossed her stuff on the floor. After everything that happened today, she needed a drink. Finding a bottle of Hennessey in the cabinet, she poured herself a glass over ice.

"Well, I'm glad you made it out of that safe." Jasmine dropped her glass in shock. She quickly went inside her drawer to grab a butcher's knife. She turned on the lights intending to run her knife through the idiot that decided to break in her house. When the lights came on, Jasmine was surprised to see her sister, Lanika, sitting on her sofa chair.

"Lanika." Jasmine whispered, dropping the knife.

"Wow, were you planning on stabbing me with that? You sure as hell know how to make a sis feel welcome. So, how's the job going for you?" Jasmine surveyed the area. Her doors and windows were locked, so how did Lanika get in here? Looking around, she saw that there was no indication that she broke into her home. Everything was at the exact place she left them before she left this morning. Even the screen door was still locked before she entered, so how? Facing Lanika in suspicion, she spoke up.

"What are you doing here Lanika?" She asked

"That's it? We haven't seen each other in years and all you care about is why I'm here? That voice mail you sent me was all about me giving you a chance and everything. Well, here I am just like you wanted."

"Yeah, but that was before today."

"Oh, and what makes today any different?"

"The Panthers." Lanika sat up straighter on the chair while crossing her arms.

"What about The Panthers?"

"This morning with what happened between the protesters and police; I can't prove it, but I know they have something to do with it, that's if they did not instigate the whole thing. I know you're one of them."

"That's some accusation, and what makes you think I have any affiliation with these Panthers?"

"You still haven't answered me. Why are you here?"

"What? Is it wrong for me to check on my big sister after you went through such an ordeal? Frankly, I'm hurt that you would think otherwise." Lanika said with feigned innocence.

"Cut the bullshit! Stop playing with me Lanika. You didn't think I have been keeping tabs on everything that you've been doing all this time? I know that you have been keeping contact with those people and if you're not going to say it, then get out before I call the cops." Lanika gave an amused chuckle at her threat.

"I highly doubt that even if you were able to call them, they would show up in time before I leave." Jasmine wondered what she meant by that. She took her phone out to see that she had no signal. Impossible! This area is a hot spot for her carrier and she never had a problem with the signal. Not a single bar. She then tried to connect to her Wi-Fi, but somehow that was disabled too. She paid the bills; both are on autopay so what is going on? Then she remembered what Lanika just said.

"What did you do?" She accused.

"Don't worry," Lanika shrugged off. "It's only temporary. It's not often that we can get reunions like this and I don't want any outside annoyances getting in the way. Every single communication signal is blocked, so come on and sit down. Let's talk." Despite the alarming situation that she's in, Jasmine knows that the only other person here with her is Lanika, and if she wanted to try something, she would have done so by now. Cautiously, she made her way to the living room and sat on the couch.

"See, that's better. No need for hostility between family, especially since you were so eager to help me find my son." Jasmine stared at her for a moment digesting how casually Lanika made that statement before coming to her conclusion about the matter.

"He's not lost...is he?"

"No. He's alive and safe." Jasmine took a deep sigh at her answer.

"I knew it," Jasmine murmured. "The moment I saw that guy in the video, I knew that The Panthers were involved somehow. If that were the case, then you would be a part of it as well, and you being here is a testament to that. Now you involve your son in this game of yours!"

"It's no game, Jasmine." Jasmine stopped at the change of Lanika's tone. It wasn't the playful dismissal one she was using earlier; no, she's dead serious.

"Since you already know so much, guess there's no point in denying it. We may not have been able to be as active in the past, but that time is over. The Panthers are on the rise and there's nothing any of us can do about it. It's too late. I came here with a warning as your sister. Leave this city." Jasmine stood up in alarm. Leave the city?! Just what the hell are they planning? Is her life going to be in danger now?

"I know," Jasmine started to speak, but took a breath to calm herself. "I know that every event that you were a part of was on behalf of that organization you're so proud about. They hide themselves in the shadows, but I know."

"Glad to know I have a stalker." Lanika scoffed.

"What are you trying to achieve by being with these people?!" Jasmine yelled. The room became deathly silent when Lanika got up from the chair. Jasmine was tensed as she walked past her and stopped at the front of the door.

"To take back everything that was taken from us." Lanika answered as she opened the door.

"Lanika!" Jasmine called out before she left. Lanika stood at the entrance but didn't turn to face her. "I'm sorry. I'm sorry for abandoning you. I should have come back for you."

"It's in the past. For the record, I never resented you for that. Think over with what I told you. Things are going to be hazardous around here soon. But if you're persistent in staying, then as you know, the mayoral elections are coming up. There's a candidate named Alex Williams. You should look him up, maybe even give him an interview. Take care sis." Lanika closed the door, leaving Jasmine alone in her apartment.

A few minutes later, she started receiving text messages and notifications again. Thinking over the conversation she just had with her sister, it looks like it's about to be a bit more dangerous in L.A.

Ronald Regan Medical Center, Los Angeles, CA

7:00 PM

Travis stared at the ceiling of the hospital room that the nurses set him in as he was being treated. There was nothing else to do since all of his possession had been confiscated and looking at the metal cuffs attaching his wrist to the bed, he was reminded of his situation. He's a suspect of murder! Travis couldn't fathom this being a possible scenario for him. He was never one to be in the center of attention and was simply fine being on the sidelines, under the radar.

That's how he was able to live his life somewhat peacefully. How could all of that crash down like this? Him? A murderer? All forms of communication, entertainment, and electronics were removed from the room where he was. He overheard that the bullet that was in his leg didn't do any severe damage to his nerves or anything like that, so they're planning to discharge him later tomorrow.

That's way too quick in Travis' opinion. Shouldn't he need to stay for another couple of days to at least let his leg fully heal? Or physical therapy? More than anything, Travis dreaded leaving the hospital and could only imagine what's going to happen to him once he's in custody. It would be nice to have a lawyer in this situation, but since they took all forms of communication from him and because they practically snuck him in through the back door, he figured the police wants to keep this as "hush, hush" as possible.

The nurse would come in to change his bandage and give him food but wouldn't say a word to him. She did her duties as quickly as possible as if spending another minute alone with Travis would endanger her life. It seemed that the police had told the staff not to interact with him unless it was necessary, so he had no one to talk to since he got here. He was fine being alone.

Always had been, but to have people be deathly afraid of him wasn't something he enjoyed. He looked out to the door to see the shadows of two people. It looks like they're guarding his room. He's chained to the damn bed where the hell is he going? Travis found sleep to be impossible due to his fear of what tomorrow brings.

That following morning, the hospital deemed him fit to be discharged after they had him put pressure on his leg, which hurt like a bitch. He could barely walk, but the staff just put it off and had him immediately placed in the LAPD's custody. They wasted no time escorting him to the police station. Travis was thankful they were secretive about it since that meant the news media hadn't caught wind of him yet.

Considering he's a suspect for killing a cop, they would eat him alive. The officers that were escorting him took him to the station through the back entrance just as they did when they brought him into the hospital. Guess they don't even want their colleagues to know about this as well. They took him into an interrogation room and left him alone after handcuffing him to one of the chairs. From being handcuffed to a bed, now to a chair, it's not much of an improvement and his leg still hurts. The hospital only gave him enough painkillers to last till he left and unfortunately for him, as soon as he was in the car, it wore off.

Time passed as Travis just sat alone in the room; just as he was beginning to think he would be dead of boredom before this whole questioning starts, the door opened. Travis watched as two officers came in and read their name badges as Woods and Clyde. The one named Clyde came into the room and sat on the other chair in front of Travis while the other one walked over and stood behind him.

Travis didn't understand why the other officer went behind him as he couldn't fight, or escape being handcuffed to the chair. Travis thought of several reasons why he was behind him, and if any of those were the case, then this is going to get rough. The officer in front of him sat in silence, staring at him. Travis responded with the same and not breaking eye contact because he refused to show any weakness. Their staring contest ended with the officer looking up at his partner then back to Travis.

"I don't know what grudge you had with Officer Peeves," Peeves? So that was his name. "But I'll tell you this. I'm going to make sure that your final moments on this earth are hell!"

"I didn't–." Travis tried to speak but was interrupted by the force of being hit in the face.

"Shut up!" Officer Clyde yelled as he slammed his hands on the table. When Travis was able to focus again, he felt movement from behind him and peered to his right to see the other officer's right arm beginning to twitch.

"You don't speak, got that?" Travis turned back to face Officer Clyde but didn't answer. His silence was short-lived as his head was slammed on the table. He groaned in pain and felt more pain as his head was pulled back up to face the officer again.

"Answer him." Officer Woods whispered dangerously to Travis.

"Got it." Travis gritted through his teeth.

"Good! Here's what's going to happen. You sit, shut up and listen. Speak out of turn, move, or do anything to piss us off and I promise, what just happened will feel like a vacation. Are we clear?" Travis gave the officer a cold glare.

"Do you want me to bust your head again?" Travis smirked at Officer Woods' threat.

"First you said shut up now you want me to talk. Make up your mind officer." Travis knew that being condescending was not going to help him in the situation, but he was not going to let these assholes have any satisfaction on what they're doing to him. He braced himself when his head was slammed on the table again.

"Let me give you your only warning. Being a smartass will piss us off." Officer Woods growled. Travis could only groan in response. He prayed that this doesn't last long because having your head repeatedly slammed on the table is not something one would call relaxing.

"It's okay, Woods. I think our friend here knows the rules and consequences. Don't you?" Travis only gave a glare as a response.

"So, you can learn. At least enough to know when you're being asked a rhetorical question. I'll give you this; it was pretty smart to use to the smoke and confusion to your advantage. We know you did it, so there's no use of denying it. We have multiple witnesses saying you were the only person near Officer Peeves when he died, including the SWAT team that found you. Denying it will only make it harder for you. Soon everyone will know that you're a cop killer."

"I didn't kill anyone!" Travis blurted out. He was rewarded with another slam against the table. Travis couldn't take it this time as he yelled out in pain. He was surprised that he didn't have a concussion at this point, but he could feel himself starting to slip in and out of consciousness. Sitting back up, he could feel a cold liquid running down his face. He heard small droplets hitting the table and looked down to see that it was blood...his blood. Officer Clyde sighed in frustration.

"It's straightforward instructions, and you can't even do that! It's like you people are just born stupid, huh?" Travis bit his lip to prevent him from lashing out, knowing exactly what he meant by saying 'you people'.

"Peeves was a good man, a family man. Everyone liked him. He helped the elderly, played with kids on the streets, tried to educate you, young people, even gave a portion of his check to Children's Hospitals. Everyone loved him. He was one of the friendliest people you can know, and you killed him. Let me tell you, kid. You pissed off a lot of people, especially the man behind you." Travis felt a hand on his shoulder and slowly the pressure of his hand would increase. More and more, Officer Woods squeezed his shoulder. Travis tried to brave it but soon it was beginning to become too much as he buried his nails into the palm of his hands to distract him from the pain on his shoulder.

"You see that officer you killed was this man's partner and he would love nothing more than to tear you apart. The only thing that's stopping him from doing so is me. You should consider yourself lucky. Once the whole city knows about this, everyone is going to want a piece of you, but I can make sure that nobody hurts you. I can do a lot to protect you, but the only way for me to help is for you to admit your guilt. Now, this is where you get to speak, and the only thing I want to hear coming out of your mouth is: I killed Officer Peeves."

Travis couldn't believe this. A forced confession. Five minutes ago, they were banging his head hard enough for him to get an aneurysm and now he's talking about wanting to help him? Does this officer think that his little show would scare Travis enough to be that stupid?

By looking at him in the eyes, Travis knew that he was entirely serious and would have no problem with leaving him alone with the other guy that wants to kill him. Not a lot of options for Travis: either confess to murder or get the crap beaten out of him. At that moment, he knew he was screwed either way. He chuckled, knowing that his next course of action would probably be the stupidest decision he has ever made. Both officers looked at him in confusion. Has he lost it? Travis stopped laughing as he looked straight into Officer Clyde's eyes.

"Go fuck yourself."

Chapter

5

"I should go fuck myself, huh? Well, you have balls. I'll give you that," Officer Clyde complimented half heartily. "It seems your head is a bit messed up from earlier. I'm going to go for a smoke, so you can just stay comfortably there and clear your mind. Hopefully, when I return, we'll have a better understanding of each other. Oh, and don't worry, Officer Woods here has volunteered to stay with you, so you don't get lonely. I'm sure you two will have lots to talk about." Travis gave Officer Clyde a death glare as he chuckled his way out of the room.

Travis closed his eyes, mentally preparing himself for what's about to come. He's no idiot. Nobody is coming for him, so he'll have to do his best to resist as long as he can. With that determination in mind, he waited for the inevitable as a fist knocked him on the ground. Considering that he's still cuffed to the chair, the landing wasn't at all soft.

Officer Clyde closed the door just as his partner knocked Travis to the ground. He smirked to himself, knowing the kind of quality time those two will be spending. Thankfully, these rooms are soundproof, so nobody is going to know what's going on. He walked away with his hands in his pockets. Fifteen minutes should be more than enough for the bastard to rethink on his generous offer.

His thoughts of enjoying those fifteen minutes were put to a halt as he heard a commotion going on in the office. He hurried to see a black woman in a red mini skirt suit. *Great!* groaned Officer Clyde. *What the hell does she want?* The other officers were trying to calm her down, but the lady was only getting more agitated. Deciding to put an end to this so he could go back to his break, he walked up to her.

"Ma'am, what seems to be the problem?" The woman snapped her head towards him. He stepped back a bit because of the intense look she was giving him.

"Are you in charge here?!" She questioned loudly.

"Yes. I am Captain Clyde. Now can you tell me what your business is here?" Capt. Clyde asked as nicely as possible.

However, dealing with these people, especially their women, is extremely exhausting for him. His little break is about to turn into a full-length movie if he has to deal with her for long and from the way that she was looking at him, he will bet his left arm on it. The woman narrowed her eyes at him.

"I'm only going to ask this once. Where is he?!" Capt. Clyde looked at her in confusion. What is this woman talking about?

"I'm sorry ma'am, who?" He tried to clarify.

"Don't play stupid with me!" She fired back hotly. "Where is my client?! I know he's here." Client? Capt. Clyde couldn't believe this. When they took Travis into custody, they took all his records from the hospital and had him locked up. The kid was in the foster care system his whole life. He has no family, barely had any friends for that matter.

There's no way he would have a private lawyer. Of course, he was planning on bringing one in for Travis, after they had an understanding between each other. A lawyer that he personally knew that would be more than happy to make sure Travis never gets set free.

Just who is this chick? Giving a quick sweep around the room, the rest of the officers there were giving him questioning glances. Well, most of them will shut up since he's the captain, but some will open their mouths to the commissioner if they hear that he held Travis in custody through means that weren't exactly by the books. The kid is a cop killer, so he didn't see why it should matter, but unfortunately, some of them sport the same skin color and might try to help one of their own out. He went back to the woman who was demanding to know Travis' location.

"Look, lady, I don't know who your client is or where they might be at. As you can see, we're the only ones here. Now, you are causing a disturbance."

"Don't bullshit me!" She screamed.

"I know you bribed that staff in the hospital to have my client released earlier than what was projected so you and your little minion could take him! He was still recovering from a bullet wound. You took him without a warrant and kept him here without having his lawyer present! I swear to God if you don't take me to him right now, I'm going to have your ass and everyone else's in here in allegations! Try me!" Capt. Clyde's blood boiled at the audacity that this woman had to threaten him of all people! He had to calm himself. The woman is a lawyer who apparently has knowledge of what had transpired in the past couple of hours. He didn't understand how she could have gotten that information.

How could she have known that they didn't have an arrest warrant when they came to collect Travis? Besides, the staff was readily happy to turn him over to them once Capt. Clyde mentioned that he allegedly killed a cop. The others were now looking at him with suspicion, but all it took was for him to give them the back-off stare for them to mind their businesses. He needs to control the situation now and somehow get this woman out of here.

"Ma'am, please follow me into my office where we can talk further about the issue." He tried to persuade her. He needed something to distract her and get her out of here. If he could get her in his office, he would be able to stall her and warn Woods to move Travis somewhere else.

"No need," She declined. "The only reason why I asked was to give you the opportunity to show me yourself and save us both the trouble. It's ok; I know exactly where he is. Move!" She said as she shoved Capt.

Clyde out of her way and marched herself into the hallway that led to the interrogation rooms. The captain quickly ran to catch up with her. The lawyer wasted no time finding the right door. He made a smug expression when he caught up to her, all the doors have keyboard access panels, so unless she knew the access code, nobody is going inside.

"Lady, there is no one in there. You need to leave." The lawyer ignored him as she pulled her phone out. Capt. Clyde could not believe the level of disrespect; that's why he can't stand to deal with lawyers. They think they can do whatever they want.

"Lady!" He was cut off when the lawyer put her finger up in front of him as if telling him to shut up while she made a call.

"Hey girl, it's me. Just like you said, these cops ain't no damn help. Yeah, it's the third door in the right hallway past the main office. Thanks." Capt. Clyde stood in confusion. Is she calling for backup? Little that's going to do for her. His confidence in handling the situation was quickly destroyed as the green light on the panel appeared and the door opened.

Impossible! Capt. Clyde shouted in disbelief. There are only two people who know the access codes and that was him and the commissioner, so what did she do?! The lawyer walked into the room to find the surprised face of Officer Woods. Travis, covered in bruises, was in too much pain to see her walk in and was only able to hear the clicking of her heels as she walked. She looked at the sight of Travis cuffed to the chair and shook her head.

"Get. Out!" She emphasized each word, staring at Officer Woods who was too stunned to comprehend what she just said as no one else, especially a lawyer, should be in here. He looked behind her to see Capt. Clyde's expression and knew that he didn't let her in. So how did she get in?

"Did I stutter?!" She yelled at him. Capt. Clyde got over his shock and made his way to stand in front of her.

"Now, look here, I don't know what you just did, but this is trespassing, and I can detain you for it unless you leave now." He said, hoping his threat would work on her.

"No, you leave now before this becomes ugly! I have more than enough to haul both of your asses in prison. My client is still supposed to be in the hospital recovering from injuries and you somehow were able to obtain his records. You took him without my notice and by the look of things, you assaulted my client!"

"Now hold on lady, before you start pointing fingers around here, everything we did was by the procedure."

"Procedure my ass! I recorded everything since I came here." Capt. Clyde looked at her in panic. He didn't think was recording everything considering the show she put on. If people found out about this, he wouldn't be able to talk his way out, especially with the commissioner. He studied her to see what she could have possibly used to record him.

She didn't take her phone out until they were at the door, and he's still trying to figure out how the hell she was able to pull that magic trick off. Wait, her phone. He looked at her again to see that her phone was still in her hands. She must have set it up to record before she entered. It's the only explanation that makes sense. If he can get his hands on it and destroy the phone, then this will all be over. He made a move to grab her phone, but the lawyer dodged his advance.

"Nice try, even if you got my phone it won't matter. The recording is already being sent to somewhere you will never be able to find. One word and all of this will go to every news station in the city! I will blast this on every social media platform! So, here's what's going to happen. You're going to uncuff him, get out, and when I'm done talking to him, you're going to release him back to the hospital. If they find more damage was done to my client, you are going to pay for it. Are we clear?!"

Capt. Clyde's nerves were hitting an all-time high at the fact that this lawyer was controlling the situation that he carefully set up. If that recording gets out, the whole unit will be in the deep. This is something that he has to keep away from the commissioner. With a heavy sigh, he motioned for Officer Woods to do as the woman said. He went over and uncuffed Travis and followed the captain out of the room.

"Don't think we're finished here." Capt. Clyde tried to sound as threatening as possible, but the lawyer rolled her eyes at him.

"Yes, we are. Bye!" The captain grumbled under his breath before closing the door. The lawyer turned around to face Travis, who was finally able to focus on his surroundings to get a clearer picture of the person in front of him.

"Hello, Trav- "

"Who are you?" He cut her off. Taking in her appearance and listening to the rant that she put on it didn't take Travis much to guess who the woman was, but as far as he knows, he doesn't know any lawyers.

"Nice to meet you too," She said sarcastically. "My name is Kiana Summers. I'm your lawyer." She said as she went around the table and sat on it. Travis rose his eyebrow and scoffed to himself.

"Isn't that funny? No one told me I had a lawyer when they brought me to this death trap. It's not like I know any, but the gesture would have been nice."

"Well, you have one now, and from the pathetic state you're in, you definitely need one."

"How did you know I was in here? I figured asshole one and two wouldn't let anyone find out about me until they were done with this interrogation." Kiana looked at all the bruises that showed on Travis's face and body, it didn't have to take a genius to figure out the kind of interrogation he went through.

"What can I say, it's good to have friends. Now, on to more pressing matters. What exactly did they say to you?" Travis took a minute to stretch himself out. Being handcuffed for the past twenty-four hours had made his body unbearably stiff. In that time, he recollected his ordeal and decided to start from the beginning, right from the protest. Kiana sat and listened to Travis' story till the part where he ended up here and where Capt. Clyde tried to get a forced confession out of him.

"And what did you say back?" Travis gave her a self-satisfied smirk.

"I told him to go fuck himself." Kiana roared in laughter. She was beginning to like this kid.

"Hope did say you were an interesting one." The moment Travis heard that name, he went back to be on full alert. Hope? As in Hope Carter? In hindsight, it would make sense since she's the only person he had any contact with that could afford a lawyer. Does that mean Kiana works for Hope? Even if that's not the case, the fact that she mentioned Hope's name implies that they are associated with each other and that also means that Kiana is probably affiliated with The Panthers as well.

"Wow, what's with the hostility? I'm here to help you." She pointed out as she saw him staring at her.

"That woman sent you here. That means you're with the..." Kiana quickly covered his mouth with her hand before he could finish. He tried to pry her hands off of him, but the woman had a surprisingly firm grip.

"Be careful with what you say," She whispered in his ear. "Just because it's just us two here doesn't mean that no one is listening to our conversation. Thought someone as smart as you would know that already. When I let go, don't mention them, understand?" Travis nodded his head. Kiana slowly moved her hand away and sat back on the table. Travis stared at her in suspicion. If she's one of The Panthers, then she knows how he got here in the first place.

"Why are you here? Your little group is the reason why I'm stuck here." He growled out. Frustrated couldn't even describe how Travis felt right now. Just what do they want from him?

"I'm sorry," It wasn't the apology that threw him off, but the genuine regret that was in her voice. "None of that was supposed to happen. We didn't foresee any of that happening. That's why I'm here. I want to help you, and the first thing we are going to do is get you out of here and back to the hospital." Travis couldn't honestly believe the words that she was saying. However, everything from her tone to her body language was telling him that she wasn't lying to him. At that moment, all of the emotions that he locked in during this whole ordeal came back all at once. His anger, desperation, sadness, and fear all swarmed at him that he couldn't hold back the tears that were flowing down his face.

Besides Janaye, there's now someone else on his side.

"Thank you."

Westlake, Los Angeles, CA; 1:52 PM

Jasmine drove to a grey building that was across McArthur Park. Looking around the area it seems that Candidate Williams doesn't want his campaign headquarters to be widely known. Even so, it wasn't hard for Jasmine to find the place after doing some research. The building itself looked to be three to four stories tall, and Jasmine doubted that there would be a guide that can take her to Alex. *Well, there goes my luck on trying to find this guy.* She sighed.

She walked inside the building and to her surprise there was a receptionist desk in the middle of the walkway. *Scratch that.* If the building has a front desk clerk, then they might know what floor and room Candidate Williams is lodged in, since he's a high-profile individual now. She walked up to the clerk, who was busy working on the computer. The woman looked up when Jasmine approached her.

"Yes, can I help you." She asked.

"Um, I'm looking for a Mr. Alex Williams." The desk clerk looked at Jasmine with some hesitance, as if trying to discern what her motives were. The staring was making Jasmine extremely uncomfortable and it must have shown as the clerk quickly dropped the look.

"Oh, I'm sorry," The clerk apologized. "It's just that we don't get many new faces around here to see Mr. Williams. You must be new to his campaign team."

"Yeah, I just got on board last week." If the clerk is going to assume that Jasmine is a part of the team, then let her, no sense in making this visit more complicated than it needs to be. She hopes that the clerk won't get in trouble once they find out who she is. Jasmine rode up the elevator to the third floor per instructions that the clerk gave her. Getting off, she saw two signs with one of them pointing left that had rooms 300-320, and the one pointing right had rooms 321-350.

The room she's looking for is 345, so, right it is. Walking closer to the door, Jasmine became more nervous. What exactly is she supposed to say? 'Hi, I'm a news reporter and I have a suspicion that you're involved with a possible extremist organization.' Yeah, that'll go well. When she reached room 345, she stopped to calm her nerves before she entered.

Once she opened the door, Jasmine took a quick look inside the office. It was moderately big, and she could count about fifteen people in the room. All of them were busy answering phones and passing documents to each other. On the walls were posters of Alex Williams and a couple of his campaign messages. She noticed that there was one other office door in the room, which she figured was Mr. Williams' private room. Taking in the scenery, she jumped when she felt someone tap on her shoulder.

"Ma'am, can I help you?" Jasmine turned around to see a young woman who looked to be in her early twenties. She was carrying a stack of folders and by the fact that every other table in the room is already occupied, Jasmine guessed that she's some kind of intern.

"I'm looking for Mr. Alex Williams."

"Oh, and what business do you have with Mr. Williams." *The kind that involves none of yours,* is what Jasmine would have liked to respond with but knew it wouldn't get her anywhere. Obviously, she can't just reveal herself, or they'll most likely kick her out.

"I work for an insurance company and the owner is interested in investing in Candidate Williams and sent me to meet with him." Jasmine hoped that her quick thinking would trick the girl.

"Well, he should be in his office. Follow me." She replied as she turned around and started walking to the back of the room towards that other door. Jasmine followed her to the office and was able to glance at the curious stares she was receiving from everyone else as they passed by. The young woman made a motion for Jasmine to stop once they reached the door. She raised her finger, signaling Jasmine to give her a moment and proceeded to knock on the door.

"Mr. Williams. There is someone here to see you." There was a pause before Jasmine heard a smooth voice replying back.

"Send them in." The young woman gestured for Jasmine to go in. When she entered the room, she found Alex Williams sitting on his desk. She looked around, capturing every detail. It wasn't as big as she imagined but was still large enough to accommodate someone comfortably. She looked back at Alex who focused on his work.

She didn't want to be rude, but at the same time just standing there was starting to hurt her feet. Finally, deciding not to care about formalities, she went over and sat down on one of the chairs in front of Alex's desk. Her movement didn't seem to rouse Alex out of his workaholic trance as he continued working. She stayed there for another five minutes before he finished and closed his laptop.

"Well, it's nice to see you made yourself comfortable." Even though she came here unannounced and unexpected, he didn't have to sound like her presence is an annoyance to him. The tone in his voice made it clear that her visit is not welcomed at the moment. Is this the person that Lanika wanted her to meet? They say first impressions are everything, and if this is how he talks to people, then he's already on the low opinion poll. If this is how he wants this conversation to go, she can play ball too.

"Well, being a woman wearing high heels, you can agree that having me just stand there waiting until you were done with whatever it was is a little inhospitable."

"That's interesting coming from someone that came here uninvited. So, tell me, what is a news reporter is doing snooping around in my office?" *Damn!* Jasmine cursed. How did he find out? She made sure not to expose herself when she made her way up here. Alex responded to her shocked expression with an amused smirk.

"Don't act so surprised, Ms. Jasmine Jones. I've seen you enough on channel 4 at night to recognize you. It seems that no one else here pays any attention to the news lately since it's all on everyone's phones nowadays. Regardless, what brings you in today? I highly doubt it's to get something on me." Well, the cat's out of the bag now, considering he knows her name as well. The real problem is how to answer his question. She honestly doesn't understand why she came here. Lanika was the one that told her to go and see this guy, but for what purpose? She couldn't think of a single reason why she came to see this man.

"To be honest, I don't know myself." Alex rose his eyebrow at her answer.

"You don't know?" Her expression was telling Alex that she wasn't lying. If she wanted to spy on him, she could have done a lot better at it and would most likely not bother trying to show up at his office while he was at work.

"If I weren't as confused as you are, I would find the irony in a reporter not knowing why she's here to be very amusing." He joked half-heartedly.

RISE OF THE PANTHERS

"A friend told me I should come to see you."

"A friend, huh? Well, that's interesting. Lanika did say for me to expect a visit from someone she is acquainted with, so I assume that's you. I wonder why she brought you to me?" All other thoughts stopped for Jasmine. Does he know Lanika? How? Well, it would make sense since Lanika was the one that told her to go see him, it shouldn't be a surprise that he knows her. But if that's the case, why didn't he know that she would come? During this whole conversation, Alex made it painfully obvious that he had no clue that she would arrive today, hell, she didn't give the chance to tell Lanika that she would even go and see the guy.

However, that's not the main issue. Knowing the group of people that Lanika is associated with, why would someone that's running for mayor be involved with an organization like The Panthers? Is this some kind of trap? It can't be, he even said so himself that he had no idea why she showed up at his doorstep, but he did say that Lanika told him that someone she knew was coming to him. Maybe he's lying. It's a possibility, but Jasmine is starting to believe otherwise. Alex may be a sarcastic asshole, but he's not giving her any vibes of being deceitful. Still, he's a politician, and it's in their blood to be manipulators.

"How do you know Lanika? What kind of relationship do you have with her? Did she mention my name at all? What connections do you have with The Panthers?!" Alex was taken back at the questions being fired at him but composed himself none the less.

"I see we've switched to full reporter mode. Since these aren't any political questions and I can assume that you're not recording me, I suppose I can humor you." Jasmine nodded her head. She never had any intention of recording anything about her visit here today.

"I met Lanika about three years ago during one of her community outreach events. Ever since we've kept in contact with each other. Nothing much of a relationship, just acquaintances and as I said, she only mentioned that someone she knew would see me. She didn't give a specific time, date, or name. And sorry, The Panthers? Who are they?" Jasmine studied his face carefully. It's true that her sister and Candidate Williams may know each other and Lanika didn't tell him anything about her or The Panthers, but something is telling her that's not the case.

His face isn't giving anything away either, so he doesn't know what she's talking about. Before she could question him some more, her phone rang, and when she looked at it, the caller was the director. What could he possibly want from her right now? It is sporadic for the director to call anyone. She looked up at Alex apologetically. He nodded his head, letting her know it was okay, and she stood up to answer her phone.

"Hello, Jasmine Jones speaking."

"Jasmine! Thank God! Remember the park where that kid died a few days ago?" Of course, she knows and didn't appreciate that Jerome was being referred to as "that kid" by the director.

"You mean Roger's Park?"

"Yeah, that one. Listen, you need to get there now!"

"But sir, I'm kind of in the middle of something right now."

"That can wait! Get to that park now!" Jasmine didn't get a chance to protest further before he hung up on her. Why now? Jasmine was sure that whatever the director was tripping about isn't all that serious. She was about to sit back down on the chair when the door burst open. Both of them turned and saw the same young woman that had escorted Jasmine to Alex. She had a panic look on her face.

"Sir, something terrible has happened in Rogers Park in Inglewood. The phones are going crazy. Ms. Knox is there right now and is requesting that you meet her there immediately." Alex stood up from his desk and took his blazer that was hanging on his chair.

"I do apologize Ms. Jones. It seems our conversation must be cut short."

"Well, if it's any consolation, that call was from my boss telling me to go to Rogers Park as well."

"Ah, well it's a date then." Jasmine rolled her eyes at his joke. She quickly made her way out of the building with Alex right behind her and both of them sped off to the park. However, as they got to the park, there was already a huge crowd that was surrounding the basketball court. Jasmine knew that the residences here set up a memorial for Jerome at the basketball court where he died. Did someone vandalize it? That would be terrible, but not nearly enough for the director to be calling her in such a dire manner.

They fought their way through the crowd only to stand shell shocked at the scene in front of them. Jasmine gasped as she held her hands to her mouth at the gruesome image of Officer Smith that was tied to the fence. He had cuts and bruises all over his body. His clothes were torn to shreds and she could see burn marks all over him. The most haunting thing was the symbol that was engraved on his chest. A paw was branded on the right side of his chest, and the words 'We will rise' was carved on his stomach. Just by looking at him, one knew it was too late. His eyes were still open, so you could see the terror he had as he died. Jasmine turned to see the disgusted look that Alex was showing.

"You wanted to know who The Panthers are? That's who they are."

Chapter

6

"The Panthers," Alex whispered to himself. "Just who are these people?"

"To be honest, I was hoping you would be able to tell me. I only know rumors that are being passed along in the streets. Some of them aren't good" Jasmine explained.

"Does this have to do with Lanika? is she one of them?!" Jasmine took a deep sigh.

"I'm not sure if she's a member or how deeply associated she is with them, but she's somehow involved with them. that's all I know."

"My God." Jasmine could tell by his shocked face that she won't be getting the answers that she wanted. It's more than possible now that Lanika is using Alex for whatever plans that The Panthers have. The director said that her team was here, but she didn't want to do any segment on this.

"First Officer Peeves, and now this. What in God's name is happening in this city?"

"Officer Peeves?" Jasmine asked, wondering why that name sounded so familiar to her.

"Yes. During Officer Smith's trial, there was a large gathering of people that came to protest. This protest turned into a confrontation with the LAPD. There was only one casualty, and that was an officer by the name Peeves." That brought back the memories of that horrible event to Jasmine. It's something that she could never forget.

Her reminiscence of that day brought an image back to her head, the person in all black with the golden paw Insignia. She has no substantial evidence, and Lanika didn't do anything that made her suspicion concrete, but somewhere deep down, her instincts are telling her that The Panthers are the reasons why it escalated to that point. Now they have another police officer dead. Is this some kind of hit?

"It seems that they already have a suspect in custody." Jasmine turned her head back to Alex. She remembered trying to get information from the hospital staff that mentioned it to her, but they wouldn't budge. Since then no one has heard anything about the apparent suspect, so it surprised her that Alex knew about it.

"Looks like you have better informants than I do."

"Knowledge is power."

"Well, does your knowledge have a name for this so-called cop killer?"

"From what I've been told, his name is Travis Miller."

"Interesting, do you have anything else on this Travis Miller?"

"Aren't we the curious ones?" He joked.

"As you said, knowledge is power."

"Using my own words against me, huh?" He asked, shaking his head in amusement. "The only thing I have is that he's currently being treated at the Ronald Reagan Center." *The Regan Center? That's not too far from here.* Jasmine mused to herself thinking that after this she could go and see this Travis for herself, but her train of thought was interrupted by loud sounds of sirens.

The LAPD has shown up and was preparing to break up the crowd so that they could get to Officer Smith. The people, however, we're not making it easy for them to enter by shouting at them. She could hear the words "child killer", "keep him up there", and "justice for Jerome" being thrown out as they refused to be moved. Jasmine was starting to have flashbacks from that day, and she didn't want to get stuck in another riot. Alex saw the pale look on Jasmine as she started backing away.

He realized that this could get dangerous extremely fast if someone doesn't try to defuse the situation. He saw that one of the officers was holding a microphone and trying to instruct everyone to depart from the park but was not making any progress as the crowd became more disorderly. He noticed that the LAPD was becoming tenser as if preparing for a confrontation. More than enough lives have been taken, and Alex refused to stand still and watch as this happens. He turned back to Jasmine and firmly grabbed her shoulders to calm her.

"Don't worry, I'll stop this." He promised as he went off into the crowd. Jasmine tried to stop him, but the words would not come out of her mouth and it was too late as he already dashed off. He pushed his way until he was face to face with the officer that had a microphone.

"Sir, you need to give me that." The officer glanced down at Alex.

"Get back! Unless you want to be apprehended for interfering you will back down and leave the premises." The officer warned him. Now, Alex looked back at the crowd and could see that their methods would not move these people. He knew if he doesn't do something, the situation will become very hazardous. Deciding that he had to take a risk, he went up to the opposite side and grabbed the microphone.

"Everyone, please calm down!" He yelled. At first, it didn't do anything, but some other people noticed that it wasn't a cop that was trying to talk to them, and soon the crowd started to calm down to see Alex. He surveyed over the people, silently thanking God that at least they're willing to listen to him.

"Like many of you today, this is not a scene that I imagined seeing here today at Rogers Park. I know that most of you feel that what had happened to Officer Smith is retribution for what he did to Jerome Washington. We must not drive ourselves to another scenario that would lead to more bloodshed.

Jerome has paid more than enough to see his people die at the same place where he has fallen. I plead to everyone here to go home back to your families, hold them tight, and keep them safe. That will be the best way to honor Jerome's memory. Do not let today be another reason to mourn. We must stay strong in times of adversity because that is when our true merit will shine. Division and chaos will not improve our environment. It is only when we are truly united that we can change for the better. For Jerome Washington and all of our lost brothers and sisters! We must unite and rise!"

He ended his speech by raising his fist in the air. This message was met with silence, then little by little, he could hear soft clapping. The sound soon spread as the crowd roared in applause. Alex could only feel relief as he was able to sway the people to calm down. He jerked though when he felt the microphone being snatched out of his hand. It was the same officer that he took it from, and he was glaring at Alex. The officer wanted to say something, but as he looked at the crowd, he decided not to bother and only shook his head as he left Alex. The rest of the officers followed his example and went off to get Officer Smith down and direct the people out of the park.

Alex stood still to see as the people beginning to disperse and saw Jasmine still standing at the same spot that he left her. Jasmine was amazed at how Alex was able to tame the people as she also took part in applauding him. The people were starting to clear, and she was able to have more space. Jasmine stared at Alex and any doubt she had in him at that moment melted away. Even if Lanika would be interested in him, this is a person that she can support. Someone for the people. Someone that this city needs.

"Jasmine!" She turned around when she heard someone shouting her mane to see her camera crew rushing towards her.

"Where were you guys? Didn't Mr. Stan tell y'all to meet me here?"

"We should ask you the same thing. We got here as soon as we could but by then that big ass mob was already here, and we couldn't get in closer!" They must have been on the outside and wasn't able to see Jasmine since she was right in the middle of it. She looked around the park and saw that other news stations were there talking to some people that were in the crowd.

"Did you get any good stuff?" Since that was their entire purpose of being here. The cameraman had a huge smile on his face.

"Oh, yeah! we got some great stuff and the whole speech."

"Good!" she said in approval. "Let's get all this stuff back to the office." Her crew went off to get back to their van. She followed them but stopped when she remembered that Alex was still there. She turned to see him talking to another woman. That must be Ms. Knox. Alex looked over and waved at Jasmine. She smiled and waved back before she turned and followed after her crew. Maybe she can revisit him on another day.

Ronald Regan Medical Center, Los Angeles, CA

3:30 PM

Travis watched as Candidate Alex Williams made his speech in Rogers Park. Before that, he saw the mangled body of Officer Smith that was tied up to the fence of the basketball court. Karma is one hell of a bitch. To die at the same spot where you killed someone, if that isn't some poetic justice, then Travis didn't know what it is.

The startling thing about Officer Smith's display was the marking on his body. The words 'we will rise' sent a chill down the soul. It was the same words that were in the invitation to that gathering and the same thing that Hope said in her speech. If the paw mark on his chest wasn't more proof, then Travis should have the staff here check on him for brain damage.

One thing is abundantly clear, The Panthers killed Officer Smith just like they murdered Peeves. Are they trying to kill every officer in the city? Or is this some kind of hit list? Hearing the door being open, Travis quickly changed the channel as the only physician that is willing to treat him, Dr. Quanisha Grant, walked into his room.

"Hey Dr. G." He greeted waving at her. She is the only one other than Kiana that would visit him and he came to appreciate the conversations that they had. Besides the physical therapy, there wasn't much to do around here, and it isn't like the staff lets him get out of the room. Kiana casually mentioned to him that they wanted him chained to the bed again. It's great to know he has some people on his side even if it's only two of them.

"Nice to see that you're in high spirits. How's your leg?"

"Not bad. Not much to do here since everyone thinks I'm a cold-blooded killer."

"You shouldn't mind them. Ignorance is a part of human nature. Unfortunately, it's not our strongest characteristic." Travis rolled his eyes. While he enjoys Dr. Grant's company, she has this tendency to talk like she's discussing the very fabric of the universe. It gets tiring at some point.

"How philosophical of you." He jabbed. Sarcasm was pouring out of his mouth like rain and Dr. Grant didn't seem to mind, in fact, she found his comment amusing as she laughed a bit. She came over to the front of his bed and looked over the medical files.

"How has your therapy been doing? Any good progress?

"You tell me, aren't you my doctor?"

"Yes, but I like my patients to tell me themselves."

"It kinda stuck, But I can say I prefer this place to where I was."

"I was informed about that unfortunate event. The people who were responsible will face punishment. Justice will find those who deserve it."

"I wish justice could tell me who they are, and then I can quicken the process for them."

"Yes, I'm sure," She said in amusement. "But I doubt it would make your rehabilitation faster. Focus on your healing."

"Hard to focus on that when you're facing life in prison. My trial is in two days." Travis didn't want to think about it, but the moment that he was readmitted to the hospital, his trial date had already been set. Since then, that was the only thing on his mind. Kiana has been coaching him on what to expect and what to say. If anything by the conversation that they had, Travis knew he was screwed, especially when Kiana told him about the Judge.

Judge Jessica Mathews is well known not to have high opinions of cases that involved African Americans, and there have been talks about favoritism, especially towards police. She was the judge in Officer Smith's trial as well as the other officers that killed Marcus, Linda, Nicole, and Trevon. Travis can already tell that this lady is going to gun for him so whatever Kiana is planning to do, it's going to have to be a miracle.

Kiana reassures him every time to trust her and that she won't let him go to prison, but with what they are up against, he can't help but feel pessimistic. Dr. Grant noticed how quiet Travis was and saw how stressed he looked.

"Stay strong, young warrior." She comforted him as she placed her hand on his shoulder. He nodded his head giving his thanks and she smiled at him before leaving his room. The next day, Kiana came in again to discuss the procedures that Travis will be going through for the trial the following day.

"Remember, as soon as you set foot in there. They're already going to label you as guilty. No matter what they say, you can't let your emotions run wild. It'll be the end for us if you do that. Remain calm and don't bite into their bait." This is the third time that they have been running through everything that is going to happen. For Travis, this was more tiring than his actual physical therapy. The court has deemed that he had enough time to rehabilitate. At first, they tried to have the trial as soon as possible, but once Kiana pointed out what happened between him and Capt. Clyde, they reluctantly backed off.

"Travis!" Kiana snapped. Travis quickly looked up at her angry face. Well, he couldn't help it! They went over this again and again till it got to the point where he could recite it by heart. Besides, what's the point if the judge has a bleeding heart for cops? He's screwed either way! Kiana must've read his mind as she sighed and dropped her annoyed expression to one who is concerned.

"I know that the odds are against us and that you think this is pointless cause you're bound to lose. But that's exactly why you have to fight! Don't just sit there and let them make a monster out of you! We will fight this and win. Believe in yourself and believe in me, ok?" Travis tried to digest the words that Kiana said to him.

He wants to have faith, but it's hard to believe that when the system is out trying to destroy you without giving you a chance to fight. Still, Kiana is right, and he can't let them win. He won't go to jail over something that he didn't do. He looked back at Kiana with newfound determination and let her know that he hasn't given up. Kiana smiled that she was able to get through to him, suddenly she jumped up.

"Oh, I almost forgot. Since I figured you don't have anything to wear tomorrow, I got you something." She said as she got a bag out and handed it to him. Travis looked inside to find a suit. While the gift touched him, there was something about it that made him curious as he took the cloths out and looked at the tags.

"So, how exactly do you know my size?"

"A girl has her ways." She said playfully.

"That's creepy as hell."

"I'm your lawyer. It's my job to know everything about you."

"Does that include spying on your client's body?"

"If need be," Travis rolled his eyes at her answer. "Now get some rest; you're going to need it." Kiana said as her parting words and left his room. The rest of the day was spent watching TV and the occasional visit from Dr. Grant. Tomorrow, he'll be fighting for his life, his freedom, and his innocence. No one there will be there to help him except for Kiana. Everyone else is the enemy.

The day finally came, and he woke up to flowers and a card that said good luck. He thought that it was Dr. Grant, she is the only one in the hospital that would talk to him, but she denied sending them. He knew it wasn't Kiana, so that left Hope as the primary suspect. Or maybe even Janaye? But that would be wishful thinking, but who else would give him flowers and a card? He got dressed in the suit that Kiana had given him and waited as she entered his room and smiled in approval.

"It looks good on you."

"Um... Thanks." Travis said awkwardly. Kiana saw the flowers in the note on the table.

"Aren't these lovely! Who sent them to you?" Travis looked at her. If Hope was the one that sent them to him, Kiana should've known.

"I figured that Hope did. Thought you would have known that."

"I highly doubt Hope sent these."

"What makes you say so?"

"She left the country a few days ago." That fact didn't necessarily surprise him since her company is located in the UK. But if the flowers weren't from her then it could have only been that Janaye sent them! That means she somehow knows that he's in the hospital, which also means that she has to be somewhere in the city.

"Well, you can figure out your secret boo thang later. You, my friend, have a trial to beat. Are you ready?" Even though he knew that this day would come, in his heart, he wasn't ready for what is about to happen. Unfortunately, life doesn't allow you to adjust to the next challenge fully, so he swallowed his fear.

"Yeah, Let's do this." The drive to the courthouse was painstakingly slow for Travis. His heart pounded louder in his chest as they got closer. Kiana saw the state that Travis was in and hoped that he could keep his composure, or he'll be ripped apart. When they arrived at the courthouse, they were greeted by photographers, news reporters and pissed off protesters.

Travis could see various placards saying, 'cop killer', 'protect our streets', 'death penalty', and all sorts of signs basically telling him to go to hell. The moment he got out of the car he was bombarded with reporters trying to talk to him, Kiana reached over to grab his shoulder and directed him to keep walking. Passing through the crowd, he couldn't decipher from all the starting, but he could guess what they were saying.

They entered the courtroom and sat down on the bench. The prosecutor came in after them and gave Kiana a smug smirk before sitting on the other side. The courtroom was a buzz of noise that it was distracting Travis from concentrating. He has to be on his A-game. Everyone in the room began to quiet down as the bailiff approached the middle of the room.

"All rise!" He said with a booming authority. Everyone rose from their seats as the judge made her way to her bench. Travis prepared himself for the most crucial battle that he's about to face. He won't back down. He won't lose. He'll show everyone here that he's not a killer. He's going to give everything he has to win, and hopefully, that'll be enough.

Chapter

7

Judge Matthews gracefully entered the courtroom and observed her surroundings. She took a seat and went over the files that were on her desk. Looking through the case, she looked up at Travis and narrowed her eyes at him. When Travis made eye contact, the glare that she was giving him was more than enough to tell him that he was already on edge. Kiana gave him reassuring looks, but the pressure that was directed at him was making it hard for him to calm down.

"Travis Miller, you are charged with second-degree voluntary manslaughter. Do you understand?"

"Yes, Your Honor." Luckily for him, Kiana drilled court etiquette to him during his time in the hospital.

"And how do you plead?"

"Not guilty, Your Honor."

"Very well." To everyone else, that may have sounded like a confirmation to Travis' answers, but he knew that the undertone of her statement was a dismissal; she doesn't believe a damn thing he said and already considers him guilty. Kiana was right; everyone here had judged him as the murderer before they even started. What kind of crap is that?

"The prosecution may make the first case."

"Thank you, Your Honor." Just hearing the sound of his voice pissed Travis off; the prosecutor was making his grand speech on how Travis had plotted to hide and use the riot that had happened during Officer Smith's trial to his advantage to assassinate Officer Peeves. Travis sat there in shock at the elaborate bullshit story that the prosecutor was presenting to the jury. To make it worse, they were eating up the man's word like a drunk guy devouring fries.

Travis couldn't believe what he was hearing. How can this guy that wasn't even there paint this lie to these people with such confidence? When he was done, Kiana got up to dispute every claim that the man made. She went on saying that though Travis was at the protest and was seen at the time when Officer Peeves was shot, that did not prove that he did anything. She explained to the jury that no weapon was found on Travis and that he was shot by the SWAT team before they apprehended him.

"I would like to call the forensic specialist that did the autopsy of Officer Peeves." The forensic walked up to the stand. The prosecutor sat silently mocking her when he figured she would call for the autopsy and that's why he made sure to get rid of every bit of the autopsy information. He even bribed the forensic doctor to play on his side.

"Dr. Roswell, can you explain to the court what your findings were on Officer Peeves' cause of death?"

"Of course. He was shot three times in the chest," He had a monitor to show the X-Ray of the body. "The resulting injury led Officer Peeves into a cardiac arrest. By examining the body, we can conclude that he died before he reached the hospital." *What the hell?!* Travis screamed in his head. He knew for a fact that the officer wasn't shot in the chest; he was shot in the back! Whoever this doctor took pictures of wasn't Officer Peeves. What are they trying to pull here?! Kiana looked at Dr. Roswell in suspicion.

"And are you certain that this information is accurate?"

"Of course! I am a professional!" Kiana walked back to the table and grabbed a folder. She walked up to the judge to hand her the document.

"Your honor, I would like to present to you the original autopsy report that was conducted by Dr. Quanisha Grant." Judge Matthews, at first, was going to dismiss it as she has never heard of this Dr. Grant, and Dr. Roswell is well respected in his field and has been called to perform autopsies of many murder cases. She respects his works.

"As you can see, Officer Peeves had the gunshot wounds on his back, so it propels me to question how did he receive any chest injury that led to his death? And let's not forget that during the time of the supposed autopsy done by Dr. Roswell, my client was already in the custody of the LAPD." The judge looked through the files and had to admit that the findings were accurate. She doesn't know how they were able to squeeze this Dr. Grant into performing an autopsy without the official proceedings since Dr. Roswell was already assigned to this case.

The judge also wondered how this fell into the hands of the defense attorney. She could have this as tampering with evidence, but considering the conflicting results, it will no doubt put confusion into the court. She couldn't outright refuse it, but at the same time, she didn't fully accept this.

"Can the defense provide this Dr. Grant so that she can give us her findings herself?"

"No, Your Honor. She is out of state at the present moment."

"Well," Judge Matthews said with a smirk. "It does seem that there is conflicting information in regard to the autopsy report. Since the defense cannot bring forth Dr. Grant until we are able to verify the truth, the jury will dismiss the autopsy report."

What?! Travis couldn't even speak. What the hell kind of backwater circus are they running here?! First, they lied about Officer Peeves getting shot in the front, and then when concrete evidence is presented right in front of their faces; the judge tells them to dismiss it. Travis has never in his life shot anyone, but right now, there's an individual in the room that he'll make an exception for.

"Is that all you have?" The judge asked impatiently. Kiana gave her a look that promised that there was definitely more she wanted to say to her but chose not to as she nodded her head.

"Yes, Your Honor." Kiana reluctantly said. Judge Matthews gave the prosecutor the signal for him to start.

"The prosecution calls Travis Miller to the stand." Kiana gave a questioning glare at him; however, looking at Travis' face of uncertainty, she focused her attention on him.

"Just as we practiced." She reminded him as she rubbed his back in comfort. Before the trial, she warned Travis that eventually he would be called up to the stand and if so that they would be asking very personal questions and will try to twist his words. She coached him to keep a level head and be collected no matter what they say to him or about him. He sat on the bench to have all eyes in the room on him. It was very unsettling for Travis to have all this attention focused on him. All of these eyes are staring at him, waiting for him to say something stupid and mess up.

"Travis Miller." He switched his attention back to the prosecutor. If at all possible, he would prefer to never talk to him, but Kiana told him that staying silent would not help him.

"Yeah, that's me. Otherwise, I wouldn't be here right now." Travis would have continued if it wasn't for the judge banging on the gravel.

"Young man! Mind your tongue!" She said sternly to him. Travis paid her no attention, but when he saw Kiana giving him the "behave or else" look, he sighed and turned his head back to the judge.

"Yes, Your Honor." Judge Matthews motioned for the prosecutor to continue.

"Thank you. Now, we have been talking about that dreadful day, but we have not given you the chance to tell us your side of it since you were there and all. Please enlighten everyone what transpired that day." Travis wondered what kind of trick this was. What point is there for him to tell his side of the story, considering that this jackass already made it obvious that he did it. God, he wishes that he can just grab the judge's mallet and knock the prosecutor the hell out. Travis controlled himself. He had to remember what Kiana said and not let his emotions run rapidly. Once he had calmed himself, he began retelling the events that took place on that day.

Everything from walking up to the courthouse in the crowd to getting shot by the SWAT. He didn't leave anything out, but still thought it was pointless. Still, even though the judge told the jury to overlook the evidence from the autopsy, he hoped that the fact that there were no other concrete findings that could point towards him being the killer would influence their opinion of his innocence. Also, the fact that the majority of the people in the jury box are minorities, he should have a fair shot here. He was honestly surprised when he saw them because

P a g e | **107**

he assumed, by who the judge was going to be, that the jury would be predominantly white.

"Thank you, Travis. Now can you tell us why you decided to go to the protest in the first place?" Travis prepared himself to answer the question. This is what Kiana has warned him about; the prosecutor is going to ask question after question and try to play his words together to confuse him.

"I saw what happened to Jerome Washington on the news, and when I learned that there was going to be a protest on the day of Officer Smith's trial, I decided to go myself."

"So why didn't you leave as soon as you noticed that there was going to be violence?"

"I didn't think it would have turned out that bad."

"You didn't think? It's well known that when you have a large group of people like that, it will turn violent." The prosecutor said, facing everyone else. Travis paused for a second. What the hell did he just say?

"Excuse me," The prosecutor turned back to Travis.
"Just what do you mean by people like that?"

"Order!" The judge demanded. "Young man, I will not have outbursts like that in my court."

"No!" Travis shouted, ignoring the judge as he stood up. "Tell me what you mean by that. You're saying that black people are just violent by nature?!"

"Order!" The judge yelled. "One more outburst and I'll see you removed in chains!" The prosecutor gave Travis a satisfied smirk. Damn, he played right into that bastard's hands.

"Thank you, Your Honor. Now correct me if I'm mistaken but the defense says that you were taken in without any kind of weapon on you."

"Yes." Travis confirmed. He had nothing except for his phone, keys, and wallet that day. He wondered how they were charging him with killing someone by shooting them when he didn't even have a gun on him at the time. It's not like they can just make one magically appear.

"Interesting," The prosecutor said as he went over to his bench and retrieved a bag. "Then tell me what this is." Travis was looking at a black pistol inside the bag, but it wasn't his. He doesn't even own a gun.

"A gun." He answered with a tone that said, are you stupid? However, there was something wrong with this picture. The prosecutor wouldn't bother with a trick like this unless he was sure about something. Looking closer, Travis thought that it looked exactly like the one that the real culprit used. That Panther person, but they were wearing gloves at the time, so it's not like there are any fingerprints on them if that's even the case.

"Thank you for clarifying," The prosecutor said. He pulled out a sheet of paper, showing it to the courtroom. "This is the weapon that was found at the scene of Officer Peeves' murder and has been verified as such. This right here, on the other hand, is the registration for this weapon. Can you please read the name in the register." He placed the paper in front of Travis.

Travis stared at the paper in front of him wondering what kind of game the man is trying to play until he saw the name on the register. *What the hell is this?!* These were the words that were racing in his mind as he saw his name on the registration paper claiming that he owned the weapon in the bag.

"Can you please read the name on a registration?" Travis looked at the prosecutor with so much hatred and if it wasn't for the fact that he was in the courtroom, he would have jumped across the bench and dropkicked him. How the hell did they get his name on a gun registration?! Why?!

"Travis Miller." He said quietly, trying to conceal his anger.

"I'm sorry, but can you repeat that?" Travis knew that the prosecutor was only trying to goad him, but how can he not get pissed off over this?

"Travis Miller!" He said louder.

"And is that your signature on the registration?"

"Yes." They even somehow copied his exact signature to perfection.

"And we also have fingerprints on the weapon verifying that it was in his possession at the time."

"What?!" Travis screamed, jumping off his seat. His patience is at its limit with these people and he's about three seconds from leaping off and tackling the prosecutor. The courtroom came alive as everyone was talking amongst themselves and Travis could hear some of them saying that he really killed Officer Peeves if the gun is his and has his fingerprints on it. How and when did they even get his fingerprints?

"Order in the court!" Judge Matthews bellowed. "Young man I have warned you about out bursting here, but I will let it slide this last time. I believe for the sake of everyone here; I will administer a five-minute recess." She finished her decision by banging on the gravel. Travis was led off the stool and followed Kiana out of the courtroom. They went into a small room and by looking at Kiana, he knew he screwed up.

"What was that?" She said exasperated. "All that time we spent prepping and you just throw it all out the window."

"What the hell was I supposed to do?!" Travis fired back.
"Just let him say all that?! You know that gun isn't mine!"

"Do you want to go to jail for the rest of your life?"

"Of course not! Who wants to go to prison?"

"Then you need to calm down and answer me right now.
Did you tell me everything that happened that day?"

"Yes, I did!"

"You didn't leave anything out?"

"What? No, why would I?"

"That registration and that gun aren't yours?"

"No! Why the hell are you asking me this?! You're my lawyer, aren't you?!"

"Calm down Travis. I'm asking this because now they're going to use this against you, and it'll be damn near impossible to convince them otherwise. The fact that you were caught right at the scene and that the weapon used is in your name with your fingerprints is more than enough to indict you."

"So, there's nothing I can do?" He said as he leaned against the wall. "That's it? What was all that crap you said about fighting and not letting them win, was that just bullshit too?"

"We will figure something out." She promised him, but before Travis could retort to her declaration, the door opened to reveal the prosecutor. The response was immediate as Travis bounced off the wall to rush at him but was stopped by Kiana.

"Travis stop!" She yelled as she was able to push him back.

"Sit down!" she ordered. Travis stood glaring at the prosecutor, not moving an inch.

"Travis, sit down now!" Travis continued to stare at the man until he reluctantly turned his attention to Kiana's face telling him to do as she said. With a loud grunt of frustration, he kicked the chair over and walked back to his original spot to lean on with his back facing the other two in the room.

"I guess that's as good as I'm going to get." Kiana murmured to herself.

"Well, well. You need to do better to control these clients of yours Kiana. So violent." Travis snapped his body around, staring angrily at the prosecutor.

"I'll show you violent, ass-hat!" Travis promised as he got off the wall.

"Travis!" Kiana yelled as she went in between them, prompting him to go back to the wall. At first, Travis stood there but grumbled as he slowly walked back. Sighing in relief, Kiana focused her attention back to the other problem in the room.

"What do you want?" She demanded.

"I came across and heard your little pep talk and while I would love nothing more than to crush you in the courtroom. In fact, I have more than enough to do so, but this dance that we've been doing for the past couple of years is beginning to be a pain in the ass. So, I came here with an offer that I'm sure you won't refuse. Instead of life, you'll only get thirty years." Thirty years?! To Travis, that might as well be a life sentence. If he agreed to this, then he won't be out until his fifties. Travis questioned if this man really thought that he's going to accept going to prison for thirty years happily. And what did he mean by "dance" with Kiana? By the sound of it, they have a history together. Travis turned to see Kiana; he knew the look on her face meant that she was considering it.

"You can't be serious?" He pleaded.

"Look, Travis, we don't have anything to disprove that you don't own that gun and you were the only one that was seen together with Officer Peeves when the SWAT found you."

"I didn't kill him!" Travis screamed. "You know that! You know who did!" The prosecutor had an excited look on his face when he heard Travis but decided to keep that little piece of information for later.

"While this is amusing," He butted in. "We don't have much time. This is your only offer." Kiana stared deeply into Travis's eyes.

"Travis, this may be your only way out."

"It's for thirty years!"

"I know, but it's either that or life and never get out. Do you want to spend the rest of your life in prison?"

"No," Travis said quietly, looking to the ground.

"Then, please, trust me," Kiana begged. "Do you trust me?" Travis looked back at her. How could he trust her if she's letting him take thirty years? But still, if it's that or life, then he really doesn't have many options.

"Yes, I do." Kiana nodded her head in approval and turned back to the prosecutor.

"Fifteen years." She negotiated.

"What?" He said, taking a step back in surprise. "You are in no position to bargain here. I'm already more than generous with my offer."

"You take fifteen or I'll bring up the fact you hid and conspired to fabricate forensic evidence in this case with that doctor of yours."

"That's some bold accusations, but you have nothing." He said confidently. She smirked and handed him a folder that was in her bag. He took out the contents inside and his eyes widen in shock as he read what the documentation entailed. He quickly schooled his face while narrowing his eyes at Kiana.

"Fine, fifteen. However, this will be our last one against each other." He said. Kiana nodded, agreeing to his terms and he responded the same as he walked off. Travis slid down onto the floor, covering his face with his hands. Fifteen years. He just agreed to spend fifteen years in jail over something he didn't do. In hindsight, it's better than thirty or life, but still that fifteen years! Where's the justice in that? Kiana knelt to be at an eye to eye level with him.

"I'm so sorry," She whispered. "I know, but this is the best outcome. I'll make sure that they won't put you in some God-forsaken hellhole like the Twin Towers." She promised, but Travis tuned her out. He just accepted to going to prison, how is he supposed to respond to anything now? His life is ruined and it's all those damned Panthers' faults! They're the reason why he's in this situation, and now he'll never know what happened to Janaye or even see her again. The time for recess ended as everyone went back to their seats.

"I believe the defense has accepted an offer from the prosecution." Judge Matthews said looking at Kiana, who was about to confirm her statement but was cut off by the prosecutor.

"Your Honor, there's no need," He said, confusing everyone in the room. "I have just gotten a confession from Travis Miller." The courtroom shot up in shock and disbelief. Travis didn't fully comprehend what just happened or what everyone was saying. He heard the word confession, but who confessed? He noticed that the prosecutor took out a recorder from a folder. The folder looked familiar to Travis, like the one that Kiana gave to him earlier.

"Will the court please listen." He played the recording and it was exactly as he said it was. Travis recognized his voice in the recording, but he didn't confess to anything! The recording sounded wrong to him, as parts of it were cut off and edited because the words sounded like the exact ones he used when he was talking to Kiana in the room. However, it was the last part that finally broke Travis.

"Do you admit that you killed Officer Peeves?" That was the voice of the prosecutor in the recording.

"Yes. I do." Travis knew that was the voice of him in the recording was when Kiana asked if he trusted her. How is this even possible?! How could the prosecutor make something so elaborate if he wasn't even there the whole time that he and Kiana were together to record anything? Unless he didn't. There was only one other person in the room with Travis and that was…

"I believe we have heard enough," Judge Matthews concluded. "I don't think that the jury needs any more time to make a verdict, do you?" She asked, looking at the jury expectantly. One of them stood up.

"No, your honor, it is unanimous. We find the defendant, Travis Miller, guilty of second-degree voluntary manslaughter."

"Very well. Travis Miller, I hereby sentence you to life imprisonment with no possibility for parole to be served at the Twin Towers Correctional Facility." Travis could only stare in horror. The Twin Towers Correctional Facility, or better known as the Twin Towers, is known as one of the worst prisons in the state. How could this happen to him? He looked at the jury wondering why they would do this to him; they should have been on his side or at least given him a fighting chance.

While he was staring at the one that stood up and sat back down, he noticed something that he didn't see at first. The person was wearing a golden necklace and hanging from it was a small golden paw. A golden paw? Travis immediately turned his head at a woman who was sitting behind them and saw that she was wearing golden earrings that were in the shape of paws too. Then he turned to another person that was on the other end of the jury bench and had a tattoo on his neck. The tattoo was a paw mark.

Something's not right. None of this is correct! Travis couldn't believe this. They're Panthers... all of them! At that moment, he knew that all of this was set up. They were all in on this! He played right into their hands like a damn puppet from the very beginning! He paused for a moment and remembered that there was one more Panther in the room.

The one that was sent to him and saved him when he was getting beaten by those cops and made him believe that she was on his side and trust her. The only person who could have had recorded his voice like that. He turned to that same person that he genuinely thought was his only ally and showed all of his weakness to, staring at him with a straight face. That face told him everything he needed to know.

"You bitch." He growled.

"I'm sorry Travis," Kiana whispered. "For us to rise, some must fall. This is the part you must play."

"You BITCH!" He screamed as he thrust his fists on the table. Kiana got up and backed away from Travis as he was prepared to jump at her.

"Guards! Get him out of my court!" Judge Matthews ordered. Two officers came in and restrained Travis before he was able to follow up on his actions. They cuffed Travis and started dragging him away from the courtroom.

"I trusted you!" Travis yelled as he was taken away. "I trusted you!"

Chapter

8

London, United Kingdom; 6:25 AM

Waking up, Hope stretched out in her bed and walked out to the balcony of the penthouse that she's currently taking resident in. A beautiful place right in the heart of London. She always loved getting up early to catch the sunrise as it touches the London Bridge, illuminating the sleeping city. Dealing with dignitaries and other distinguished guests from all over the world made sure that she never stayed in one spot for long, but she was fine with it and liked to be on the move even if Black Diamond's headquarters is here. However, the Cheval Three Quays in London is one of her favorite places to stay.

She sat in a chair and overlooked the image in front of her while reminiscing over the events that took place during her visit to the United States. It's been years since she last set foot there and honestly, it didn't really give her any nostalgia. It's still the same hypocritical place as it has always been.

If it were up to her, she wouldn't have bothered to step a single foot on that land, but she had a mission to complete. Speaking of missions, Hope had gotten a notice that Kiana should be wrapping up part of hers soon. It's only a matter of time now. The die has been cast and there's no stopping what's coming, thinking about it sent shivers down her spine. The time of hiding is about to come to an end.

Hope took out a cigarette, lit it, and took a deep inhale before expelling it to the chilly morning air. She can't believe that it's finally here. Every plan and hardship they had to endure is all leading to this moment, and they're almost ready to begin. She looked at her phone to see that it was 6:45, just in time for sunrise. Hope looked over the horizon as the sun appeared.

Today will be their last annual meeting. After today, there will be no going back. Heading back to her room, she got dressed and called for her chauffeur to be ready to pick her up.

As she walked out of the building, she was greeted by her chauffeur that was driving a black Rolls-Royce Phantom.

"Good morning, ma'am." Her chauffer said as part of his daily greeting.

"Morning, Jefferson. Thank you for coming to get me." She replied as she got in the back seat. Driving through the city made Hope remember the struggle that she and Black Diamond had to endure when they were chased out of America and took refuge here in the U.K. It took grueling years of hard work to pick up the pieces that they had to leave behind in order to establish the powerhouse shipping company that it is today. Years of pain, heartache, blood, tears, and today will mark that their sacrifices were not in vain. The light that she and the others seek is almost in their grasp. They will obtain their Eden.

She arrived at the headquarters of Black Diamond. Walking through the main lobby area, she was greeted by the vast employees that she passed by. She would smile and give them a warm reply. She may be one of the CEOs, but that doesn't mean she's so heartless to just ignore the people that helped make this company rise to power over the years.

Their hard work and loyalty paved the way for Black Diamond to grow and dominate the shipping industry. She would be a fool not to acknowledge them. She continued walking to the elevator and was met by her personal aid. A short woman, who sometimes can be a little dense, but was a great manager. Hope was never one for administration, so it was a great relief for her to have her current aid that was a master at it.

"Good morning, ma'am." The aid greeted cheerfully.

"Good morning Clair." After being acknowledged, Clair immediately went over the items that Hope has to go over for the rest of the week. From documents to meetings with investors and other business partners. They reached the top floor which contained the offices of the two CEOs and the office of the founder and chairman of the company, Lucas Turner. Hope walked to the door that leads to Lucas' office. It was time. Before entering she stopped and faced Clair.

"Clair, I have an important meeting with the chairman. Hold all of my other appointments until I am done."

"Yes ma'am, and when should I expect you to be available?"

"Not sure Clair. This might take more than a minute."

"Then I shall reschedule all of your appointments for today." That was why Hope hired her. She was able to adapt to new situations easily.

"Thank you, Clair." She said as she pressed her thumb on a panel next to the door. The panel scanned her thumb for a few seconds and another screen appeared where she entered a code. The screen disappeared as the panel glowed green and the doors opened. Hope walked in to see Lucas standing behind his desk, overlooking over the city, with his back facing her. The room itself composed of a long conference table that can comfortably seat sixteen people in the middle. A huge crystal chandelier hangs over the table that lights up as the sun rises and encompasses the whole office like mini stars.

"Hope. It's good to see you." He greeted while he kept his back facing her. It was no surprise to him that it was her since she's the only other person besides him that has access to this office. The panel on his door is one of the most sophisticated finger index scanners in the world. It traces every single detail including the heat signature of the index as to keep it in a file and use it as a reference in case if someone had obtained either of their prints, they would not pass the heat signature test. If the scanner finds a single fault, it shuts off all the rooms on the floor, including the elevator, and traps the individual until security arrives.

"It's good to see you as well as, Chairperson." Lucas turned around to face her and made an annoyed face when she called him that.

"Don't call me that. Honestly, it should be you who should be Chairperson, not me. You made this company what it is."

"Yes, but you are the one who founded this company. So, deal with it, Chairperson." Hope laughed at him. She always found it amusing to annoy Lucas. He just shook his head, knowing she was trying to rile him up for fun.

"Anyway, how was your time back in The States? Worthwhile, I hope?" She rolled her eyes at his attempt to be funny by using her name in a pun.

"Well, it wasn't as I expected. Still, I fulfilled my role. Meeting Travis was interesting, though." Lucas looked at her in interest.

"Oh, and how was he?"

"A bit of a smartass, but interesting, nonetheless. I believe he'll do just fine."

"Wow, that's something, if it's coming from you."

"What can I say?" She shrugged. "He's got my attention."

"Let's pray that attention doesn't get him killed." Before she could respond with a rebuttal, Lucas' watch started going off.

"It's time." He said. All jokes were put to rest, and both of them prepared themselves. Lucas flipped a switch under his desk and a long screen appeared that screeched to cover the entire length of the windows. There was an extra lock that was placed on the door and both the table and chandelier disappeared. The screen that covered the windows split into eleven sections. One of the screens lit up to show a young woman in glasses. She had light brown hair that was braided and put into a bun on top of her head and wore a green sweater with a golden pin on her right chest in the shape of a paw.

"Erica, it's nice to see you." Hope greeted the young woman.

"Hey, guys. It's been a while, huh?" She responded brightly. Lucas nodded his head and waved back at her. Another screen lit up to reveal Lanika.

"Lanika!" Erica exclaimed excitedly. "Hey, girl it's been so long."

"I know," Lanika responded calmly. "And thanks for letting me use The Ark."

"Oh, no problem."

"Speaking of," Lucas chose to interrupt. "What reason did you have to use The Ark for? It must have been something important." He questioned Lanika.

"My reasons and mine alone." Lucas shook his head at her answer.

"Lanika, The Ark isn't a toy for you to play with. Just because Erica has a soft spot for you doesn't mean you can abuse her inventions for your personal whims."

"Shut up Lucas! Nobody asked for your opinion, you overrated taxi driver."

"It's nice to see everyone is as lively as usual." Three more screens lit up. Lucas and Hope turned to the one that spoke out. It was an older gentleman that was in a U.S. Naval blue-uniform. Though one would wonder what someone in the armed forces would be doing in this particular meeting, looking at his uniform, you can see the distinctive three stars showing his status as a top official in the United States Navy.

"Admiral Lamar. A pleasure, as always, to see you." Lucas chose to greet him, completely ignoring Lanika.

"And it's good to see you and everyone else." The other screens that appeared revealed Dr. Quanisha Grant and Kiana Summers.

"Just as I thought, Lanika and Lucas are always arguing. Y'all might as well stop pretending and get engage already." Kiana joked. It is well known within the small group that Lanika and Lucas never got along with each other and would bicker between themselves every time they would see each other. While their antics are a source of entertainment for the rest of the group, Hope found their childish arguments to be more than annoying. Unfortunately, nothing she does or say will stop them, so she just lets them go after each other's throats.

"Shut it, Kiana!" Lanika fired back. Hope ignored Kiana teasing Lanika and noticed that the remaining screens were still blank. Two of them she knew was not going to come on because they had no means of this kind of communication where they were at, but the others should be available. This meeting was well communicated to everyone, and everyone was notified well ahead so as not to have anyone absent, especially since this will be their last one before they begin.

"Where are the others?" Hope questioned. All other conversations ceased.

"They will not be able to join us today." A new voice popped up. It was a very distinctive deep voice that they all immediately recognize. They all stood straight and placed their right fist over the left side of their chests. An image of a man appeared in an all-black suit, and though he had a relatively young face, his eyes bore of that of a war veteran that has seen real horrors of this world. A scar can be seen that stretches from the top of his right eyebrow down to the left side of his nose. Another feature that was very distinctive was that a portion of his right ear was missing as if it was bitten off.

"Sir." Hope heard Admiral Lamar greet the man.

"Everyone. It is good to see you all again." The man responded. Everyone broke off from their salute and went back to a relaxed state.

"The honor is all ours sir," Lucas spoke up. "But it seems that we are missing a few attendees."

"Yes, they are off completing their missions and as such, they will not be able to be here with us today." The man answered Lucas.

"Of course, sir. Forgive me." Lucas apologized.

"Kiana," The man addressed, turning his attention to her. "Has the message been sent to our two incarcerated friends?"

"Yes sir! Both "Blue King"' and "Red Devil" will be receiving your message soon."

"Good," The man nodded in approval. "Dr. Grant, are the serums prepared?"

"Yes."

"Excellent. Your patients will be arriving soon, be prepared when they do." Dr. Grant nodded her head. The serums that the man spoke of have been something that Dr. Grant has spent her whole life researching on and has finally completed in the past few months. One of them is a disease that she had worked on as a new strain. One that is resistant to penicillin and antibiotics. A true monster in the making, but not her masterpiece.

The other is her crown jewel that she has spent absolutely no expense to complete, a drug that was only to be believed in theory and science fiction. It's a drug that puts the subject in a trance-like state and attacks the nervous system. It goes after the connecting points between the neurons and the cortex that contains the user's memories and forcefully brings them out.

The trance-like state is the result of the drug that releases a chemical in the body that makes the subject only focus and is stimulated by the sound of a particular pitch, a pitch that only Dr. Grant knows, and that forces them to speak when asked a question. In other words, a truth serum. The only known truth serum in existence.

"Erica, is The Ark ready?"

"Of course!" She said proudly. "Thanks to the cooperation of Prime Minister Ivanov, those idiots still believe that it's a Russian satellite."

"Make preparations to have it in full operation."

"Finally!" She shouted in excitement. "It's time to show what my baby can do."

"We are drawing close, my friends. The time for us to come out of the shadows is near."

"We will follow you even to the depths of hell, Sir." Lucas proclaimed.

"Be prepared, my disciples. For the voice that can't be heard, for the justice that is never seen and for the truth that is not spoken. We are here."

"We will rise!" Everyone finished as they saluted the man.

"Lucas, Hope, prepare to have the forces move out. It's time for you to return home permanently."

"As you command." Lucas responded.

"As you wish, brother." Hope said firmly. The man nodded his head.

"You know your assignments. Failure is not an option." Everyone knows what will happen if they were to fail in their missions. "It's time to start with operation Hunter."

West Hollywood, CA; 10:47 PM

It was a chilly night in the secluded residential neighborhood of Judge Jessica Mathews, who tiredly entered her home. The past few days were extremely tiring for her, especially having to deal with the Travis Miller case. It didn't matter to her that the upstart lawyer Kiana Summers that had been making record winnings of cases for felonies was on the defense. She already knew that Travis was guilty and even when presented with proof, the prosecutor decided to go for a bargain, which took some convincing on his part for her to agree. However, he made a deal for her that she couldn't refuse.

Who would have thought that he would have gotten a confession? She knew though that it was either forced or fabricated. It didn't matter to her since she wanted that murderer locked up and out of her city. It's like these people were bred for only violence, especially towards the police that risk their lives to protect the people.

She vowed that she would toss every single one of them in prison. However, after the trial, some people have been calling her a racist who would only do cases where it involved sending black people to jail. She doesn't care what those people say. She knows where the criminals are and it's her job to protect the rest of the populous from their filth.

She did her usual rituals before going to bed. Because right now, that's what she needs, a comfortable bed to take the stress away. She might not even go to the courthouse tomorrow, depending on how she feels. She got in her bed and made herself comfortable so that the sleepy bliss could take her away. Her quiet night, however, was interrupted as she felt a hand covering her mouth. She popped her eyes open to see a shadow looming over her. She tried to move but found herself somehow restrained on the bed.

"The Panthers send their regards." She heard the shadow whisper to her. *Oh God!* she panicked. Who is this? Why are they targeting her? Why is this happening to her?! She didn't do anything wrong! She fought for the peace of this city to make sure nothing like this happens. She could tell by the sound of the person's voice that it was a male and from the accent, it sounded like one of those hoodlums in South Los Angeles.

This is why she couldn't defend these people. They're all nothing but a bunch of murderers, rapists, and drug dealers. They all need to be eradicated before they infest the city with their poison! And just who the hell are The Panthers? Her fear was only made worse as she felt the barrel of a gun resting on her forehead. Uncontrollable tears fell down her face. No, not to her! She doesn't want to die, not like this!

"For the light of the revolution." Those were the last words that Judge Matthews heard as the figure pulled the trigger, ending her life. The figure pulled back as he looked at her dead body.

"Is it done?" Came a female voice from across the room. He turned to face his partner.

"Yeah. We should hurry up and get this done." The weapon the man used was a silencer, so there were no worries of being immediately discovered, but still being on the side of caution propelled him to get the job done as soon as possible. He moved into the living room where multiple barrels of gasoline waited for him.

"Let's finish this quickly." He said as they covered the entire residence in gasoline. They saved the bedroom for last and made sure that the body was covered from head to toe. Once finished, the man took a lighter, lit it, and tossed it on the bed. The room was immediately ablaze with fire. The two assailants quickly made their escape as the entire house caught on fire.

Since it was late at night, there wasn't an immediate response. About thirty minutes passed until someone saw the burning home and called the fire department. By the time they came, the house was starting to fall apart due to the fiery flames. The firefighters, paramedics, and police showed up to try to stop the fire. Residences in the neighborhood that recognized whose house it was cried out in horror.

The two individuals hid in the shadows as the firemen tried to save the judge and put out the fire. Unfortunately for them, they won't be saving anyone in there. Both of them stood in silence until the man felt a buzz in his pocket. He took out his phone to see an unknown number was calling him.

"Hello?" The man answered. "Yes. We were able to take the documents. They won't find anything else there. I will spread the word to others. Operation Hunter is in full effect."

Chapter

9

Twin Towers Correctional Center, Los Angeles, CA

2:30 PM

Travis sat in his cell, staring at the wall. It's been about a week since he was sentenced to life in prison for the murder of Officer Peeves. The death of a person that he didn't kill. Hell, Travis was more than positive that the officer would have shot him instead, and no one would have batted an eyelash over it. Well, none of that matters now. Nothing matters now. Ever since he came here, the only thing on his mind was Kiana and how she betrayed him.

Travis laughed at himself for being a fool to trust her when she popped up out of nowhere while he was interrogated at the police station. He just had to let her pretty words reach out to him to give him hope. He now realizes that everything was planned from the moment he decided to go to that little party. The second that he caught Hope's attention, he was already a sacrificial pawn to their game.

But the only thing that he couldn't find an answer to was why go through all that trouble just to send him to prison? He doesn't know these people and hasn't done anything to provoke them. He's just an orphan; no parents, no family, and no friends. So, what is it that The Panthers want from him? Well, he can't precisely say no friends, there's Janaye, his best friend. The only person that pulled him out of his lonely solitude life when he first met her in middle school. She was the only one to approach him and talk to him.

The only friend he made. She even welcomed him to her home and her family has treated him like he was one of them. He can never repay their kindness and vowed that he would do everything in his power to protect Janaye.

What good is that promise now? He got played like a damn marionette. He knew that when he read that invitation at Janaye's house that she was involved with something dangerous and that chasing after her would put him right in the middle of it. However, he never thought that she would be involved with an organization that kills people. He hopes that wherever she is somewhere safe and that these people won't force her to attack anyone.

After they dragged him away from the courthouse, he was transported immediately to the Twin Towers. Everything in his possession was taken from him. Going through the process, he could feel the hatred from all of the guards. Apparently, word spreads fast in this city. He didn't have any time to be adjusted to his new environment as the guards manhandled him the entire time.

They put him in an isolated room to change into the customary uniform for inmates. As he was changing, three of the guards decided to "initiate" him by beating the shit out of him. Once they had their thrill, they left him on the ground and told him to change quickly.

He noticed when he looked around that there weren't any cameras or anything and figured that it's where the guards would normally take the prisoners for their initiation that they just displayed to Travis. When the guards came in, they roughly grabbed him and shoved him to walk through the cells. The other inmates heard of what Travis did and was calling out "pig killer" as he walked by. Travis stayed silent throughout the whole ordeal up until they pushed him into his cell. Even now, about a week later, Travis hasn't said anything to anyone, inmate, or guard.

The guards like to harass him to get a reaction, but he never uttered a word. It seems that not giving them any reaction to their pestering pissed them off more as they always tried harder to goad him. His silence had some effect, though, as it unnerved some guards and inmates to make them believe that he's either retarded or crazy. Most of the inmates call him a mute and leave him alone. Others took a liking to give him the nickname 'silent P.K', for silent pig killer, or 'P.K'. He didn't care; they can call him whatever and do whatever they want. He's powerless and stuck in this hell hole. What's the point of fighting back? A bang on his cell disrupted his self-pity.

"Hey, you!" One of the guards addressed him. "Get up!" Travis looked at the guard for a few seconds then went back to staring at the wall.

"You're going to ignore me, you damn mute?" The guard growled. He entered the cell and took out an extendable baton. He raised his arm and struck Travis to the ground.

"You listen when I tell you to do something!" He yelled as he repeatedly stomped on Travis. Travis didn't bother to fight back or protest against the guard's treatment, as it stands, there was no point doing so. The guard grabbed him by the arm and dragged Travis out of his cell.

"Now, walk!" The guard ordered as he shoved Travis forward. Travis stumbled from the force but found his balance and started walking down the hall. When Travis first arrived at the Twin Towers, he didn't eat or willingly move out of his cell; he preferred to stay there for as long as he could. It came to the point where they had to send in someone to forcefully retrieve him and make sure he got out and eat at least one meal. It wouldn't look good if people found out that he died there because they were being negligent.

It's not like Travis is forcing himself not to eat, but he just couldn't hold anything in his stomach at the time. Even looking at the food made the bile in his stomach wanting to come back up his throat. Now, though his appetite has got better, they still send in someone to get him to make sure he eats. He walked into the eating area and found an empty table in the back corner.

Considering how overcrowded this place is, he counted himself lucky. If all the tables were occupied, he wouldn't bother sitting anywhere and would just stand eating his food and continue standing, not moving until it was time to go back. Making his way to the empty table, he sat with his back facing everyone else, trying to block out the noise.

"Hey P.K." Came a greeting that interrupted Travis' peace. He looked in front of him and saw an inmate that he met on his first day here. He introduced himself as Devante, and even though Travis never responded to him, he took it upon himself to always sit next to Travis every day. Travis thought that after the first three days of not receiving anything verbally, Devante would lose interest and leave him alone, but apparently not, since he continued to be with him.

A stubborn bastard, but Travis would be lying to himself if he said that he didn't appreciate the company of another person. Travis nodded his head at Devante. Even though he won't talk doesn't mean that he wouldn't at least acknowledge Devante. Travis gives the other man credit for sticking around to constantly talk to a so-called mute.

"Still not saying anything, huh?" Devante asked as he started eating. "You know being mute isn't gonna help you here. Most just think you're retarded and some of these freaks here prefer the silent type, so I would be careful." One needs not to be a genius to understand what he meant by that. Travis had heard more than his share of horror stories of prison, especially what goes down in the Twin Towers. So far, nobody has tried to come on to him like that, but for how long? Travis and Devante sat in relative peace until a group of men surrounded both of them.

"Hey, Pig Killer, get up, someone wants to talk to you." One of them demanded. Devante looked at Travis in confusion and was about to get up.

"You sit your ass back down!" One of the other men shouted in such a way that quickly made Devante obey him. All of them were huge as hell, and Travis was more than positive that only one of them was needed to kick both his and Devante's asses at the same time. Having these many people surround them was a bit overkill. Travis decided to get up and hoped that whatever they wanted from him would be quick and painless.

As Travis walked, he noticed the distinctive groups that separated themselves in different areas. The two most prominent groups were The Bloods and The Crips. They sat across from each other. Devante told him about the feud that they had here in the Twin Towers and were not to cross since that could be seen as an act of aggression. It's astounding to Travis how this is supposed to be a maximum-security facility and the inmates can still have gang paraphernalia. Passing by, all Travis could see were red and blue flags, in fact, now that he thought about it, the group of guys that were escorting him all had blue flags.

They arrived at a table where only one man was sitting and was surrounded by other Crips. When Travis looked at the individual, he immediately recognized the man.

Benjamin Jackson, or better known as "Blue King" Ben, the boss of all the Crips on the West Coast. When he was out in the streets, no one knew his real name or what he looked like. The only thing that people had was that alias and the authorities only had information that his main base of operation was located in the heart of Los Angeles. A couple of years ago, the LAPD got tipped off about a drug smuggling deal and was able to bust it before the exchange. During their investigation, they somehow got the information that one of the suspects that were in custody was, in fact, the notorious Blue King.

For unknown reasons, he was transferred to the Twin Towers and not somewhere outside the state since he was the leader of one of the most infamous gangs in the country. When Ben reached the Twin Towers, he immediately established his rule within the facilities, even though at the time, the prison was filled with more Bloods than Crips.

He made everyone; even the guards understand who was on top and has not been challenged. Ben studied Travis as he was brought before him. He looked closely at Travis' face and though he looked like a lifeless doll, Ben could see a different story in his eyes.

"Sit!" One of Ben's men ordered. Travis sat in front of Ben and put his head down, thinking it wouldn't go well for him to unintentionally disrespect the leader of The Crips, especially when the said man's entire entourage is surrounding him.

"So, you're the pig killer, huh?" Ben started off. Travis looked up as he was being addressed but didn't answer. Before he knew it, the back of his neck was grabbed by one of his men.

"He asked you a fucking question! Unless you want your tongue ripped out, I will find whatever voice is in there and you will answer." The man threatened. The few seconds that Travis took to consider speaking up was apparently too long as his head was slammed on the table. He felt a hand reach into his mouth and took out his tongue. Travis shivered as the man pulled out a small switchblade and knew that he was serious about cutting his tongue off.

"Enough!" Came out the commanding voice of Ben. The man stopped and backed off from Travis. Travis slowly sat back up, shifting his eyes fearfully back and forth to see if anyone else was going to attack him.

"Calm down. No one's gonna come at you," Ben reassured. "I only wanted to confirm something. That's all." Travis gave Ben a questioning glance.

"Confirm what?" Travis whispered when he finally found his voice. What could he possibly want to confirm from Travis about? Him killing Officer Peeves? Seeing as he runs The Crips, something like that shouldn't be anything special.

"They said that they would send someone here at a certain time to me as the signal. I thought those Panthers were bullshitting me but seeing you here confirms that it's finally starting, I'm convinced our long wait is about to be over, boys!" Ben roared as the others around them lit up in excitement. Travis tuned out everyone the moment he heard Ben said The Panthers.

Them again! Just what the hell are they planning? Ben said that they told him that they would send them a signal. Was it supposed to be him? Is that why those bastards set him up to rot in prison? To be a fucking errand boy?! Lost in his thoughts, Travis almost forgot the last part that Ben said. Their long wait was about to be over, and that something is starting.

"What is starting?" Travis couldn't but ask. Ben looked at him with a confident smirk.

"Operation Hunter."

Downtown, Los Angeles, CA; 2:30 PM

Within the walls of City Hall, one can hear shouts coming from the office of the man who is the head and Chief Executive Officer of the city, Jonathan Lambright, the mayor of the city of Los Angeles. He paced behind his desk as an older gentleman sat and patiently waited for him to calm down.

"Five!" Jonathan yelled as he slammed a folder on the desk. Five photos came out. The older man looked over the desk to see the image of Judge Jessica Mathews, Dr. Roswell, Capt. Clyde, Officer Woods, and two other young women.

"Five people, dead in a week! How could this happen? Not only did we lose Judge Matthews, but you also lost two of your men, Commissioner." The elder man Jonathan was conversing with is the commissioner of the LAPD force, Stuart Greenfield.

Recent events after the death of Officer Peeves have been hectic for Commissioner Greenfield as the mayor has been calling his office nonstop. Though it irritates him that the main reason for him being here was just to hear the mayor bitch and complain, however, the man had a good reason to be concerned. Not only are two of his officers dead, but a judge as well. The city won't stay quiet about this.

"Mr. Lambright, I understand your concerns."

"Do you now?" Jonathan fired back sarcastically. Commissioner Greenfield decided not to answer the man. However, his patience is starting to wear thin and he might slip and say something condescending.

"Believe when I say that my best man is handling this." He tried to reassure the other man.

"I don't doubt your men, Commissioner, but with the state of things, they're going to need more support in this. That's why I called in for a favor." That caught the commissioner's interest.

"A favor, Sir?"

"From New York. I was able to pull some strings to have someone come here that may know what exactly we're dealing with. Ah, here he is." Commissioner Greenfield stood up as a young man walked into the office.

"Commissioner, this is NYPD detective William Pope." Both men greeted each other as they sat down.

"Detective Pope, I've just been told that you may have answers to what is happening in the city. I take it you've already read the files that were sent over before coming." While the commissioner didn't like the idea of having any outsiders strolling into his jurisdiction, dealing with the mayor is a bigger pain in the ass. He'll entertain this for now, but if this guy proves to be useless, then he'll ship him back to New York. He has enough trigger-happy idiots here in L.A. and doesn't need another one to add to the mix that needs to be babysat.

"Yes, in fact, that's why I agreed to come here. This reminds me of a similar case that I was working on a couple of years ago. I believe the suspects, in that case, maybe the same one here."

"The same one?" The commissioner asked. "You mean to tell us that whoever is doing this here was out in New York killing people? Is this a serial killer we're dealing with here?"

"You misunderstood me. I never said it was just one person. I believe, no, in fact, I know what we're dealing with is not a person but an organization. Tell me gentlemen have either of you heard of a group known as The Panthers?"

Chapter

10

"Pardon me?" Jonathan asked. Both men gave Detective Pope a confusing glance. They've never heard of a group that went by that name.

"Apparently not," Detective Pope whispered to himself. "It was a name that I first came across in passing about two years ago when I was doing an undercover investigation."

"And you believe that these Panthers are responsible for these deaths?"

"Yes, I do."

"What makes you so certain?" challenged Commissioner Greenfield. "I've never heard of them."

"There have been numerous disappearances and deaths that have been happening in New York and each time I heard that name being passed along. When I learned that five people died here in the span of a week, something told me to look further into it, and when I saw who they were, I knew it couldn't have been a coincidence."

"So, this gang that you have been chasing in New York has somehow crawled their way over here?"

"No, I don't think that they're your usual thugs. The whole time during my investigations, I have only been able to find out two things. Their names and that they're affiliated with a corporation that you should be familiar with, Black Diamond Shipping Industry." That was a name both the commissioner and Jonathan had heard of, especially after the scandal that forced them to flee the country. Last Jonathan has heard about them was that they took refuge somewhere in the U.K. The company's asylum was all over headlines for weeks, but soon, they faded out and were able to reconstruct the company to be a powerhouse all over Europe.

If what detective Pope suspicion about this group is correct, then he would be right. Having the backing of a corporation like that, with the money and resources that they could utilize, then these people are defiantly more of a threat than some gang. Even more now if they are responsible for these deaths. The only thing that stifles Jonathan was that even if this organization was operating in hiding, why hasn't he heard anything about them? He should have at least heard their name.

Jonathan prided himself on being able to have the vast connections that he has. From politicians to school officials, and even have some with various organizations that the public would deem unethical, though that piece of information is a well-guarded secret. In all of his years in office, he has not even once come across a mention of these people. That fact alone sent a shiver down his spine. If they were this discreet, that even he could not take notice of their presence, then what else are they capable of? And is this only the beginning? He feared the answers to those questions but feared more that these people are unknown to him.

If this is the case, then Jonathan concluded that he needed to find every last piece of information about this group. Where did they come from? Who is leading them? What are their capabilities? Where are they hiding? And most importantly, what are they after? Jonathan prayed that detective Pope is as good as he was advertised, for the sake of his re-election.

"Detective, I hope you will be able to work with the LAPD on this matter. Whether or not it is these Panthers that we are dealing with, we will require all of your cooperation, for the peace of this city. I look forward to good results, gentlemen."

"Of course." Detective Pope responded as he got up. He took that as being dismissed and nodded a farewell at the Commissioner as he walked out of the office. Walking out of the building, he pondered on how the victims were connected. This wasn't just a random pick in the slot, and he knew from experience that The Panthers don't do mindless murders. They kill for a reason. He has been keeping up with their trail ever since he came across their name while he was doing an investigation back in New York a few years ago.

The victims at that time were similar to the ones here. A judge, lawyer, and police officers and they all died in a week as well. During his investigation, he couldn't find a thing at first. After months of undercover work and searching, he was finally able to obtain one piece of information, A name; The Panthers. Soon after, an anonymous informant tipped him off that they are a group that prioritizes the welfare of African Americans. It made him curious; most groups that focus on the lives of black people are usually very vocal about it. These people, on the other hand, are making it very clear that they don't want to be seen or known.

That same informant mentioned that they might have connections with a shipping company called Black Diamond. He was suspicious about the timing of the information; it was too convenient. However, when he looked up the company and what happened to them, he realized that if it was true, then they could be a dangerous entity. A secret organization, with the backing of a multibillion-dollar company, is not a good sign, especially if they are in the business of murder.

Now, the same thing happened here and only a fool would say that it is a mere coincidence. That's the whole reason why he agreed to come to Los Angeles. His instincts are telling him it's them and for some reason, they decided to come all the way to the other side of the country, but why? What are they after? And why kill these people? None of it made any sense. There are too many questions and not enough answers. He fears that when he finds those answers, more people will die.

There was another thing that puzzled him. Out of the victims, two of them were nurses. How exactly do they fit in this pattern? Looking at their files, both of them worked at the Ronald Reagan Medical Center. Other than that, they were both ordinary civilians, but he knew that there was more to it than that. He decided that the first thing he should do is to head down to the medical center and talk to the staff that worked closely with the nurses. Hopefully, he'll be able to find a connection.

When he entered the building, he immediately went to the front desk and asked if there was anyone that last saw the nurses the night before they died. Luckily, he was provided with the name of three physicians that each nurse worked closely with Dr. Michael Stone, Dr. Sara Waters, and Dr. Quanisha Grant. He searched the entire hospital but was disappointed when he learned that Dr. Stone was out of the country visiting family, and Dr. Waters was on vacation. That left him with Dr. Grant and fortunately, he was told that she was in her office. He made a beeline straight to her.

Quanisha sat in her office, waiting patiently for her guest to arrive. She had predicted that once they started Operation Hunter, that the mayor would request external help. They prepared to make sure that the person the mayor sent over was the one that The Panthers needed. Quanisha never doubted the tactics or their leader and as planned, that person came and all she has to do was wait for him to come to her. There was no surprise on her features as she saw the detective enter through her door.

"Dr. Quanisha Grant, I presume?" He questioned as he walked in.

"You would be correct in your assumption seeing that my name is outside the door. I wasn't expecting any visitors today."

"I apologize for barging in, but I'm detective William Pope from NYPD." He introduced himself as he pulled out his badge.

"All the way from New York? What brings you to the other side of the country?" He answered her by placing two photos on her desk. When she inspected it, she recognized the two as the nurses that worked in the hospital. Specifically, these were the nurses that first took care of Travis Miller when he first came to the hospital after getting shot by the SWAT team. They were also the ones that worked with those two officers to forge documents that allowed them to take Travis into custody in the first place.

Of course, all of these were pre-planned. Conniving with the ambulance team to make sure that they were at the courthouse before the riot was child's play. As soon as Travis was admitted to the center, she made sure that those two nurses would be the ones to care for him. Both have family in law enforcement, so she knew they would have great resentment for someone who was a suspect for killing a cop.

Quanisha casually shared that information about Travis to one of her colleagues who had an interest in one of the nurses and would have only taken mere seconds for him to pass it to her. It was easy enough to bait Capt. Clyde when one operative made an anonymous call that Travis was being treated in the Reagan Medical Center. Everything went according to plan to make sure Kiana was able to meet Travis, and now he's exactly where he should be. After that, those nurses served their purpose, and well, as they say, loose ends need to be cut. It wasn't anything personal.

"Do you recognize these two?" He asked her. "I was told that they worked closely with you."

"That's correct. Not too long ago, I heard that they were treating a patient that had a shot wound from that riot that happened on the day of the trial of Officer Smith." Detective Pope saw footage of what happened that day. It amazed him that during all that chaos, only one person died. If he remembered correctly, it was a police officer that died. In fact, the reports said he was murdered during the whole ordeal and that the SWAT team had apprehended the one who did it but injured the individual.

"By any chance, was that person involved with the death of Officer Peeves that died on that day?"

"He was actually the prime suspect that was taken in and was sent here because he was injured during his capture. I believe his name is

Travis Miller. He only stayed in our care for about a day then somehow was discharged and was put in the LAPD's custody. Then the most curious thing happened; he came back the day after." Detective Pope pondered on the information that was given to him. He was slowly putting the pieces together. Capt. Clyde and Officer Woods had taken a leave of absence for un-procedural interrogation of a suspect before their deaths, and it seems that they collaborated with these two nurses to obtain Travis.

The judge that foresaw Travis' trial was Judge Matthews. They were all connected and in the center is Travis Miller. He could be the key to all of this and if he's lucky, this will give him a clue about The Panthers. Detective Pope is certain that they're responsible for all of this.

"Would you know where I can find Travis? Where is he being held at?" Detective Pope figured since he was treated here, she may know where he can find him.

"From what I have heard, he was sentenced to the Twin Towers Correctional Center."

"The Twin Towers, huh?" He's heard rumors about that place. Many know how overpopulated they are with inmates and how short-staffed they are. Threats of prison riots are a norm over there, definitely not somewhere you want to work or get sent to. However, if Travis is there, he has to go.

"Thank you for your time, Dr. Grant."

"My pleasure, Detective, I hope I was able to provide you with what you needed."

"Yes. You were of great help." He gave her a slight nod in appreciation and exited her office. He knew where he needed to go, The Twin Towers Correctional Center. It wasn't hard to find the place, considering how tall the building was. He took note of the beaten down exterior and could only summarize that the interior was most likely just as bad in shape.

Walking inside, he found that his assumption was correct. He was told that this place had seen better days but thought that those rumors were exaggerated. Looking around, it was absolutely filthy, and it seems that no one cared in the slightest. He went to the front desk to see if he could speak with Travis, but they were not helpful at all. He can now see how those rumors were stirred; not only the building itself but the correctional officers here are trash too.

Luckily, the assistant warden, Captain Burns, came to assist him. Detective Pope showed his credentials and informed him that he needed to speak with Travis Miller. He was curious when Capt. Burns told him that someone was already here visiting Travis and was escorted to a waiting area. When Capt. Burns came back out, a woman was behind him. She was wearing a red suit with a black jacket. Her head was covered in curls like a lion's mane. She strolled behind him when she looked up to catch Detective staring at her and raised her eyebrow.

"Good afternoon ma'am. I am detective William Pope from NYPD." He took the initiative to introduce himself and pulled his hand out.

"NYPD?" she asked curiously while shaking his hand. "Jasmine Jones. If I may ask detective, what brings you all the way to California?"

"A case that I've been working on brought me here. I'm trying to gather as much information as I can, starting with the person that you just talked to."

"Travis Miller?"

"Correct. Are you perhaps, family?"

"Oh, no. I'm just checking on him."

"And now it's my turn to ask if I may. What kind of relationship do you share with Travis then?" Jasmine looked at him in suspicion. In L.A., a cop asking more than one question is never a good thing.

"If you must know, there is none. In fact, this was my first time talking to him. I hope you find what you're looking for." She said as her parting words as she walked away. Detective Pope stood and watched as she went away. There's more than what she led onto; that was obvious. For some reason, he had a feeling that she wasn't lying to him, but there was something hidden in what she said. Or better yet, what she didn't say.

"Detective Pope," He turned around to face Capt. Burns. "The room is ready for you."

"Captain, who was that woman?"

"She's a local news reporter. She's actually well known around the area."

"A reporter, huh?" One wouldn't look too much into it; a reporter trying to talk to a convicted murderer for a story, but he had a feeling that that wasn't the case. The fact that he didn't see any kind of recordings or folders on her. She wasn't carrying anything, so that leaves the question of what was she doing in one's mind? He couldn't just ignore that and if he lets her go now, he may come to regret it.

"Actually Captain, there's something else I need to look into first. I'm sorry, I'll have to come back at a later date. Sorry for the inconvenience." He apologized as he ran out in the same direction as Jasmine exited. He hoped that he could catch up with her. Travis can wait since he's not going anywhere. His instincts are telling him that what Jasmine is hiding is something important. When he exited the building, he caught a glance at Jasmine entering into a vehicle with another person at the driver's seat. Before they drove off, he was able to catch the image of the person that was driving.

He recognized the face from the billboards and signs he saw on his way to The Twin Towers. It was Alex Williams, a candidate for the upcoming mayoral elections. What kind of relationship do they have, and how are they related to Travis?

Chapter

11

Jasmine exited The Twin Tower Correctional Center after running into Detective Pope. She wondered why a cop from New York would come here, but from what he implied, he's here for Travis. Speaking of which reminds her why she went to that place to see him.

That day when she played that footage in the office, she was told that somebody died during the riot, but didn't know that it was a murder until she heard that there was a suspect in custody. She then later found out that the suspect was the same young man that she saw at the courthouse that day. She couldn't believe it; the kid was dead frozen when all of the craziness happened.

She couldn't believe that he could just go and kill someone. Jasmine's thoughts went back to her sister and The Panthers. She knew that they were working behind the scenes of that event. That whole protest was their doing; they organized it. What if the entire thing was just a ruse? But why kill a police officer?

Travis could have been an innocent bystander that was, unfortunately, at the wrong place, at the wrong time or he could be one of them. If he is one of them, that means he could give her a clue to what The Panthers are after. All of these are only speculations, but she has to know, and Travis is possibly the only one that can give her the answers that she needs.

It wasn't difficult to find out where he was being held after his trial. The only thing she wasn't expecting though was a surprise visit from Alex. The man just arrived right in her office and offered to take her out for lunch. She was wary at first, thinking this was going to be some campaign propaganda or trying to enlist her for information on other candidates. However, she didn't get that vibe from him. She told Alex about needing to go to The Twin Towers to talk to an inmate that was being held there.

Surprisingly enough, the man actually offered to drive her there and didn't ask any further questions, but she knew he was curious about it. She was able to easily set up a visitation without prior reservation. Usually, prisons wouldn't do any popup visits, but the guard was more than cooperative. He led her to a private room and asked her to wait for him to bring Travis in.

Jasmine was nervous as she inspected the room; it looked like an interrogation room. It had a simple desk with two chairs and no windows. She guessed there would be a camera of some sort in there, but she didn't see any when she sat down in one of the chairs, she only had to wait for a couple of minutes for the guard to bring him in.

She felt so bad for Travis when she saw the guard manhandling him in the room. He looked so confused and terrified. It was like watching a frightened animal that was caught by the hunter. The moment Travis sat down, and the guard left, his entire demeanor changed. Gone was the scared child. The switch-up completely caught Jasmine off guard that she forgot what she was going to say.

Once she put herself together, she tried introducing herself but was cut short by Travis when he said that he knew who she was. The conversation continued as Jasmine explained why she came to see him and that she wanted to hear his side of what happened between him and Officer Peeves. Jasmine observed that he was on edge. He didn't trust her as he kept quiet the entire time she spoke. She hoped that if Travis can recollect what happened in his own words, that she might be able to find something. At first, Travis asked her why she wanted to know and of what use would it be.

She didn't want to divulge her true purpose to him since he might be part of the same organization that Lanika belonged to. She thought of different things that she could say that wouldn't reveal her true intentions, but in the end, if she wanted to obtain the information that she needed, then she had to take that chance. Jasmine told him that when she saw him at the courthouse when everything first began, she didn't believe that he would do something like killing someone.

The moment she asked him about The Panthers, all color drained from his face. He became infuriated and started accusing Jasmine as being one of "those bastards". It took a minute for Jasmine to be able to calm him down so he could listen to her. She explained that she wasn't a part of The Panthers, but that someone she is close to is and that she's trying to find and stop them.

Luckily, that did the trick as Travis began to open up to Jasmine little by little. He eventually told her everything that happened that day, and she could still tell by the tone of his voice that he didn't trust her, but at least, he let down his guard to tell her his story.

Everything that he said wasn't out of the norm until he got to the part where Officer Peeves confronted him. When he told her who killed him, she jumped up in shock. She knew it! They orchestrated the whole thing and framed Travis, but why? Travis went on to tell her about his time in the hospital and the trial and what his lawyer, Kiana, did. Jasmine had never heard of her, but she made sure to remember that name.

After Travis was done, she told him that she believed him and that she'll do anything she can to make sure that he gets out. He stopped her when she made her promise to say that it didn't matter anymore. She could see that he was already registered with his fate to be stuck behind bars. She couldn't believe that he would prefer to stay in prison for a crime that he didn't commit. Instead, he asked her that if she was going after The Panthers to look for his friend that disappeared, he could only provide a name, which wasn't much to go by, but the desperate look that he gave her made her promise him.

Jasmine truly felt pity for Travis. An innocent young man that was used as a sacrificial pawn. She then thought of Alex and grew worried.

Lanika was the one that first mentioned him, so that means that they have their eyes on him as well. She wondered if they are planning on using him as a sacrifice too?

Their time was up as the assistant warden came in to inform her that there was another person who needed to see Travis. She said her farewell to him, encouraging him to stay strong. When she exited the room, she was introduced to Detective Pope. She was, of course, curious about why he came here from New York, but then he started asking questions that were beginning to make her feel uncomfortable.

Relationship with Travis? That question made her wary. After everything that Travis told her, now a cop from the other side of the country is here to investigate. All of this has to do with The Panthers. She has to find Lanika and slap some sense into her before this grows out of control. She made her interaction with the detective brief and quickly made her way back outside where she finds herself right now, in the car with Alex.

"Did everything go well?" He asked as she got in the vehicle.

"Yeah. it was definitely worth the trip," She answered, as they drove off. "So, where are we going?"

"Don't worry, I know this great spot." Jasmine rolled her eyes as he answered her but didn't say where they were heading to. Alex parked on the street and Jasmine looked across to see that they arrived at Roscoe's House of Chicken and Waffles.

"Roscoe's?" She asked with a hint of surprise.

"What? You were expecting some five-star joint?"

"Shut up." She responded as she playfully pushed him out of the way and walked towards the restaurant. There was a long line at the door, which is what you would normally expect during the lunch rush hour. Jasmine didn't mind waiting, but as she was about to walk to the back of the line, to join the queue, Alex grabbed her hand and started heading towards the front.

"What are you doing?"

"Don't worry, I got this." When they got to the front, the host recognized Alex as she already had the menu and said that their table is ready. Jasmine raised her eyebrow. This place doesn't make reservations during the rush hour. Must be the perks of running for mayor. When they entered, many of the patrons saw Alex and greeted him as they passed by.

"Well, look at you, Mister Celebrity." She commented when they sat at the table.

Thankfully, the waiter quickly came because Jasmine was starving. They ordered their food and began talking about their day. She was sure that Alex will try to bring up what she spoke to Travis about, but he never said anything about it. For that, she was thankful because it was a subject that she didn't want to open up to him, not yet at least.

Besides, he's running for mayor, so right now, the less he knows about this, the better.

Their food came in and Jasmine couldn't have been more thankful, realizing how hungry she was. The time passed as Jasmine and Alex enjoyed each other's company. She gave a small smile as Alex went on telling a few stories from his childhood. She found it funny that Mr. Future Mayor wasn't as innocent as a kid as she pictured him to be.

Alex was more than happy when Jasmine accepted to go out to lunch with him because there was something about her that drew him closer. At first, it seemed that she was wary of him, but she later warmed up to him, and now he's able to see this other side of her. The way her eyes light up in amusement when she laughs at the stories he's sharing. Like a moth to a flame, he doesn't care if he gets burned. Their time together was put to a halt when Alex felt his phone vibrating. He saw that it was his assistant.

"Hello?" Alex answered when he picked up the call.

"Alex!" His assistant yelled out. "Thank God, where are you?!"

"Whoa, calm down. what's wrong?"

"I don't know how, but you need to get to the office now!"

"You're not making any sense. Why-"

"Alex just get here now!" She yelled and hung up. Jasmine looked up at Alex in concern.

"Is everything ok?"

"I don't know." He answered unsurely.

"What was it?"

"I don't know just that I have to go to the office." They quickly paid for their food and rushed to the building where his office was. When they arrived, Jasmine got out of the car and covered her mouth at the condition of the building. Practically all the windows were broken and there was trash everywhere.

Alex rushed inside with Jasmine running after him. The reception area was completely demolished, with broken glass littering the entire floor. Ignoring the elevator, Alex went straight towards the stairs and climbed up as fast as he could to his level. Once he came to his hall, he saw that the door leading to his office was ripped open. He walked to the door and froze at what he saw inside.

Jasmine finally catching up with him and watched as he stood still in front of the office and then slowly walked in. She wondered how bad the condition of his office could be for him to act like that. Considering how the rest of the building is faring, she had an idea of what it might look like. When she entered, she couldn't believe what she saw.

It was worse than she imagined. Broken chairs, desks, and glass everywhere. However, that wasn't the most alarming factor. All over the walls were drawings of swastikas and the word "NIGGER" in large bulking red letters. Jasmine couldn't comprehend why Alex's office, the whole building, was vandalized by Nazis! Where did they even come from? Why target Alex?

Speaking of Alex, she searched around to see where he could be and found him in his private office. She navigated her way, being careful not to step on glass or trip over the broken furniture. When she entered, she saw that everything was in tatters. The bookshelf was kicked down, and all the books were torn to shreds. The walls and desks were also covered in swastikas and other racial slurs.

Jasmine saw Alex standing in the middle of the room and she was worried as he has yet to move from his spot. She walked closer to see that his head was down and that he had something in his hands. Whatever it was, he was staring at it hard. Jasmine went around him to get a closer look at what he was staring at. When she was able to see it, she realized it was a picture, a picture of what looked like a young teen with a white bag over their head.

"Alex, what is this?" Now she was getting scared. What does that picture have to do with the people that vandalized his office? A few seconds passed by as Alex finally registered that Jasmine was in front of him and looked back at the picture.

"This is me. "

Chapter

12

It took close to an hour for the police to finally arrive. Jasmine and Alex sat on the sidewalk across the street as the LAPD taped everything off around the building. Jasmine later found out that the person that called him was his secretary. When she came to the building, the receptionist was outside, on the floor, severely beaten, so she took her to a nearby hospital which is why they didn't see either of them when they entered the building. Curious enough, no one else was inside the building.

Alex hasn't spoken another word and only stared at the picture in his hands. That picture unnerved Jasmine to no end. Just what the hell happened to him? She wanted to ask, but his pale face stopped her from saying anything. One of the officers came to question them, but it was Jasmine that did all the talking. After the officer left, they sat in silence. Finally, Jasmine had had enough.

"Alex, talk to me." He didn't respond. Frustrated Jasmine got up and snatched the photo from his hands.

"Alex!" She said forcefully. "What is this?!" Her sudden movement snapped him out of it. He looked up at her, then closed his eyes and took a deep breath.

"I was born in Alabama. My father was a superintendent in a school district that was mostly white. No surprise, a lot of people didn't like that a black person was in charge of their kid's education. He would always push for notions to help minorities, which didn't give him many friends. Many wanted him out of his job and some even threatened him, but he stood strong." Alex paused his story for a moment and took another deep breath.

"One day, I skipped school and was walking home. This van just showed up out of nowhere and three men came out and grabbed me. It happened so fast; I couldn't even scream or understand what was happening. They blindfolded me and tied me up. When I was able to see, I was in some basement. I don't know how long I was trapped down there, but it felt like days. They tortured me." He got up and took his shirt off. Jasmine gasped as his torso and back were littered with scars and burn marks.

"Those sick bastards taped the whole thing and took pictures. I don't even remember being rescued; at some point, I blacked out from the pain. I remember waking up on the same street that they took me from. They sent the video to my father and threatened to do worse to me if he didn't leave. After that, my father immediately resigned and took us as far away as he could. That eventually led us here, where I've stayed ever since." He finished his story as he covered himself up. Jasmine stood, trying to digest the dramatic tale that Alex shared with her. No wonder he was petrified when they were in his destroyed office. He was just reminded of a horrible childhood experience, but there was something missing.

"What does this have to do with what happened in your office?"

"The investigators never found out who took me, but they were able to pinpoint the location where I was being held. Inside, they found nothing but swastikas and neo-Nazi propaganda. Who would have thought that they would have followed me here too?" Jasmine still couldn't believe it. Neo-Nazis in L.A.? She shouldn't be so surprised, considering she heard rumors of several members of high society that is still a part of the Klu Klux Klan. It seems Los Angeles is a nesting field for white supremacists. Still, the fact that these kinds of groups exist scares her.

"What are you gonna do?"

"What can I do?" Jasmine narrowed her eyes at Alex. Why did he sound so defeated? His whole demeanor right now is of someone that's already given up. She might not have known Alex for long, but it was long enough to know that this isn't him. The Alex that she has gotten to know wouldn't have said something like that.

"What you're going to do is to get yourself together," She ordered, walking up to him. "You're not going to let these cowards control you like this! You have an election to win. The people here need you, Alex, get it together!"

"But-"

"No! It's just a building. You can go and find another place. What happened to you was in the past, they don't have power over you! If you lose your drive now, then they'll win, and I will never forgive you if you let that happen." He took a step back and thought over everything that Jasmine had said. She was right, what happened to him is in the past, he has to focus on the now and if he was to give in, then all of his work and sacrifice will be for nothing.

"You're right."

"You're damn right, I am. People are going to hear about this so what you need to do is show that this will not stop you. You know what? We'll do an interview and you can show the city that you're still standing as strong as ever."

"Thank you." He said with gratitude.

"Come on, let's go! We got work to do." Alex nodded his head as they went back to the car. He drove them back to the news station and dropped her off. Jasmine told him that she'll call him once she gets everything set up.

Word of what happened traveled fast because as soon as she entered, everyone swarmed her to get as much information as possible. Luckily, the director came in and saved her.

He brought her back to his office, she told him everything that she saw except for the picture. What Alex told her about what happened to him was extremely personal and she won't betray his trust. She brought the director up to speed with it and went on to mention her proposal to interview Alex which the director was more than excited and wouldn't pass up this opportunity.

He told Jasmine to make sure that Alex would be ready and that they could do it tomorrow morning. When she called Alex to inform him about the arrangement, he agreed to meet her at the station in the morning. She went back to her apartment that night and poured herself a glass of wine. She collapsed on the couch as all the energy from the hectic day was drained from her.

Collecting her thoughts over the events that transpired the past twenty-four hours, she couldn't help but compare Travis and Alex. Both of them were victims of a ruthless organization; the only difference is that she doesn't know The Panther's motives. At that moment, she put all of her thoughts about The Panthers aside. Right now, her focus should be on Alex, who in her opinion is the only person that can truly change this city for the better. This will be her first time being in the actual anchor room, so she needs to be on her A-game.

The following day approached faster than anyone could predict. Jasmine was in the female dressing room, looking over the notes she wrote the previous night. She went through those notes over and over again to make sure that she didn't sound stupid. She thanked God that the director gave her full control of the interview and she was going to use this opportunity to the fullest. She went over questions one last time until she heard a knock on the door.

"Jasmine," Her cameraman called her as he pulled his head inside. "Everything is set and ready. We're all waiting for you." Jasmine nodded in acknowledgment and calmed herself before she headed out. The moment she entered the room, all eyes were on her. She saw Alex sitting on the other side where they would do the interview and quickly made her way over to him.

"You ready?" She whispered to him.

"Yeah, more than ever." When everything was in place, the main cameraman held his fingers up in a countdown for the show to start. It went off as it usually did with three main anchors. This made her remember the time where she practically begged a director to give her a chance to be one of them when the position was open. He never gave her a chance, but she realized later that she rather be out where the people are and see the action firsthand.

She saw the second camera guy that was pointing at them was signaling them that their session was about to begin. She started doing a quick five-second breathing exercise as she prepared herself. Their camera guy did the same countdown as the first one. The moment when she saw the red lights on the camera, she knew it was their time.

Everything was proceeding without a hitch. She didn't mess up on her greeting and wasn't nervous. She asked questions and gave Alex enough time to respond to them while thinking of the next one. It was all going completely smooth, for which she thanked God. One of the questions that she asked was if he was suspecting that it could have been one of the other candidates.

That was the strategy that she was using. In the election, there are only six candidates, including the current mayor and Alex is the only African American that is running. There is one Latino, another that was Native American, the other three are white. She knows that if the people start to suspect those three of a possible hate crime, then it could help Alex in the long run. Is it a dirty tactic? Yes, but sometimes you can't always play fair. Alex played his part magnificently as he answered the question.

"I do not believe so. I trust in the integrity of all the candidates. I'm just happy that no one was seriously injured. However, these individuals will not deter me from fixing this city. I was insured by our police force that they will find them and bring them to justice. With this, I hope-" His speech was interrupted by the flickering of lights. Everyone in the room looked around nervously as the lights continued to switch from on to off. Then all the lights shut off, which caused some in the room to scream in shock.

"Jasmine, what's going on?" He whispered to her.

"I don't know." She replied nervously. She was about to say something else when another voice entered the building.

"I applaud your optimism, Candidate Williams, but I seriously doubt it." The voice spoke in a deep tone. The room was too dark for Jasmine to see where it was coming from. The light suddenly came back on and everyone froze. Surrounding them were people in black combat gear holding rifles. Jasmine looked around and counted at least fifteen of them. Most stood at the back while there was one behind the other three news anchors and behind each cameraman, a pistol aimed at the back of their heads. Jasmine was about to get up when she heard a voice behind her.

"Don't move! Stay seated!" She turned her head to find one of them suddenly behind her and Alex.

"Everyone remain calm." It was the voice again. Jasmine swerved back around to search the room to see who the owner of that voice was to see a tall man in a black suit at the front entrance. He had two others that were behind him and followed as he walked into the room.

"I promise you if you stay where you are, no harm will come to you. We are only here to deliver a message." Everyone held their breaths as the man talked. The director, unfortunately, decided to confront him.

"Who the hell are you!" His approach was stopped as he was shot in the leg. Collective screams could be heard as the director fell on the ground, moaning in pain.

"No one gave you permission to speak," Jasmine turned back to the man to see him holding the gun that shot the director. "I don't need anyone to talk. Just stay where you are." He motioned for two of his people to drag the director out of the room. Everyone was petrified, thinking of what is going to happen to them. Jasmine's fear increased as the man who shot the director started walking towards her and Alex. She gasped when she saw his full appearance as he got closer. His face had a huge scar that ran across one side to the other and part of his ear looked like it was bitten off. Her eyes followed his movements as he approached her from the side.

"Sister. May I borrow that chair?" It wasn't what he said that surprised her. It was the tone of his voice when he spoke to her. When he shot the director, he sounded so cold as if he was talking to an insect, but to her, it was completely different. His voice to her was gentle and warm, like a mother comforting a child. It took her completely off. She quickly brought herself back to reality and to the present situation she was in.

She slowly nodded her head as she got up from the chair. Alex sat still in anticipation. Jasmine looked back at Alex as the one that was initially behind them was escorting her away to the back of the room. The man who is now sitting in her chair watched as she was guided to the other side, then focused his attention back to Alex.

"There's no need to worry; she's in safer hands than you know. It's a pleasure to meet you, Brother Williams." He said as he stretched his hand out to Alex. Alex was too stunned to even form words, but he looked at the man in front of him and slowly shook his hand. No further words were exchanged between them, but it seemed that the man was satisfied enough with just a handshake. After he let go of Alex's hand, he turned around to face the camera.

"City of Los Angeles, I am Huey Carter. We are The Panthers." The cameraman moved around the room to show all the members that were present.

"There's no need to panic. There's no immediate threat to your safety like a bomb or mass shooting. We are here to give a message that I hope you take to heart. To my brothers and sisters, on behalf of The Panthers, I apologize. For years we have heard your cries in the shadows, as your children were taken from you by the same people who are supposed to protect you. We have witnessed as you were belittled and discriminated in the society that does not value your existence. We stood by as injustice was imposed on us by those who decide what justice is. No longer will we stay silent. My brothers and sisters, The Panthers are here. We will hear your voice. We will see your justice. We will tell your truth." The man now revealed as Huey got up from the chair and nodded at Alex before walking around the table to face the camera.

"And for those who stand in our way, there's no place for you to hide."

Chapter

13

The man, who identified himself as Huey, studied the terrified faces of all those that were in the room after he finished his speech. Everyone but two. Alex and Jasmine were the only ones that pushed their fear aside to pay attention to what Huey had just said. Both of them were startled, but for different reasons. For Alex, it was the fact that this man was crazy enough to bring a fully armed entourage just to deliver a speech, which sounded more like a rallying call.

Jasmine, on the other hand, was slowly realizing who this person was. She was looking at the man that's responsible for the change in her sister. Right in front of her is the person that will lead her to Lanika.

Satisfied with the impression that he left with, Huey turned back to Jasmine. He gave her a smirk and a slight nod before making his way out of the room. The soldiers in black followed him out of the door. Everyone continued to stay where they were, frozen in their fear. The room was blanketed in silence until someone finally snapped out of it and yelled out to find the director and called an ambulance. After that, everyone started springing into action.

While everyone was moving frantically, Alex and Jasmine didn't move a muscle. Both of them had the same thought in mind. What just happened? It was obvious that Huey and his entourage didn't care about being incognito since they just stormed into the building in broad daylight. What was that speech about? Both of them couldn't get over what Huey had said. Though he was addressing the whole city, it was clear that he was only talking to certain groups in parts of his message. There was also something else in it that he said... something dangerous.

Speaking of Huey, Jasmine couldn't help but notice how the soldiers that surrounded them acted when he showed up. It was very subtle, but she saw how they all stood straighter the moment he walked in. there's no doubt that he's their leader. His whole demeanor gave off one of authority. Even if that's not the case, it didn't matter to Jasmine; he is probably the only one that can lead her to Lanika.

With that thought, she knew that this would be her only chance, and she had to act now. She ran out of the room, exiting via the same door that Huey left. She rushed down the stairs and out to the main floor. Considering that the back entrance required a key and code to get in, she highly doubted that's where they left, which left her with the front entrance. It's incredible to think that they would have the balls to just stroll in through the front door like that. When she passed through the main floor, everyone that was there was tied up on the floor.

Well, that explains how they got in like they practically owned the place without anyone calling the cops. She chose to ignore them, seeing as none seemed to be injured. She's more than confident that the others will come and untie them. She ran outside to see five black vans and Huey as he was about to enter one of them.

"Wait!" She shouted. Huey stopped and looked at her.

"Ah, Sister Jones. A shame that our time together had to be short. Lanika told me much about you."

"Where is she?! What did you do to her?!"

"I didn't do anything. She saw the truth on her own. One day you will as well, and when that time comes, I'll be there waiting for you." Both of them turned their heads in the direction of where they could hear police sirens. Huey waved his hand to her and went inside the van and all five of them drove off. Jasmine stood and watched as eight police cars came into the vicinity.

Three of them drove off to where Huey and his group sped off to while the others stayed. All of the officers came out and swarmed the building, rushing past her. She didn't pay them any attention because of one individual that was standing across the street. It was the detective that she ran into yesterday when she visited Travis. He crossed the street and approached her.

"I heard everything," Jasmine held her breath. "I think it's time we talked."

"Jasmine!" She turned around to see Alex exiting the building. When he came out, he saw her and another person in front of her. He recognized Detective Pope as he saw him staring at Jasmine when he picked her up from the Twin Towers facility. It worried him at first, but he didn't say anything about it and now it came back to bite him in the ass. He immediately went up to Jasmine and put his arm around her shoulder.

"Is there something I can help you with?" Alex may have sounded polite, but Detective Pope could clearly hear the underlying hostility.

"There are things that I need to discuss with Ms. Jones. That's all I need to say as it doesn't concern you." Alex raised his eyebrow. What does a cop have to talk to Jasmine about? He also didn't like the fact that he was being dismissed. Whatever it is, if it concerns Jasmine, it's his business too. Looking at her, it was obvious that the last thing she wants to do is be anywhere near this man.

"Does it have to do with what happened here?"

"I'm not at liberty to say so."

"If it is, what does that have to do with Jasmine?"

"Again, that's none of your concern. Are you going to continue to be in my way? Because I can make this difficult for everyone." Alex didn't like the sound of that. The way he was dodging his questions implied that he's accusing Jasmine of something and is trying not to have others involved and the fact that he's here alone made Alex's suspicion more positive. He has a fairly good picture of what the detective is thinking, and it made him more guarded.

"You think she had something to do with this? That's crazy. Even if that's remotely true, you have no grounds to go on that can allow you to question her. But I get the feeling that you're the stubborn type and won't let this go. If she goes, then I go with her and after that, you leave her alone." Jasmine didn't want to talk to the detective but knew that Alex was right. She would constantly be pestered by him if she didn't. If she had to, then she would much rather have Alex by her side. Detective Pope was weighing his options. He could just say that she's a possible assailant and force her to come to the station. However, Alex isn't just an average citizen and has a political pool in the city. He could make things exceedingly difficult for the detective.

"I can agree with that. If both of you can follow me, please." Detective Pope waited for both of them to enter Alex's vehicle and drove off to the station. They reached the building and followed the detective inside. They passed a couple of desks and into a hallway where they entered a private room.

"I believe that there's no point beating around the bush," Detective Pope started, as he sat down. "What relationship do you have with that man?" Alex looked at Jasmine in confusion. That man? Was the detective referring to Huey?

"A relationship? This was the first time I saw him when he had all of us hostage."

"Don't bullshit me. I heard you yelling at him about someone that you obviously know that is involved with him. A Lanika if I'm correct."

"I don't know what you're talking about."

"Do you now? I found it strange how you were acting when we first met. It was like you were trying to leave as soon as possible before you said something that you didn't want to. After that, you got me interested and I found out you have a family member that lives here. A sister. Dr. Lanika Jones, a professor at UCA who recently resigned her position and after that just disappeared. It also came to my attention that one of her students disappeared not too long before she resigned and that you were the one that talked to the student's family."

"That student's name is Janaye, and it was only a segment I did so that her mother would have a chance to find her son. As for Lanika, we haven't talked in a while, so I don't know where she is or what she's doing."

"I know. It's been about thirteen years, hasn't it?" Jasmine's eyes popped open. How did he know about that? "Curious how two sisters that live in the same city for more than a decade had no form of contact with each other."

"And where would you get that speculation from?"

"Ms. Jones, please don't insult me. It's quite easy for me to obtain information like that. However, there has been none between you and your sister since both of you came to this city. I wondered what could have happened between both of you?"

"My relationship with my sister is none of your damn business and has nothing to do with what happened today."

"You're right. Unless whatever happened made her join a terrorist organization, an organization that is familiar to you. You know what they're up to and where they're hiding. I. Want. Answers!!!" Jasmine was about to fire back at the detective. He must have lost his mind if he thought he could yell at her like that. Before she could pop off, her phone started to vibrate. It was an unknown number, so she ignored it. She pressed the cancel button, but three seconds later, a text from the same number popped up, telling her to answer. The phone rang again, which she hesitated to answer. Alex saw her staring at her phone and became worried.

"Are you ok?" Detective Pope was getting more frustrated that he was being put on hold like this.

"Yeah, I...Um." She paused before accepting the call. She didn't hear anything at first, but then a voice came out that she didn't think she would have heard again.

"Put me on speaker." It was Lanika! Detective Pope curiously watched as Jasmine slowly placed the phone on the table. Is this some sort of joke? Or was there someone that wanted to talk to him?

"Detective Pope," Came out the voice of a woman, but he didn't recognize it. "I see that you have been taking care of my sister." Her sister? He looked up to Jasmine and realized that this was Lanika on the other end. He didn't think that she would actually call here. Is she an idiot or just absurdly overconfident? It doesn't matter because right now, he finally has something. All he needs to do is keep her on the line long enough, and once he receives the recording, he could use that to pinpoint where the call came from. It may not be a precise location, but a general one is better than none and he can work with that.

"I wouldn't bother trying to track the call. I promise you that it won't lead you anywhere." It looks like she was able to read his mind while not even being in the same room.

"Oh, and how are you so sure about that?" He challenged. He needs to keep her on the line for as long as possible.

"Do you really think I would call here and be put on speaker and not be confident that you have no chance in hell in finding me? But by all means, you're more than welcome to try."

"I will find you. Whatever The Panthers are doing, I will find out and all of you will never see the light of day for all the lives you've taken." He heard laughter coming from Lanika.

"We welcome your pursuit detective. Be assured, though, that nothing can stop this, and no one can put out the flame that we will ignite. Our time is on the rise and all will know what happened when you get in our way."

"What do you mean by that?"

"You will see soon enough." The phone hung up, leaving everyone in the room speechless. Jasmine couldn't think why Lanika would call her now of all times. All that just to provoke Detective Pope. The better question is, how did she know that she was with him? Is Lanika watching her? When? And for how long? That's not a good feeling to have. It's downright creepy.

Alex sat in confusion and Detective Pope was trying to collect everything that was exchanged between him and Lanika. He wondered why she would call him, knowing the risks. He assumed that Jasmine would have warned her about him, but the way that Lanika spoke was like someone that already won. She has no doubts about The Panthers' capabilities. What was more troubling is the last thing she said. He didn't need to imagine what would happen to the poor souls that get in their way. This has to stop before more people die.

"Detective," Alex spoke up for the first time. "Are we done here?" Honestly, Detective Pope got more from the brief conversation with Lanika than he has ever gotten from anyone else. Everything he needs is on the phone right in front of him.

"For now." Alex and Jasmine got up from their seats. When she tried to reach for her phone, it was quickly snatched away.

"I'm afraid that I will have to confiscate this. It is now a piece of important evidence of a possible terrorist organization. You have my word that I will not go through anything personal only at the recording and I will return it back to you." Jasmine couldn't believe what she was hearing. Could he really just take her phone like that? She felt Alex's hand on her shoulder and saw him shake his head. It would be more troubling to fight him over something that he had a legit cause on, so she reluctantly let Alex guide her out of the building.

East Los Angeles, CA; 6:34 PM

Lanika stood in an abandoned building, staring at her phone. She wished she could have said more, but she had to follow the plan and do her part. She put the phone in her pocket and sighed as she observed her surroundings. Of all places to hide, she wondered why it had to be in this sketchy place. Five others were guarding the room that she was in. It was Huey's policy; no one stays alone. His paranoia sometimes grates on her nerve, but she understood his reasoning. Still, she hated being always guarded and not having any personal space.

She left the room and entered the hallway. The hall was filled with soldiers who saluted her as she passed by. Lanika was never a person who was a stickler for formality so the militaristic mannerisms that

Huey has the soldiers do annoys her. It was a culture that she knew wouldn't change so she learned to get used to it.

She reached the end of the hallway to a door that was guarded by two soldiers who opened the door once they saw her coming. She entered an empty room except for a chair in the middle that faced the window which stretched throughout the room overlooking the city. She could see the figure of Huey sitting on the chair. She turned her head to the sound of moaning to see four men that were tied up against the wall. Each one had a swastika carved on their forehead.

"I take it that the bait has been set?" She turned her attention back to Huey when he spoke.

"Like a worm on a hook."

"Good. He's an important guest, make sure Quanisha knows to take extra care of him."

"Of course. While we're on the subject of taking care, what were you thinking pulling that stunt earlier today?" Lanika made an irritated sigh hearing Huey chuckle.

"Sometimes, one must take a risk when trying to make a statement."

"I wish you wouldn't be so reckless. You preach about us being careful while you go off and pull crap like this on your own. And now we're stuck in this poor excuse of a construction site, hiding like rats, again. I thought we were done hiding?" Huey found amusement in her rant. He stood up from his chair and walked towards the window.

"Patience, my sister. All things will come to those that wait. Besides, I enjoy the view from here. No need to worry, our promise land waits for us." The promised land. That is what all of them are fighting and risking everything for. She would gladly give her life to see even a glimpse of it. Her musing was interrupted by the sounds of the men on the ground.

"They sure are noisy. What are you going to do with them?" Huey turned around to face the four individuals. They immediately stopped their moaning when his eyes landed on them.

"I almost forgot about them. I'm sure that our esteemed candidate will appreciate the gift that we are going to present to him." The men shivered as Huey's gaze intensified. It was like looking at the eyes of a demon. They didn't know what he meant by the gift but knew that they wouldn't live long enough to find out. While the others were too focused on their dear lives, one of them took the time to try and get out of his bonds. For some reason, they didn't tie their legs together, only their arms. He waited patiently for his chance to escape.

While he knew that he wouldn't be able to take out Huey or any of the armed guards, the woman, on the other hand, is another story. He figured he could use her as a hostage to get out of here alive. He waited as Huey turned back to look out the window. He got the final restraints off and made his move. He rushed to Lanika and tightly wrapped his arm around her neck. Huey looked back at the noise to see Lanika being held in a headlock.

"Let me go!" The man shouted when he ripped the cloth from his mouth. "Or I swear to God that I'll break this bitch's neck!" Huey stared at the man that held Lanika and almost pitied him. He has no idea who he's trying to hold hostage. He turned back to face the window.

"Are you deaf?! I said let me go or I'll kill her!" He yelled, tightening his hold.

"You can leave anytime you wish," Huey responded, confusing the man. "That is if you can, ignorant fool." Huey left the man speechless. He has one of his follower's hostage and he doesn't care? Does he not think that he'll kill her? What's wrong with him?!

"You think I'm playing here?! I'll-" His threat was replaced by a scream as he fell on the floor, holding his side that got stabbed. Lanika stood calm as the man withered in pain, holding the knife that's dripping in his blood. The man looked up to her and held in his breath at the cold stare that she was giving him.

These people, they're all insane! He screamed in his head. The only other thought that crossed his mind was to escape and to do it now. He tried to get up, but the pain was too much for him to walk. He got on his knees and tried to crawl away while holding his side to prevent bleeding out. Lanika slowly walked up to him and pulled out a gun. The man looked on horrified as she approached him.

"No! Please!" Lanika kept coming closer. There was only one thing he could do now.

"Someone help-" His cry for help was silenced as Lanika shot him three times in the back.

"I don't see why you don't have them tied up properly." She casually told Huey and three soldiers came in and dragged the body away.

"The predator never fears their prey," He responded nonchalantly. "A pity, though, I was hoping to deliver all four of them." He said, but his voice had no trace of regret. He looked back to the remaining men on the ground and all of them huddled closer in fear.

"Oh well, three will work just fine."

Chapter

14

Harvard Heights, Los Angeles, CA; 7:15 PM

For the rest of the day, Jasmine didn't have anything else on her mind than what happened at the police station. After they left, Alex drove her back to her job, in which she was silent for the entire ride. When they reached her job, the police cars were still there, and people were crowding the front entrance. The director was still in the hospital, so Jasmine didn't bother to stay any longer and decided to go home. She drove back to her apartment and was surprised to see a gift bag in front of her door. She carried it inside and when she looked inside, it was a new phone that had a note attached to it:

Figured you would need another one since that asshole took yours.

-Alex

Jasmine smiled as she read the note. She was extremely grateful that he came with her earlier today. It sent shivers down her spine at how much Detective Pope knew about her and her past, thankfully not all of it. That piece of information luckily will still stay between her and

Lanika. Thinking about her sister revived some unwanted memories that she buried long ago.

Her attention was brought to the door when she heard knocking. She opened the door and to her surprise, it was Alex standing outside.

"Hey, sorry I got lost and my fine as hell compass pointed in this direction." Of all things to say, she wasn't prepared for that. When she fully comprehend that he just used a pick-up line, she couldn't help but laugh.

"Are you serious?" She said through her laughter. "That is probably the corniest thing I've heard. What are you doing here?"

"Well, it got you to laugh, so I call that a win." Alex replied, sounding satisfied. Jasmine shook her head and invited him inside. While it was unexpected, she won't say that the visit is unwelcome. Right now, some company is what she needs. She offered Alex a seat on the couch while she prepared some drinks. She came back to the living room and handed Alex a drink.

"Thank you for the phone." She said, sitting on the sofa next to him.

"I didn't know if you would have gotten one yourself, but I like to be on the safe side."

"So, what brings you here?" Alex paused as he finished taking a sip. There were a lot of things on his mind ever since they left the station and after what happened earlier this morning. He didn't say anything when he drove Jasmine back to her job since he felt that it wasn't the time or place, but that doesn't mean he couldn't stop thinking about it.

"I wanted to see how you were doing. If everything is alright."

"Thank you. I appreciate it, but I'm okay." If there was one thing that he knew, it was that she was not ok. She couldn't be, not after everything that happened today. He had this feeling that Jasmine knows more about the situation with The Panthers than she's letting in on. He couldn't get it out of his mind that her sister is Dr. Lanika Jones.

From what he's seen so far from these Panthers, they are a ruthless organization. He views them as nothing but thugs willing to use fear and killings to get what they want. To think that someone that he looked up to like Lanika is roped in with a crowd like that, and the fact that she's Jasmine's sister was a bit much for him. Jasmine never mentioned anything about her family to him.

"Jasmine." He spoke up. Jasmine turned her attention to him and saw that he was struggling to find the right words to say. She knew that eventually, he would ask about her and Lanika, especially now that they had an encounter with the very group that she's in.

"I need to know. What exactly is going on? Why didn't you say anything about your sister?" All these years, Jasmine did her best not to remember about her past. It is something that she would have never revealed to another soul. However, when she looked at the genuine concern that Alex was showing, she felt the wall that she built starting to crumble. She remembered when his office was vandalized, and he shared the horrific event of his childhood. If he had enough strength to tell her his story, then she can too.

"Lanika and I were born in Macon, Georgia. We were like any other family with loving parents. We didn't have much, but we had each other. I can still remember those days. They were wonderful." Alex could see the pure joy that Jasmine was showcasing. The remembrance of a precious childhood memory, but her expression soon morphed into terror.

"Everything changed when our mother became sick. She had breast cancer. No one knew, not even her, and when we found out it was already at stage four. There was nothing they could do. Lanika and I were devastated, but our father took it the hardest. After her passing, everything about him changed." Alex sat as he listened to the horrors that Jasmine had to live in. How her father turned to alcohol and drugs after their mother's death. He blamed them for the loss of his wife and began tormenting them. Jasmine went to say that at first, it was only verbal lashing, but it later turned physical.

Their father would regularly beat them and say how everything is their fault. Jasmine, being the oldest, would make sure that she took the brunt of all the assaults in order to protect Lanika. For years, they endured endless abuse from their father, and through it all, Jasmine held on with the hope that when she turned eighteen, she would take Lanika and go away.

"But-," She paused in her story. Alex could see her body starting to shake. "That all changed one night. I was sixteen and at that point, I was used to him coming home drunk, and since both of us would be in our rooms by that time, he usually left us alone. That night, he came into my room and-" Jasmine couldn't complete her sentence as she broke down and cried. This was a side that Alex never thought that she had. Ever since they first met, she had this air of confidence and strength. She was a woman that is unapologetic about herself and her opinions. To see her break down like this unsettled him.

He inched closer to her, not sure how to comfort her. She had her arms wrapped around herself, trying to stop shaking. Alex couldn't just sit and watch while Jasmine was suffering like this. He got up and held her close to him, not saying a thing. Right now, words weren't needed. He could feel every tremor that was vibrating off of Jasmine and that only made him hold her closer. His action paid off as he could feel her calming down. When she stopped shaking, he let go of her and sat back down.

"Thank you." She whispered

"Any time." He replied, happy that he was able to provide her at least a little comfort.

"Did he...?" He cursed himself as the question left his mouth. He didn't mean to ask that, knowing that it could make her relapse, but it was something that was gnawing at his conscious.

"No," She answered, shaking her head. Alex released a breath that he didn't know he held. "He was on top of me trying to take my clothes off. On my bedstand was a lamp that I was able to reach, and I hit him on the head. I couldn't stay after that, so I ran." Jasmine told Alex how she survived, going from city to city, doing odd jobs until she found herself in Los Angles. He listened, admiring the inner strength she had, being that young and on her own. There was still one thing about the story that's missing.

"What happened to Lanika?"

"After I left, I haven't made any contact with either of them. I can only imagine what she went through. About ten years ago, I saw her again for the first time since then. I was doing a story on the anniversary of the death of Biggie Smalls. One of the neighborhoods did a memorial and she was there. Even after all that time, I knew it was her and I tried to approach her, but she avoided me. The day after, I received a call from her to meet up." She continued to explain that when they met up, she found out that Lanika was a teacher and already had a son. She also told Alex about the agreement that they had.

It was that there was to be no contact between them and that she could not interact with her son until he turned eighteen. The only way they could be in the same room was if their jobs created a situation where it was so, other than that, they were to keep their distance from each other. Jasmine didn't have any room to interject, so she accepted

Lanika's terms. Lanika did, however, give Jasmine a number to call, in case of a dire emergency.

"A few weeks ago, her son went missing and that was the only time I have ever used that number. After that, everything else led me to you and where we are now."

"How did she get involved with The Panthers?"

"That, I don't know." *Lanika, please be alright.* Jasmine prayed sadly. A knock on the door alerted both of them. She wasn't expecting anyone else and wondered who it could be. When she got to the door, she gasped at what she saw through the peephole. At the front of her door were people dressed in the same black combat gear as the ones that held them hostage, earlier this morning. The Panthers are here! Alex quickly went up to Jasmine when he saw her backing away from the door.

"What's wrong?"

"It's them. The Panthers."

"What?!" Alex went and looked through the peephole.
He cursed under his breath when he saw them.

"Why are they here? What do they want now?" He heard her whisper to herself. He went over to her and put his hands on her shoulders to reassure her.

"We have to call the police." Jasmine nodded as Alex was about to take out his phone but stopped at the sound of a familiar voice.

"I advise you not to do that, but it's not like you could anyway." Jasmine jumped when she heard the voice. Alex pulled her closer to him. Both held their breath as a figure moved into the light of the living room to reveal the owner of the voice, Huey.

"It's you." Alex whispered.

"Brother Williams," Huey acknowledged. "A pleasure meeting you again."

"Why are you here?" Jasmine asked, stepping away from Alex and carefully moving closer to Huey. Though he gave off a dangerous aura, she had a feeling that he's not going to hurt. She's more than positive if that was the case, then both of them would have been dead a long time ago.

"To talk," Huey answered. "I was honest when I said that I wanted more time to talk to you before and to top it all off, I just heard an interesting story. Though it's one, I know very well." Jasmine was puzzled. Story? Then she realized that what he meant was what she told Alex. Has he been in her apartment this whole time?! What is with these people and their sense to not care about other's personal space? Also, this is the second time that someone was able to sneak into her apartment without her noticing. Either The Panthers are training to become ninjas, or she and the landlady need to seriously talk about her shitty security.

"What do you want to say to us?" Alex questioned. Huey didn't give an immediate answer and started walking to the living room. While he moved, Alex made his way to put himself in front of Jasmine. Whatever Huey wanted; Alex was sure that he had an interest in Jasmine. Huey sat on the sofa that was once occupied by Jasmine. He looked back at the pair calmly and motioned for them to sit on the couch.

Alex was too apprehensive to move any closer to Huey. He has no idea what the man is thinking, and the fact that his goons are outside didn't make the situation any better. Jasmine, on the other hand, adjusted to the scenario rather quickly and grabbed Alex's hand while heading to the couch.

"Now," Huey started as both Jasmine and Alex sat down. "I believe that there are some missing blanks in that story you just told Sister Jones. I can fill in the rest if you wish." Missing blanks? She wondered what he meant by that. What missing blanks could he be referring to? It didn't take long for her to realize what Huey was offering. He knows what happened to Lanika after she left. When they had met all those years ago, she never mentioned what happened and only said that the past should stay dead. Jasmine didn't push any further.

It shouldn't be a surprise that Huey would know. The real question is, is Jasmine ready to hear it? Or rather, should she at all? She abandoned

Lanika with that monster. She doesn't even deserve to be called her sister. Huey could see the inner turmoil within Jasmine.

"She doesn't blame you." She snapped up to Huey. Is that true? Even though Lanika said the same thing the last time she saw her she didn't fully believe that. How could she? But, if so, then maybe, maybe they could reconcile.

"Why are you so interested in Jasmine?" Alex spoke up. He didn't like the effect Huey was having on her.

"Not just her, Brother Williams. You as well." That wasn't an answer that Alex was expecting to hear. What could Huey want from him?

"You two are important assets to us. As for why I'm invested in sister Jones is because I see Lanika as my blood. In that same sense, I consider you part of me."

"What plans do you have that involve us?" Alex figured that they could try to get as much information from Huey as they could.

"All in due time," Huey said leisurely. "First, as a show of good faith and that we, The Panthers, are on your side." Both of them turned their heads at the sound of the door opening, and three men that were tied up were shoved in. All of them had bruises all over their bodies, but the main thing that stood out was the swastikas that looked like it was carved on their forehead.

"What is this?" Alex whispered.

"These are the rats that were in charge of destroying your office. We have their entire group in our custody, but I felt that you should be able to see justice with your very own eyes." Alex didn't know how to respond—seeing these men brought painful memories and bitter feelings.

Besides the men, there was something else that Huey had said that Alex knew had an underlying meaning.

"What are you planning on doing to them?"

"Those who follow the path of evil shall be judged." Alex knew by that phrase alone what the man intended to do. And while the world will be better off without men like them, Alex couldn't agree to what Huey had in mind.

"Is that what you are? Some bringer of justice?! You're nothing more than a murderer coated in sugary words."

"You're right, I am." Jasmine and Alex were confused that he would outrightly admit it. "There is no sense in denying what is. Sometimes, to defeat evil, one must do evil. Vermin like these have been allowed to roam free while our people live in fear. That ends."

"Not like this!" Alex interjected. "This is why we have a process. What you are doing is no different than any other tyrant."

"If that's what it takes to protect my people, then I'm fine with being one."

"Wait," Jasmine spoke up. "What do you mean by your people?" Jasmine wondered if he was only referring to The Panthers or was there a larger entity?

"To all my brothers and sisters, we, who have suffered the most and longest of any race in this country. Every day, I hear the cries and pain of my people, yet nothing is ever done." He motioned for the soldiers that brought the tied-up men to take them back outside. They cringed as they heard muffled plea as the men were dragged away.

"I believe in all of my people. My brothers and sisters, which includes you both. You may not see it now, but someday you will."

"You still haven't said what you want from us." Alex said.

"As I said before, all in due time. Now, Sister Jones, back to the main topic. Would you like to know? I'll tell you everything. About Lanika and The Panthers."

"Why?" Jasmine pleaded. She was so confused about everything that was happening. Lanika. The Panthers. Just what the hell is going on, and why does Lanika have to be mixed into it?

"Once again, I see Lanika as family. Therefore, I see you as a family. The trust I have in Lanika extends to you as well. The same goes for brother Williams. So, I will tell you everything."

"Are you sure?" Alex questioned. "Either of us could go to the authorities about this and you." Huey chuckled at the attempted threat.

"I'm sure you can, but you won't. Not after you listen to what I have to say; about The Panthers and what we seek." The rest of the night, they sat and listened to what Huey had to say. Time passed, and they began to understand everything, but their hearts stopped once Huey spoke on the ultimate goal of The Panthers. Jasmine could feel her blood run cold as she listened to Huey's insane plan. The Panthers and what they're after could only lead to one thing. The one thing which terrified her down to her soul and never thought she would ever have to experience. War.

Chapter

15

Downtown Los Angeles, CA; 2:15 PM

"Damnit!" Detective Pope yelled as he knocked a stack of papers on the ground. Nothing! He wasn't able to get anything out of the phone that he confiscated from Jasmine. He did everything that he could, even taking it apart. The only thing that the ITs were able to dig up was that the number that Lanika called from was from a payphone, so they couldn't even track that. Still, they should have been able to get the background noise and should have been able to pick up something of use.

Nothing. They went through the phone's entire history. Calls, Facetimes, text, email, social media, and every app that was on there. Anything to give him some sort of lead. His hopes were dashed when they came back to him, saying that they couldn't find anything that was related to Lanika or The Panthers. The only thing he has left is a useless phone. Now that he has no further need of it, he could return it to Jasmine as he promised, but he's too frustrated right now, so he decided to pull it off on another day.

He sat in his chair and looked over the various notes and articles from news and blogs he found online. They were scattered all over the walls with arrows connecting to each other. If nothing else, he gives these people credit for being crafty. This whole time that he has spent here, and the only substantial evidence he has of The Panthers' involvement of those deaths is the relationship between Jasmine and Lanika, which isn't much to go by in the first place. He sat back, scanning the room. There must be something he's missing. Something left that he must have forgotten or overlooked. He realized what it was when he saw the article about Travis Miller.

Travis! He jumped off his seat. How could he have forgotten about him?! He was the entire reason why he went to that prison in the first place. It just so happened that he ran into Jasmine and after that, he became completely sidetracked. He called the Twin Towers Facility to schedule a time to talk to Travis, and luckily, he was able to work it out to see him today. Hopefully, this will be his second wind. He drove with haste to the facility and quickly made his way to the receptionist area.

Captain Burns was there waiting for him and escorted him to the same room where he first saw Jasmine walk out from. Inside was a simple desk and two chairs with no cameras or windows. He wasn't here to do an interrogation, so he wondered why they chose such a room. He knows there are other, more open areas that they could have their discussion. It was honestly a bit depressing.

He put those thoughts aside as the door opened, and a guard shoved Travis inside. When he sat down, he was cuffed to the table. The guard left without saying a word. This left Detective Pope a bit perplexed. Is

Travis really that dangerous? And if so, why leave him alone with him? Something about it didn't sit well with him, but he put a hold on his suspicions until after he got done talking to Travis.

Speaking of, Detective Pope could immediately tell by Travis' body language and facial features that he would rather be anywhere else than here with him. Hopefully, he will be more cooperative than the vibe he was giving off. The detective didn't want to resort to any drastic measures, but he was getting desperate. Before he could introduce himself, he was silenced.

"Another one, huh?" Travis said in a monotone voice. "You people can't just leave me alone, and by the looks of it, you're a cop. What the hell do you want with me?" Detective Pope went on to introduce himself and explain to Travis why he came to see him. He left out a few details since he didn't know if Travis was a member of The Panthers. He did his best to play the role of the good cop who wants to clear Travis's name and bring the real culprits to justice.

The entire time that Detective Pope spoke, Travis didn't utter a single word. He only stared at him. Travis was giving him the look of someone who didn't believe a single thing he said. That didn't deter the detective from trying. Any information that Travis can deliver to him will be of great help. He just has to convince Travis that he's on his side and wants to help him. He promised Travis that he would do everything in his power to proclaim his innocence.

He urged Travis to tell him everything that happened to him on the day that he was apprehended, stressing on the importance to spare no detail. The detective tried to persuade him that anything that he could give would make capturing the real murderer that much faster. He prayed that Travis believes him. He doesn't want to get forceful, but he needs this kid to talk. After he was done, Travis didn't give him an immediate response. They sat in silence for a couple of seconds before Travis spoke up.

"It doesn't matter." Though Detective Pope did want Travis to talk, this wasn't what he wanted to hear.

"Why? I can help you get out of here."

"It doesn't matter if I talk to you, that woman, or anyone. Nothing will change. I'm done."

"You're going to accept this?!" He yelled, slamming his hands on the table. "You're ok being in a cage for the rest of your life over something that you didn't do?!" Detective Pope couldn't understand what was going through Travis's head. Usually, if someone is framed of a crime, they would do everything that they could do to prove their innocence. No one willing wants to stay in prison.

Travis, on the other hand, didn't want to trust people. How could he after everything that's happened? That reporter that came to see him was an exception. He remembered her from the courthouse that day and something was telling him that she knew more than what she led on. He hopes that his decision to tell her won't come back to haunt him. He looked back to the detective that was waiting for an answer.

"I said I'm done." Detective Pope sat back on the chair with a frustrated sigh.

"So that's it? Do you have any idea what's going to happen if you don't co-operate with me? I'm your only chance!" Travis didn't answer back. Detective Pope was about to speak again when the door open. He turned to see Captain Burns.

"I apologize detective, but that's all the time we have." He thought about talking to him to allow him some more time. However, given the circumstances, there might be operatives of The Panthers hidden in prison. Hell, he's not one hundred percent sure about Travis. Pressing the matter right now may prove to backfire on him if that's the case. He'll let it go, for now.

"Fine." He sighed as he got up. He made one last look at Travis, who was staring right back at him.

"We'll see each other again. Think carefully about what I said." He walked away with those parting words. The detective left the prison more frustrated than ever. He didn't obtain anything useful. It was a complete waste of his time! That kid just had to make it difficult for him. He couldn't think of a reason why Travis didn't talk to him. Is it because he's a cop? The reason doesn't matter, but he has to make way for Travis to open up to him before the situation spirals out of control.

He got into his car, thinking about what his next course of action should be. The past days have been nothing but disappointments. He hoped that Travis would give him his big break, but that turned out to be for naught as well. He needed something to calm his nerves. He drove around downtown and found a local bar deciding that a drink is what he needs.

Walking inside, he took a seat and relaxed in front of the counter, watching the game that was on. He made a slide glance at the sound of the door opening, and a loud group of young men walked in. They sat at a table that was directly behind him. There weren't many people in the bar, so he was able to hear the conversation that they were having. He originally paid them no mind so that he could take his mind off of recent events. It was impossible to completely ignore them considering how loud they were.

"Bruh, stop bullshitting." He heard one of them say.

"I'm not, man! I'm telling you this is about to blow up."

"You talking about what happened to that news station?" Now they have gotten his attention. The detective didn't need a Doctorate's degree to know that they were talking about the news station that The Panthers stormed in and made that threatening message. He sat up, not making any subtle movements as he listened to the conversation.

"Yeah man, that was crazy! It was all over my timeline."

"Right. Now get this." This was the only time that they were quiet, but Detective Pope was still able to hear pieces of what was being said. He was able to hear the words; panthers, gather, warehouse, demonstration, and promise land. Promise land? He wondered what that could mean, but he knew that something big is about to happen, and it seemed that it's starting tonight.

He was thankful that all of his experiences made him fully prepared for situations like this, and he was a master at tailing. He waited for the group to leave before he made his move. He quickly got into his vehicle, and once he saw them moving, he followed right behind them. Their destination led him to some sort of construction site. There were many cars parked on the dirt and people walking into the area.

He parked off the grid to make sure that no one saw him and carefully made his way around the unfinished building. He crept inside and followed the sound of the people that were gathering. He found a flight of stairs and quietly made his way up to where he found a spot that had a view of the main area down below. There was a huge crowd that was filling in and in front was a long horizontal stage.

He stayed perched on the spot, not making a sound.

About thirty minutes passed, and the sun was setting. Soon, the whole building was shrouded in the darkness. Finally, a set of lights came on, illuminating the main room where he saw people in black combat gear. All of them were carrying riffles as they surrounded the area.

The crowd grew quiet but soon erupted in cheer as Huey and Lanika came on stage. The cheering lasted for a few seconds until Huey raised his hand to silence them. Detective Pope crouched in anticipation. This is it. This is the break that he was looking for. He recognized Huey as the man that Jasmine was calling out to that day at the news building and he was also the one that gave that message. One thing is clear and that is Huey is the one calling the shots. Detective Pope slowly reached for his pistol that was hidden in his right leg. He just needs one shot. One shot and he can end all of this, but he would have to do it at the right moment. He knows that once he fires, he would be swarmed, and it would be tough, and almost impossible for him to escape alive.

"My brothers and sisters," Huey's voice echoed throughout the building. "Soon, a new era will come for us. No longer will we be second class citizens of a country that never welcomed us!" Detective Pope could feel the outrage that was coming off from the crowd. It was never a secret; how African Americans have been treated ever since their ancestors were first brought to the colonies. Is that what this is all about?

"For centuries, we had to endure this country's mission to humiliate, prosecute, and exterminate us! Our language, our culture, and very lives have been in constant jeopardy of going extinct. Though we may not be slaves anymore, it doesn't mean that we are free. How can we when we are being oppressed by the very same system that enslaved us! No longer!" Huey turned around and made a hand gesture. A line of eight men was brought onto the stage in chains that were followed by a group of soldiers. The crowd roared when they saw that each of the men had a swastika on their forehead.

"The trash that you see will love nothing more than to put every one of us back in chains! Thousands of them have been roaming this country like a plague that the United States has turned a blind eye to." The soldiers that were behind the men forced them to kneel on the ground.

"For too long, they have been free to terrorize, rape, and kill our people while the government does nothing. They, this whole country doesn't give a damn about us, and sure as hell won't protect us. We have to protect ourselves!" The soldiers then pulled out their rifles, aiming at the back of each man's head. Huey took out his gun and pointed at the man that was kneeling in front of him.

"And so, we will." The only sound that was heard in the room was the bullet that was triggered by Huey's gun. The moment that the body slumped on the ground; the soldiers fired on the other men. Dead bodies now decorated the stage with their blood flowing to the ground. The people remained silent.

"They no longer have the power!" Huey spoke loudly. Everyone followed his movement as he walked closer to the edge of the stage and kicked the body that he shot onto the ground.

"Because now we are here. Believe in the light of the revolution. Believe in the promised land to come. There is nothing for you to fear anymore. We are The Panthers. We. Will. Rise!" He finished his speech by raising his fist in the air. The few seconds of silence was replaced with the roar and cheer of the crowd. Many of them were chanting out the last phrase that Huey said, 'we will rise'. Detective Pope jolted himself back to reality as he had become lost in thoughts as he witnessed what just happened. This was madness!

He knew that if he didn't do something, more people would die. This has to end now. He carefully took out his gun and aimed it at Huey. This is his one and only chance. Even if his survival will be at risk, he has to take Huey out now. He wouldn't call himself a sniper, but he was more than confident that he could land a solid hit on Huey at this distance. He aimed and put his finger on the trigger.

"I'm afraid that I can't allow you to do that." He made a snap turn to the right at the sound of a feminine voice. By instinct, he positioned himself to take the woman out.

"Too slow." Before he was able to follow with his action, he felt a sharp pain on his right arm. The room immediately began to swirl around him, and then everything went black. Two soldiers came up and took hold of the detective's unconscious body.

"What should we do with him, Sister Freed?" Janaye turned around to the soldier that spoke to her.

"Take him in. This one has something that we need. Quanisha has been waiting patiently for him." The soldiers saluted her and proceeded to take him away. Janaye walked down the stairs and passed by the outgoing people that were leaving. She walked up to the stage where

Huey was still standing with Lanika behind him. The soldiers that were on the stage were busy getting rid of the dead bodies. Huey smiled as he saw Janaye approach him.

"I take it our guest has arrived."

"He's being transferred to Quanisha as we speak."

"Good," He said, looking at Janaye and back to Lanika. "Soon, my sisters. Our moment has come."

"For the light of the revolution." Lanika responded to him.

"For the promised land." Janaye said quietly.

"Give word out to the others. It's time for our incarcerated brothers to be free at long last."

Chapter

16

Detective Pope stirred as he was beginning to wake from unconsciousness. He adjusted his eyes to the dim light that greeted him when he fully gained his sense of sight. Searching around, he took note that there were no windows and that the room he was in was empty except for a few shelves that were in the back.

He figured he must be in a basement though he didn't know whether he's in the same building that he was captured in or somewhere else. Right now, that shouldn't be his main concern, the fact that he's restrained to a chair is the real problem. He tried to move his wrists, but the straps were too tight.

"Looks like our special guest is finally awake."

"Yes, it does seem that way." Hearing those voices, Detective Pope mentally prepared himself. He had no illusions about the situation he was, and with groups like these, it doesn't take much imagination to know what they do to prisoners. After witnessing Huey execute those men, he has the impression that they're not the type to torture their victims. If they wanted him dead, then they would have done so the moment he was caught.

There's a reason why they kept him alive. But the question is, why? The two voices that spoke up, according to his analysis, were those of females. He recognized one of them as the one who was at the building, but the other one, he couldn't figure out. It was familiar, but he couldn't put a face to the voice. The two figures came out of the shadows. One was the one who caught him, Janaye. The other he realized was the doctor that told him about Travis, Dr. Quanisha Grant.

"It's good to make your acquaintance again, Detective." Quanisha greeted him.

"I shouldn't be surprised that you're one of them. So those two nurses, you killed them." He responded back.

"An unfortunate but necessary sacrifice."

"And Travis?"

"You should worry more about yourself than others, Detective Pope. Or rather, I should say FBI special agent Craftwell." His eyes popped open as Quanisha just revealed his true identity. They know. His entire mission has been compromised and the situation has become direr now that he is in the custody of his targets.

"You've done well to hide your tracks, but it wasn't good enough to deceive us."

"How long?" He asked. It would be better for him and the government if The Panthers had only recently discovered his identity.

"We've kept tabs on you for quite a while. You FBI people sure are an annoying bunch. You don't honestly believe that you're the only ones that can infiltrate another organization?" It was worse than he feared. If what she says is true, then the whole department has been breached. Who knows what kind of information they were able to obtain? More importantly, they could have the face and name of every active agent in the field.

"That's right," Janaye spoke up. "We know every one of you. It was cute that you thought you could do to us the same thing you did with the original Black Panthers. All that time, you didn't even consider that we had already planted our operatives." He doesn't know how, but he has to escape. This has become worse than what the top brass had briefed him. They're now a serious threat to national security. He did his best to remain calm, but Quanisha was able to see right through him.

"No need to panic Agent Craftwell. We're not going to do anything drastic like assassinate the President or such." Hearing that didn't make him feel any better. Even if she said that they aren't planning to do one of the worst-case scenarios, it's not like he could take her word for it. Then that also leaves the question of what they intend to do popping in his head.

"What is it that you people are after? If you already know who I am, then why keep me alive? All the other agents that we've sent to investigate The Panthers all came back dead."

"Because unlike them, you have something that we want. That alone makes you more valuable to us alive."

"And what would that be?"

"File B260." All of his clam demeanor melted away the moment he heard that. B260 is a document that is classified as one of the most Top-Secret files in the Bureau. The number of people that even knows of its existence isn't even in the double digits. The only reason he knows about it is that the previous Deputy Director was his grandfather and before he died, he passed on the information to him. If his superiors were ever to find out, there would be no doubt that they would ship him out to a completely isolated facility or dispose of him. That's how delicate the information in B260 is.

"How do you know about that?"

"B260?" Janaye asked. This was the first time she ever heard of it.

"A document that's been kept in one of the deepest parts of FBI intelligence." Janaye and Quanisha looked over to see Huey enter the room. Agent Craftwell stiffens as he hears Huey's voice. Both women took a step back to allow Huey to walk up to him.

"Sir," Janaye greeted Huey. "What exactly is it and why am I just hearing about it?"

"This information has only been shared between me and the twelve chiefs. We had to make sure nothing was leaked, even if I had to keep it from my most trusted Intelligence Officer." Janaye didn't like the fact that Huey couldn't trust her but knew that she had no right to question him. She had no choice but to let it go.

"Then can you tell me what's so important about it?" She asked. If anything, she would like to know what is so special about this B260 that even she had to be kept in the dark from it.

"In truth, B260 is nothing more than a list."

"A list, sir?" Janaye knew there had to be more to it than that. She waited for Huey to explain further.

"We assumed that the U.S government never kept records of certain organizations, especially the ones that promote white supremacy. However, we were able to discover a certain set of documents that contain not only every active organization in the country but also the names and locations of each member. A complete directory that's been put under the file name B260." That caught her attention quickly.

Janaye didn't know that the FBI had something like that in their archive. She thought of why they would even need something like that, but just put it off as part of the government's paranoia. Still, the KKK alone has tens of thousands of members, and with that information, they would be able to snuff them all out. It was one of The Panthers' primary missions; to completely eradicate every single one of them.

"I'm impressed that the FBI can hide it from us, even from The Ark." Agent Craftwell smirked. It's one of the government's most well-guarded pieces of information. Even if they know of its existence, there's no possible way for them to know where to find it or even access it. Hell, he doesn't even know of its location. No hacker in the world would be able to obtain it. Knowing that gave him a surge of confidence.

"Looks like The Panthers aren't as capable as we thought." He mocked. Janaye looked ready to murder him, and if it weren't for Quanisha, who held her back, she would have. Huey looked at Agent Craftwell with a smirk of his own.

"Yes, that would seem to be the case," He replied as he pulled out a folder. "However, we have our ways." Agent Craftwell raised an eyebrow when he saw the folder. He was confident that whatever could be in it would have no effect. Huey took out a piece of paper from the folder and showed it to him. Was he supposed to read it? What good will that do? Shrugging, Agent Craftwell read the paper, and soon, all of his new confidence went down the drain. In front of him was a letter that had the location of where B260 is hidden.

"Thanks to our good friend, Judge Matthews, who was kind enough to lend it to us. It seems that her family had very powerful individuals that were in the Klan. Powerful enough that they were able to strike a deal with the FBI at the time to obtain this information. Lucky us." Now he was begging to understand why they kept him alive. But how could they know that he knows the access codes? No one knew, he made sure of it!

For years he has done everything to make sure that no one would even suspect that he knew. What good that did! Now understanding what they wanted from him, there was only one thing he could do.

"You might as well kill me." Agent Craftwell declared. His body had endured torture before, and he would rather die than give them anything. They have nothing that will make him talk.

"There's no need to be so dramatic. I have no intention of killing you, yet. Besides, we have other methods." Huey motioned for Quanisha to come closer. Agent Craftwell could see that she was carrying a needle filled with a green fluid.

"What are you going to do with that?" He asked wearily.

"It's not poison, I assure you. It's just something that'll help loosen those lips of yours." Huey gave Quanisha permission to proceed. Agent Craftwell struggled, but the restraints were too tight. Quanisha carefully took hold of his left arm and injected the fluid into him. The moment that it entered his system, he felt the entire room begin to blur. Everything was moving as if it was in slow motion. It was nauseating. He looked up to Quanisha and Huey, and though he could still see them, he couldn't hear anything that they were saying. What did they put in his body?!

He watched as Quanisha leaned closer to him and placed her hand right next to his ears. Suddenly his senses jolted when he felt the vibration of her fingers snapping. All at once, his senses were only focusing on Quanisha. His body wasn't under his control. What is happening to him?!

"Looks like the serum took effect faster than expected." He was able to hear her speak. For some reason, he could hear her, but everything else was a buzzing sound like listening to white noise. Quanisha and Huey were talking to each other, but he could only hear her. He watched as she turned back to him.

"Special Agent Jeremy Craftwell, how do you access the archive containing file B260?" If he could laugh, he would be on the floor, rolling at the stupidity of her asking him that. He already told them that he would rather die than tell them. Did they really think that messing with his senses will entice him to reveal that secret? If the worst that they can do is make him disoriented, then they obviously don't know how interrogation works. As he was mentally insulting them, he felt something very strange. His mouth began to move on its own.

"Code 44313648." Wait. What did he just say?! He didn't just tell them that, did he? That instant, he realizes that whatever they put in him was making him talk. He couldn't stop himself!

"Good. Now how do I bypass the security?" He tried using all the strength he had not to talk. He's a special agent of one of the world's top intelligence organizations. He can fight this! However, his struggle was in vain as his mouth began to move on its own again.

"Code 158436." *Damnit!* He cursed internally. There's no telling the kind of damage that The Panthers can do with that information, and he just handed it to them on a golden platter. He hung his head in defeat. There's nothing he can do now. They got everything they needed out of him, so it was only a matter of time before they disposed of him.

"Excellent!" Huey exclaimed as he watched Agent Craftwell crumble. "Quanisha, make sure our guest is kept comfortable. Janaye, follow me." He ordered as he left the room with Janaye right behind him. As they walked, she could hear Huey chuckling to himself.

"Are you alright, sir?"

"It's nothing. I just find the irony amusing."

"Irony, sir?"

"Yes. I will thoroughly enjoy the look on their faces when we begin with our own ethnic cleansing."

Chapter

17

Twin Towers Correctional Facility, Los Angeles, CA

11:00 AM

Travis was more on edge today than when he first entered the prison. It wasn't because of the other inmates. Ben had an annoying habit of keeping tabs on him, and once the others found out, they kept their distance. Guess for once; it pays to be a pigeon. No, it was the guards that were making him this nervous. He had gotten adjusted to the harassment he would receive daily from them.

Today, however, they have yet to do anything to him. They didn't even bother him as he slept in. Usually, they would barge right into his cell and manhandle him out. Something was up, but he couldn't tell what it was. Are they waiting for when he let his guard down? Is this some new game they came up with to torture him? Either way, he's enjoying this brief moment of peace for as long as he can.

"Hey, time to get out!" Well, there goes his peace, it was nice while it lasted. He got up from his bunk and noticed that this wasn't the regular guard that would greet him every morning. Maybe it was because he killed a cop, but the guy had a personal mission to make his mornings as miserable as possible. Travis doubted that he would willingly give up a day to have his fun with him.

Everything about this was seriously suspicious. Travis looked up at the new guard cautiously as he left his cell. With the other one, at least, he knew what to expect. This was a new and unknown one, and Travis had no way of knowing his intentions. The guard didn't say anything to him; he only nodded his head, signaling Travis to start walking. Travis sighed in relief, grateful that for the first time since he's been here, his mornings didn't have to be physical.

When he entered the Dining Hall, he saw one of Ben's men waiting for him. Ben must want to talk to him again. It didn't often happen; for the most part, he leaves Travis to his own devices. Other times, he would invite Travis to sit with him, and they would talk. Despite technically being a gangster, Ben was more insightful than Travis gave him credit for.

They would have discussions about things such as politics, history, religion, economics, literature, and even philosophy. Travis would be lying if he said that he didn't enjoy the conversations he had with the man. Ben had a profound level of knowledge, and Travis found himself learning a lot from him.

The more time he spent with him, the more Travis became curious. He wonders why Ben would even spare a moment of his time with him, but the fact that the man was keen to know what Travis was thinking all the time puzzled him. Ben would always prioritize Travis's opinion on each subject. He would paint different scenarios and ask Travis how he would handle the situation. He would ask many questions just to see Travis's point of view.

Travis felt that he was being tested. No, that's not exactly it. It's more like he's being educated, and Ben is mentoring him. Every time that Travis would answer a question, Ben would interject if he felt that the answer was too narrow-minded or biased. He tried to make Travis see the bigger picture. It's almost as if Ben is grooming Travis to be some sort of politician.

Travis didn't even think of that as a possibility. Why would Ben focus his time and energy on something like that? Is it because he's bored? No, that can't be it. There's a reason why Ben has taken such an interest in Travis, but he couldn't figure out why. None of it made any sense. Both of them have life sentences; there's no escaping this place. Even if Travis was to be free, what kind of life could he have now? The whole country sees him as a cop killer. He'll be lucky even to get a job at McDonald's.

"Looks like someone enjoyed sleeping in today." Ben greeted as Travis sat down. It took only a moment for him to understand what Ben implied by that.

"I take it that was your doing."

"More or less." Travis had to control the urge to roll his eyes. That was one of Ben's most annoying qualities. The man never just gives straightforward answers.

"If that's the case, I would have been more appreciative if you just did that the moment I got here." Travis really has no right to complain to Ben, but still, if the man had such pulls, doing this earlier would definitely have saved him a lot of trouble.

"Then, you would still be soft." That was a response that Travis anticipated; he would say. Still, why should that concern Ben?

"And what's wrong with that? Not everyone is meant to be strong." This is the game that Travis has to play in order to get something out of Ben. It irritates him that he has to do this just to get the answers that he wants, and of course, Ben doesn't tell him everything that he wants to know.

"You and I both know very well that in this world, you don't have that kind of luxury."

"Even if you don't have access to the world?"

"More so than ever." Travis sighed. This wasn't getting him anywhere.

"I still don't understand what you want from me. I already served my purpose, what more do you want? I can't give you anything."

"Who said I want anything from you?"

"You know what I meant. What do The Panthers want from me? I'm already stuck here, thanks to them. What else do they want?"

"The time will come when you will find out on your own." Travis scoffed at his answer.

"You make it sound like we're going to get out. In case you've forgotten, we're both stuck here for life."

"Sometimes, the Lord works in mysterious ways." Travis had no delusions in his mind that Ben and his crew were planning to break out of prison. He knew that the second he realized that he was basically a messenger bird. The rest of the day passed uneventfully. Travis mainly spent his time alone until Devante came.

Over time, he had gotten used to the other man's company and even started talking to him. He found out that Devante kept to himself as well, so he was the only person that he would converse with. After that first day, he would always stick himself with Travis. He still doesn't know how Devante ended up in prison, but he never pushed for the subject. It wasn't any of his business anyway.

That night, he laid in his bunk, thinking over what Ben had said. Though he always knew that they were plotting to escape, Travis thought it was pointless. If they escape, then they'll forever be on the run, and what kind of life is that? He tried to convince Ben otherwise, but he would always change the subject to something else. Travis was fine with that. He wants nothing to do with what they're planning.

He doesn't want anything in association with Ben or The Panthers. Why would he since they're the ones that put him here. The only thing he wanted was to find Janaye to see if she was safe. That's all he wanted. He would give anything just to see her again. Thinking about her brought back the questions he had that started this whole train wreck.

Where is she? How is she connected with The Panthers? What are they after? He accepted that he would never find out, but with what Ben said, it seems that he may be getting those answers. The question now is does he want to find out after everything that he's been through. Of course, he wants to see Janaye again, but in finding her he will have to run in with The Panthers.

He hopes that she's not being forced to do anything. Travis put his worries aside for another day. Fretting about it won't change his situation right now. The best thing he can do for himself is to not stand out and survive here as long as he can. He closed his eyes and tried to get some rest.

His attempt to sleep, however, was disrupted by a loud sound. He merely sat up when he felt the whole room rumble. It sounded like something heavy just crashed through a wall. Only seconds passed when all the lights were turned on, and the alarm assaulted Travis. He could hear many people shouting, and he jumped out of bed to take a look at what was happening. He could see all the guards running around in frenzy. They were all armored up and wore bulletproof vests and carried rifles. What the hell is going on?

"Attention!" Travis heard the announcement over the speaker. "The facility has been breached. This is not a drill! I repeat this is not a drill! All inmates are to remain in their cells, or there will be dire consequences!" As soon as the speaker was done, Travis felt another fissure, he may not be able to see what is happening fully, but he knew one thing for a fact. Ben made his move. That realization came with another one. The Panthers are here.

Lost in his thoughts, he was startled when the door to his cell automatically swung open. He backed away; in case it was one of the less than friendly guards that opened his door. However, no one was there. He stood still, not sure of what he should do. About thirty seconds passed, yet there were no guards that approached his cell.

Counting himself to be safe for the moment, he took a cautious step forward. He immediately steps back against the wall at the sound of heavy footsteps. He became completely still as a stampede of people dressed in black combat gear rushed past his cell. He recognized the familiar uniform.

It's them, The Panthers. One of them stopped and turned toward Travis pointing his weapon at him. Travis could feel his heart almost bursting out his body as the person walked into his cell. He was petrified! The person came closer to the point where the gun was literally in front of Travis's face.

Then they suddenly stopped. They pulled the weapon away from Travis and slowly backed away. It took a minute for Travis to realize that he was still alive. He was brought out of his shock by the sound of gunfire. It honestly sounded like a war zone out there. Despite knowing that the danger was out there, and he was probably safer just staying in his cell, something was telling him that he needed to get out.

He crept out and moved towards the sound as it got louder. When he reached the main Dining Hall, what he saw was nothing short of pandemonium. Everyone was fighting, the guards, inmates, and the soldiers in black. He ducked his head as he backed up to the wall. He jumped when he felt a hand gripping his shoulder. He turned around to see Devante in a panic.

"Don't just stand there, dumbass! We need to get the hell out of here!" Travis moved on autopilot as he followed Devante back to the entrance but was blocked as more guards came out and swarmed the area. Devante cursed and grabbed Travis' shoulder herding him in the other direction.

Travis couldn't even process everything that he was seeing. Everyone was fighting in every corner of the room and blood splattering everywhere. They had to navigate through the area as bodies continued to litter the ground. Many severely injured and the rest dead. Each exit they were trying to go was being blocked.

Devante cursed even more. There was no escape; they were trapped! The only thing they can hope for now is to hide somewhere and wait it out. He instantly searched around to find a spot until he heard the click of a gun. He turned around to see one of the guards pointing his weapon at them. He looked back to Travis, but he still had that lost, blank expression on his face. He shoved Travis behind him, ready to take the bullet. He flinched when he heard the gunfire, but he didn't feel any pain. He looked up to the guard and watched as he fell onto the floor.

"That was close." Devante looked over to face the person that just saved them.

"Ben!" He shouted in relief. Ben walked up to them and put his hand on Devante's shoulder.

"Go with the others. I'll handle him." Devante nodded and ran off. Ben turned to Travis and frowned. He knocked Travis out of his trance state by hitting him to the ground.

"Snap out of it!" He shouted. Travis blinked for a moment and was able to focus on his surroundings finally.

"Space out like that again and you're dead." Travis was confused. What did Ben mean by that? He found his answer as he saw the body of a guard behind Ben that was still holding his gun. Did he almost got shot? Why? He's not a part of this. He has nothing to do with what is happening here. Ben was able to tell what Travis was thinking, his face gave it all away.

"I told you before that in this world unless you have the power, you will never have the luxury to do what you want. It doesn't matter if you're involved or not, they will still hunt you down like a dog because they have the power to do so. You have only two options; stay here to rot like this country wants you to or take freedom into your own hands. Die or fight?" How can Travis choose at a time like this? Everything was happening so fast that he couldn't get all of his thoughts together. Fight or die. Become a wanted criminal or stay caged for the rest of his life. Be free or stay imprisoned.

When he first got here, he had already accepted his fate, but now, something else is screaming at him to choose the other option. Following Ben will lead him to The Panthers, which will lead him to Janaye, and isn't she all the reason that he needs? Travis looked back to Ben, with determination in his eyes.

"I won't die." He declared.

"Good answer." Ben nodded as he walked to the dead guard behind him and tossed the gun that the body was holding to Travis.

"Stay close." Travis gripped the gun tightly and followed right behind Ben as they made their way out. Several of the guards tried to stop them but The Panthers came to cover them. They made their way to a hallway that led to the main lobby of the facility that was being heavily guarded. Ben pushed Travis to the side to avoid the bullets that were flying in their direction.

Travis stayed behind Ben, and the rest took care of the guards blocking their way. They pushed through and were able to reach the main lobby where Travis saw there was a massive hole in the wall to the outside with the back of a semi-tractor facing them. The back of the tractor was open, and there were more Panther soldiers that were waiting for them and at the same time, was having a shootout with the guards that were hiding behind the receptionist's desk.

"Quickly, go in there!" Ben shouted, pointing to the tractor. Travis was about to move when he saw something out of the corner of his eye. It was a guard down on the ground, and he was starting to move. No one was paying attention to him, probably thinking that he was dead, and he was about to aim at Ben, who backed him. Without thinking further, Travis instinctively pointed his gun at the guard and fired.

Ben snapped at the sound of the shot and saw Travis still pointing the gun at the dead body on the ground. Travis' entire body was shaking. He actually did it. He killed someone with his own hands. He couldn't help but drop the weapon in disgust at what he just did. There's no turning back now; he's a murderer. He will forever have that blood on his hands, and it felt sickening.

"Now is not the time to breakdown!" Ben shouted as he grabbed his shoulder. "Freedom always has a price, and you must be ready when it comes to collect it. Never forget this feeling, because the moment you do, you lose your own humanity. Go!" Ben pushed him towards the tractor, and he ran inside where he met with other inmates that were part of Ben's crew and Devante.

"Glad to see you decided to come with us." That right there told Travis that he was a part of this too. It honestly shouldn't surprise him, and right now, it doesn't matter. He sat next to Devante as more people started filling up, and once Ben entered, they closed it and drove off.

Seeing as there weren't any seatbelts or anything to latch on, the ride was extremely uncomfortable. Everything was rocking side to side. Though Travis couldn't see anything, he could hear the sirens of police cars that were chasing after them. He flinched as he heard the sound of bullets colliding with the tractor's metal exterior. Soon, he could hear helicopters that joined in the chase.

Now that they got helicopters on their trail, escaping will practically be impossible. They will never let them go, and the fact that they're trying to run away in a huge tractor truck makes them conspicuous and there's no way that they'll be able to lose their pursuers.

Travis slid as the truck made a sharp right turn. Everyone inside faced the back door as it opened, allowing the wind and light to rush in violently. They could see numerous cop cars and two helicopters right behind him. Both of the copters were shinning a large bright light practically blinding everyone inside. In front of everyone stood Ben, and he was holding something large. What Ben said next made Travis realize what he was holding was a rocket launcher.

"Everyone back up!" It was the only warning that they received as Ben shot off one of the rockets. It hit the wing blades of one of the helicopters and made it crash into the other one. Both copters plummeted to the ground, causing an explosion that consumed most of the police cars that were chasing after them. Only three of them were left and they began opening fire at Ben. He tried to reload quickly, but before he could, another tractor truck rushed forward, bulldozing the three cars off the road.

Ben then shut the door, and everyone set back up as they continued their escape. Travis couldn't tell how much time has passed since then, but it felt like hours. The constant bumps and shaking made it impossible for him to get any kind of sleep. He doubted that he would have been able to sleep after everything that has happened. He's a fugitive. He'll forever be on the run. There isn't anywhere safe for him as long as he's in this country.

He quickly walked away from those depressing thoughts that were creeping upon him. He made his choice. No one forced him to accept that gun and follow Ben. He can't have any regrets. The only thing he can do now is to move forward and continue to survive. Suddenly the truck came to a stop, and everyone started getting up in anticipation of getting out, but no one opened the door yet.

The truck began to shake, knocking those that were standing back down. Travis could feel that the truck was moving, but it felt like they were on some kind of elevator as he felt the sensation of them descending. Once they came to a complete stop, the door finally opened to reveal a group of people in black like the ones that The Panthers' soldiers were wearing. The moment that they have spotted Ben, all of them saluted by putting their fist across their chest.

"Chief Ben. The commander has been expecting your arrival." One of the soldiers spoke.

"Yeah, I bet. Took him long enough." Ben scoffed as he jumped down. Everyone else was exiting the vehicle. Once Travis stepped out, he stared in amazement at the place that he was currently in. They were in what looked like a large storage facility, except this one was filled with every single type of military vehicle and weapons that one could imagine. Tanks and missiles were lined up next to each other, and he could see crates everywhere and had no doubt that each one was filled with weapons. He couldn't imagine how they were able to obtain all of this and were able to hide it all. It was like Travis was in one of those spy movies where the main character was shown the secret weapons vault. Looking at all of this, Travis was surer, now than ever, that The Panthers are preparing for war.

"Impressive, isn't it?" Travis jumped. He turned to see Ben right behind him.

"Yeah, it is. But there's something that I still don't get."

"And what would that be?"

"What do you stand to gain out of all of this?" He had that question since the day that he first met Ben. What would a leader of a gang want to do with something like this? He doubted that they would be able to profit out of this? There had to be something.

"I have always dreamed of the day when we would all be united. And we are very close to achieving that." United? Did he mean The Crips? Did they ally with The Panthers? Travis looked around and saw that there were more tractor trucks than the one he rode in. The people that were coming out of them were all Crips! There were hundreds of them, maybe even thousands! And the facility was getting filled up.

"It's not just us," Travis looks back as Ben spoke. "All of the Blood will be coming here as well. For the first time in our history, we will at last be united." *Woah!* Travis thought with his eyes wide open. Not only The Crips but The Bloods as well? The Panthers were able to enlist these two who were enemies since the beginning of their cause. Now that's scary. The Bloods and The Crips are the best-known and most notorious gangs in the country. Each of them has members in tens of thousands, and now all of them are going to work for The Panthers.

"Why are you all doing this? What can possibly be the point?" Travis asked. Knowing their history with one another he couldn't see any reason why any of them would willingly join forces.

"I wouldn't worry about stuff like that right now. Besides, I believe that there's someone here that wants to see you." Travis raised an eyebrow at him. Who would want to see him? He doesn't know anyone here besides Ben and Devante. Ben pointed behind Travis and when he turned around, his heart stopped. Right there in the middle of the crowd, facing him, was the one person that he thought he would never see again. The one person he tried so desperately to find only to get caught in someone else's game as a mere pawn. The reason why he was willing to go through all that hell. The reason why he's here.

"Janaye."

Chapter

18

Ben watched, in amusement, the silent reunion in front of him. Neither had made a move or attempted to say anything to each other. It was as though both were frozen in time. Janaye looked over and saw Ben giving her a sly grin. She narrowed her eyes at him and finally made the first move by marching over to Travis.

Before Travis could realize what was happening, she was already in front of him. She didn't say anything as she grabbed his arm and started walking. Ben laughed at the stupid look on Travis' face as he was being dragged away.

"Don't hurt him too bad now!" Ben teased. Janaye responded by showing him her middle finger, which only made him laugh harder.

"Chief Ben," He stopped laughing and turned to see the same person that first greeted him. "The commander awaits your arrival; follow me please." Ben followed them to the entrance of a hallway, passing by many individuals on the way. The majority of them were soldiers, but some of them were part of the medical unit and the Science and Technology Division. They passed by a training facility, where all of the recruits were going through various drills. He chuckled internally, thinking on how Travis would fare once he gets put through the wringer too.

They reached the end of the hall, where there were a pair of doors that were heavily guarded. Once the soldiers on guard saw Ben, one of them knocked on the wall next to the door, and an access panel appeared. They entered a code and a blue light came out that scanned Ben before sliding open.

Ben gave a low whistle, being impressed at the amount of security the place has. He entered the room and was greeted with a large circular table in the middle. He took note of all of those that were in attendance. It was his first time seeing them all, well except for one. The other chiefs of The Panthers, or as Huey likes to call them his disciples, are the top executives of the organization. They all lead the various departments that comprise The Panthers.

He saw that the table was split between the genders. All of the women were on the right side, while the men were on the left. Interesting setup. He also noted that there were three empty seats. Now that he has arrived, that takes care of one, but who do the other two seats belong to? He figured that he would be the last one to show up. He walked to the left side of the table and found himself a seat.

"Brother Ben. It's good to have you with us at last." Ben turned his attention to Huey, who spoke sitting at the head of the table.

"Yeah, figured that you got too comfortable in that cage you made and bitched out." Came the taunt from one of the men in the room. Ben recognized the man that spoke as David Jackson or, as he was called throughout L.A., The Red Devil. He was known as one of the most prominent leaders of The Bloods. Everyone knew of his viciousness as a cold blooded killer, and the bloody path he made to rise to the top. Before Ben was in prison, he had met David only twice, but it was long enough to know that they were polar opposites. Their viewpoints clashed with each other, and both times, they almost ended their meetings in bloodshed.

Ben didn't bother to reply and decided to check out the other members. Two of them were clearly military men, and by the stars on their uniforms, they're exceedingly high up in the chain. The other guy looked like a regular businessman. The women on the other side didn't seem all that special, but with this organization, he knew that there was way more to them than meets the eye. The fact that they had a seat on this table was proof enough, considering that this is the war room. Huey looked around and stood up.

"Now that all of the members are present, we can finally begin."

"Hey boss," David interrupted. "We're still missing two people." Everyone now focused on the emptied seats. Though they were indeed curious about it they didn't dare to question Huey about it, luckily David was bold enough to voice their thoughts. Huey didn't skip a beat to answer the question.

"Be assured that no one is missing. Those seats are vacant at the moment but will be filled very soon. Once they are ready for their roles to be my disciples." Everyone wondered just who they could be. From what Huey had said, it could be assumed that they are not yet part of The Panthers. They were a bit concerned about that, the fact that they are all here means that they're ready for the final phase before all hell breaks loose. This meeting should have all the leaders present, but they won't question Huey on the matter.

"Putting that aside for the moment, we have other things to discuss. Now that we have brothers Ben and David here, the unification is almost complete." Everyone besides David and Ben was confused about what Huey had said. The rest of the chiefs were briefed on who they were, but that was all. They also had an understanding of how both gangs operated, and while they could bring in a good number of soldiers, honestly, it won't be enough.

"Sir Huey," Lucas spoke up. "Can you elaborate for us? What unification?"

"Of course. The reason why this was not spread to you all was that I did not think that this would work. The Bloods and Crips are overly complex organizations with many sections or sets as they like to be called. The leaders of each of these sets have such different ideologies from each other that it made it impossible for us to recruit them to our cause. However, that situation has changed."

"There are over one-hundred and fifty Blood sets in Los Angeles. Every single one of them, including the Prius, have been taken under my control. That gives us ten thousand soldiers." David spoke up to everyone.

"There are one-hundred and ninety five Crip sets throughout the county. As of right now, all of them are in my command and that brings fifteen thousand soldiers." Ben announced.

"In doing so, we are one step closer to the unity of all major gangs in the country. Their eyes are on us and what we accomplish in L.A. Once we have them in our ranks our army will be complete." No one else needed further explanation. Ben and David were able to bring in a force of twenty-five thousand strong, and that was only from the Los Angeles County. Imagine if they could incorporate not only all of the Bloods and Crips, but the other major African American gangs into The Panthers. Combine that with the current numbers in their ranks; they would have a force that easily rivals that of the National Guard.

While they knew that they originally lacked in manpower, none understood that better than the two eldest members in the room. Admiral James Lamar and General Reginald Mack. Of all the chiefs, they are the forefront in military strategy and serve as Huey's advisors in warfare. They constantly warned Huey that with the lack of able soldiers, they would still be overturned by the sheer number of the National Guard.

They did their part to make sure that when The Panthers were ready that the Navy and the Marines wouldn't swarm them. The Army had their hands full ever since that border dispute between Turkey and Syria popped up and the government feared that a terrorist organization might try to capitalize on the situation. The Air Force is still trying to decipher what The Ark is since they still think it's a Russian satellite. That took care of four major problems for them, which left them to deal with the National Guard. They both cautioned Huey, that the moment The Pentagon catches wind of their actions they would send in their full force at them.

Huey took note of their concerns, but it seemed to them that he didn't take that disadvantage as seriously as they wanted their leader to. He would only wave it off and say that he has a plan. Both of them now took a sigh of relief that he actually had something and that it succeeded.

"Commander," General Mack spoke. "With our army now having sufficient numbers for the first strike, are we finally ready?" Huey gave a predatory grin.

"That's right. The time has finally come. We are now ready to begin operation Promise Land." Everyone in the room couldn't help but feel excitement at Huey's announcement. All these years of plotting and hiding are now coming into fruition. The long-awaited Promise Land that they are all willing to sacrifice their lives for will soon be in their grasp. The beginning and the end. It all starts now. The final operation.

"You all have your assignments. Once the signal has been ignited, you may begin. My brothers and sisters, our time is now. For the light of the revolution."

"We will rise!" The collective cry of everyone vibrated throughout the room as they all stood up and put their fist across their chest.

"Prepare yourselves, my disciples. Soon, we go to war."

Location, Unknown; Time, Unidentified

Travis sat still staring at Janaye in a room that she dragged him to. The entire time he hasn't said another word and neither did she. There were so many questions running through his mind. Too many questions, and he didn't know where to start. Before entering the room, he was able to take a look at the interior of the place. It was like an underground fortress. They first entered through a hallway that seemed to stretch endlessly like a maze.

There were many sections that they passed through that had huge windows that allowed Travis to see through. Clinics, training rooms, laboratories, libraries, armories, and even an indoor temple. This place has everything that you could imagine. You would think that whoever designed this place was preparing for the apocalypse. Travis put aside his thoughts of interior architecture to focus on the present situation.

Right in front of him was the only person that he had wanted to see so badly. Thinking of her was the only thing that made him not lose himself when he was in prison. It was the only thing that he thought of when he accepted Ben's offer and escaped. All of it was for her.

"You shouldn't be here." Janaye whispered. Though she spoke in an exceptionally low pitch, Travis was able to hear. He shouldn't be here? The last time he saw her, she said to not worry about her, but did she really think that he wouldn't?!

"What are you saying? You're the one that told me about that meeting to go to, remember? That's what started all of this!" Janaye sighed before responding.

"That's not what I meant." It wasn't an answer that Travis wanted to hear as he became more agitated.

"Then what?! You tell me not to go and find you, but at the same time, leave out bits and pieces for me to find like I'm Scooby-Doo. All of that shit I had to deal with! And now this!" Travis had to calm himself down as he kept getting worked up the more, he talked. Jasmine didn't say anything while he was ranting at her. There's not much she can say that will make this better. She waited for him to settle down to explain but was cut off.

"How long?" Travis asked abruptly. Janaye didn't understand what he was asking of her.

"How long what?"

"How long have you been a part of this?" The moment that she saw Travis, she knew that it would lead to this. She prays that he can understand her reasoning and believe her that she was trying to protect him. Everything she did was to protect him, but right now, he deserves the truth.

"A few years before I first met you." Travis was shell shocked at what Jasmine said. They had their first encounter in Middle School when they were both twelve. That could only mean that she was part of The Panthers for more than a decade!

"For the past thirteen years, I have been a spy for The Panthers."

Chapter

19

Downtown Los Angeles, CA; 8:45 PM

The past couple of days have not been kind to Mayor Jonathan Lambright. Ever since the day The Panthers had stormed into one of the local news stations, their name had spread throughout the entire city. Practically every corner is filled with graffiti of their propaganda.

The tension between the people and the police force has started to skyrocket due to the numerous accounts of confrontations that left many injured. He's slowly losing control of the city, and it's because of those damn Panthers and that upstart Alex Williams.

The moment Alex's campaign office was attacked, it somehow turned him to L.A.'s golden child. Everything that he did gather all of the attention and the people ate his words up like he's the champion of the Iron Chef. Last night, in particular, gave him more of a headache than anything else. It was the night of the mayoral debate, and everyone was treating Alex like he was God's gift to the Earth.

Jonathan, on the other hand, got completely one-sided and was attacked at every angle. If there were ever a public enemy number one, then he would be the top candidate. His administration was put on fire and his leadership was severely questioned. He couldn't understand how everyone went south so fast. As if that wasn't bad enough, there was a prison break at the Twin Towers, in which they lost several correctional officers and inmates. Speaking of the inmates, they had lost their most notorious one that night.

To top everything now, it seems that Detective Pope is missing! Jonathan had the entire city searched when a week had passed since he heard an updated report from the detective. Nothing. It was like the man just vanished into thin air. Jonathan thought at first that the detective may have found a major lead and is going undercover, but if that was the case, he would have been notified about that.

The detective warned both him and the commissioner about these Panthers. Jonathan didn't take it that seriously, considering that he had never heard of them and believed that they couldn't pose to be any threat to him. What a fool he was and now he's paying the price for his negligence.

The situation is becoming dire. So much that he had to have a meeting with all of the heads of the police force in the county. He made a declaration that if anyone is caught in suspicious activity involving The Panthers, they are to be labeled as part of a domestic terrorist group and to be apprehended. He had hope that it would allow him to get a hold of the city, and that was the best that he could do at the moment.

Of course, the entire force wasted no effort scouring Los Angeles in constant patrols. Many people were placed into custody, whether they were guilty or not. This action caused a deeper rift between the LAPD and the public and Jonathan has no idea how to fix it. He couldn't just pull back the order that he issued. The Panthers are a menace and he cannot allow them to grow and infect his city.

Jonathan stayed in his office late into the night, pacing around his desk, hoping that a solution to his problems would magically appear. He wished that Detective Pope was here to at least help in providing him with information. Thinking about the detective, Jonathan thought over what the LAPD had found about his disappearance. Detective Pope was last seen at a bar that was down the street from the hotel that he was staying in. Unfortunately, none of the workers there knew where he went off to.

Before that, he was spotted at the Twin Towers Correctional Center. Luckily, the assistant warden, Captain Burns, survived the prison break and was able to confirm that the detective was indeed there and that he was speaking to an inmate named Travis Miller. If Jonathan remembers correctly, Travis was the one that was convicted in the murder of Officer Peeves. Captain Burns didn't give any information on what they were talking about, and they couldn't use any of the footage or recording since all of it was destroyed during the prison break.

Tracing back before he went to the Twin Towers, a few of the LAPD officers noted that he was seen in the department building with Alex

Williams and a woman that he later found out was a reporter. Funny enough, when they looked into that reporter, they found out that she works for the same news station that was attacked by The Panthers and that she was there when it happened.

Jonathan was curious about why Alex Williams caught the detective's attention, but he was more interested in that reporter. This is definitely something that can be used for his advantage, but he would have to play his cards carefully. If he did anything to L.A.'s new Wonder Boy recklessly, then there would be Armageddon. He had to make his moves very discreet and have that woman tracked.

Several things about that woman didn't add up to Jonathan. There were many coincidental moments between her and The Panthers but making a move too soon will invoke the wrath of Alex Williams since the man had no shame to show the whole city that she's his woman. It will be tricky, but Jonathan won't let that stop him. He's worked too hard just to stand and watch everything that he has made crumble.

"This is a nice office you have here." Jonathan jumped at the new voice in the room. He scanned the place to see a figure in the back looking through the bookshelf.

"Who are you?! How did you get in?" Jonathan's heart was pounding hard. He didn't even hear the person sneak inside. Is this an assassin?!

"Calm down. I'm not here to harm you." Jonathan took a moment to calm down, and when he was able to think straight, he glanced at the emergency button under his desk. He slowly reached over to press it.

"I wouldn't bother pressing that," Jonathan jumped again as the figure spoke. "No one will come. I made sure of that." Jonathan pressed the button anyways, but the alarm didn't go off. Well, that would explain how this person got in.

"Who are you and what do you want from me?" If this intruder was really here for his life, then he would be dead right now. The only thing that Jonathan could think of is that this is a threat. The figure started walking closer and Jonathan immediately recognized who this was as they entered into the light and sat down on a chair in front of his desk.

"I believe that a formal introduction is in order, Huey Carter." There was no need for that because Jonathan knew very well who this man is though Jonathan had only seen his face once; this is the leader of The Panthers.

"What do The Panthers want from me? It's bad enough that you're trying to turn this city into a warzone." Huey chuckled at the accusation.

"It's funny that you mentioned that. I'm here to present you an offer so that the exact scenario doesn't happen." Jonathan was on alarm. So, The Panthers do have that intention in mind. What do they gain by that? But what's more puzzling is what kind of offer Huey's trying to make.

"And what would that be?" Jonathan felt a cold sweat rolling down as he watches Huey being comfortable in his office. The overwhelming pressure that he feels while Huey is as calm as ever, it's like Jonathan is discussing with the devil. Huey gave him a predatory grin making his demonic image more realistic.

"Give me Los Angeles." Jonathan blinked a few times. Did he hear that right?

"Pardon?" Jonathan had to be sure that he didn't hear things. Huey couldn't have asked him what he thought he did.

"I do hate to repeat myself," Huey sighed as he stood up and leaned over the desk. "Surrender the city to me. You and the LAPD will leave Los Angles. That is my only offer." It was exactly as he feared. This maniac in front of him wants to take over the city like some deranged dictator. Is that what this is all about? In the first place, Jonathan doesn't even have the authority to do that. A threat to the city is a threat to the United States government. Jonathan cannot just hand over Los Angles. However, he assumes that Huey is the type to act out un-rationally if he is given an unsatisfied answer, so Jonathan chose his words carefully.

"That is quite an offer. And suppose, if I may ask, what if I am not able to fulfill your request?" It was a question he had to ask because it was an action that he definitely couldn't do.

"You'll see that we can be very persuasive." Yeah, Jonathan did not doubt that. It's the method of persuasion that worries him. He could

RISE OF THE PANTHERS

only imagine the amount of destruction and chaos that The Panthers can further inflict.

"You must understand that what you're asking is impossible for me to do. Even if I do step down from my position, the government will not take your actions lightly. With the kind of force that they'll summon to suppress you, I'm afraid that it will lead to more bloodshed on your part. I beg you; please think about this. If not for your own sake, then for the city of Los Angeles." Jonathan hoped that he was able to convince Huey. The fact he made the offer told Jonathan that they do not have the numbers to withstand a full assault. He concluded that they wanted the city so that they could operate under the White House's radar. That kind of thinking was beyond naïve and Jonathan prayed what he had said knocked some sense into Huey.

"Well, that is a shame," Huey commented as he backed away from Jonathan's desk. "Let's hope that you don't come to regret your decision." He said as he walked out of the office. At first, Jonathan was mentally patting himself on the back, thinking that he was able to persuade the man, but his self-praise was shattered by what Huey had said afterward. Jonathan didn't like the sound of that. He really didn't like what Huey had implied. He quickly went over to the phone on his desk to make a call.

"Commissioner Greenfield, I need you in my office now!"

Harvard Heights, Los Angeles, CA; 7:20 AM

Jasmine woke up feeling more mentally drained than usual. Ever since Huey came in and dropped that bombshell on her and Alex, she has been on guard. Hell, she even thought of leaving Los Angeles altogether, but Alex convinced her to stay. Alex, what a man. She remembered him trying to persuade Huey not to go through with their plans. He tried to say that if he were to become mayor that he would make sure to use his power for the people. That way, The Panthers would never have to worry and resort to what they are planning to do. Unfortunately, He wasn't able to move Huey as he said that it was too late.

After that, Alex worked nonstop on his campaign. He hoped that Huey would see his progress and have faith in him. Jasmine was with him every step of the way. She was even there at the debate, not as a reporter, where Alex crushed the other candidates. The people love him, and she hopes that's enough.

Jasmine walked outside of her apartment, getting ready to do her morning jog when she noticed smoke rising off in the horizon. Though it could be anything, something was telling her to go in that direction. She didn't know if it was her curiosity or fate that moved her. Jasmine went back to get her keys and drove off, following the trail of smoke. The closer she got; the more smoke polluted the air.

The trail led her to Beverly Hills where she entered into a very well-known prominent neighborhood. Only the wealthy lived here, and there were rumors that the realtors were very selective on who lived here, seeing that all the residents are white. As she got closer, she could see countless people running away. She parked on a nearby street and ran off to the source of the smoke.

When she arrived at the main entrance of the neighborhood, the scene before her could only be described as seeing hell itself. The fire was spreading everywhere. The entire neighborhood was in flames. Worse yet was that she could see people holding what looked like flamethrowers, torching everything in sight.

She couldn't believe what she was seeing. The heat was so intense that she could feel it as she stood across from the main gate. The gate itself was bent and broken as if it was busted through, and she could see the streets were occupied with black vans. She walked closer, ignoring the screams of the people either running for their lives or distraught that their homes are being destroyed. She passed through the gate to see a figure in the middle of the road and as she got closer, she was able to see that figure as Huey. She could feel tears flowing down her face. They were too late. They couldn't stop them.

"Huey!" Jasmine screamed. Huey turned around to face her.

"Sister Jones," He greeted calmly. "How unexpected to see you here. Be careful, or you might get burned." Is he insane? Everywhere around them is covered in flames and here he is casually talking to her like nothing's wrong?

"You have to stop! This isn't right. What you're doing isn't going to solve anything!" Huey didn't respond to her at first. To Jasmine, it seemed like he had a thoughtful expression thinking of what to say. Couldn't he see the destruction around him? How is this supposed to help the people?!

"Did you know, Sister Jones, that there was once a period in history where African Americans actually flourished? They created a place of their own that was so prosperous that it was a utopia for blacks. At that time, we governed ourselves and were able to thrive." Jasmine knew what he was talking about. In the early 1900s, there was a neighborhood in Tulsa, Oklahoma, called Greenwood. The area was also known as Black Wall Street because only African Americans lived there, but the people there were able to create massive wealth. It was a paradise for black people, until one day; everything changed. A mob of angry white men came and destroyed the entire neighborhood. Everything was burned to ashes.

"That was proof that we didn't need them. It could have been our promise land." Jasmine agreed that what happened to the people of Greenwood that day was nothing but horrific, but it doesn't excuse what he's doing now.

"How does something that happened that long ago justify what you're doing now?!"

"Because now it's their turn to experience a piece of the fear that we had to endure. The revolution is upon us my sister and with this, we have made our declaration."

"You're talking about starting a war with the United States! Do you understand how insane that is?!"

"It's only insane for those who are not willing to risk everything for freedom. For The Panthers, this is the only way." Jasmine couldn't comprehend that Huey believes that he can start to fight with the world's dominant Superpower and win. This is madness. Their conversation was interrupted by the sound of multiple sirens. Arriving at clockwork was the fire department and the police force.

Jasmine turned around at the moment of soldiers in black coming out to create a blockade at the front gate. They lined up, taking out their weapons and started firing on the incoming police. The LAPD in return hid behind their vehicles and returned fire. Fearing that she would get hit by a stray bullet in the crossfire, Jasmine chose to flee the area.

She was able to escape with her life, with luck on her side, without getting hit. She made one last glance at the struggle between the LAPD and The Panthers before running back to her car. However, before she could reach her vehicle, she was suddenly grabbed by the shoulders.

"Let go of me!" She screamed in panic. The same hand that had a hold of her turned her around, and she was face to face with an elderly man wearing an LAPD bulletproof vest. Taking a closer inspection, she knew this man to be Commissioner Greenfield.

"Jasmine Jones, in suspicion of being affiliated with a terrorist organization, you are hereby placed under arrest."

Chapter

20

Location, Unknown; Time, Unidentified

Travis laid on his bed in the private room that was given to him. His body was still sore over the drills that he had to do with the other recruits. He couldn't tell how long he has been here since being stuck inside an underground fortress has messed up his sense of time and add to the fact that there's no clock or anything to tell time made him feel like he was stuck in Purgatory.

He still couldn't get over what Janaye had shared with him. A spy for The Panthers! And even crazier is that she's been doing that since before she even hit puberty. She said that the reason why The Panthers wanted her at a young age was that no one ever suspects a young child.

That did explain some things to Travis. Like how she would go off at odd periods, especially during the summer. She would tell him at the time that she was going to summer camp or some other trip. To think that she was actually doing secret missions for The Panthers.

Everything else was toppled when she told him what her main mission was. It was him. Specifically, her main job was to look after him, like a bodyguard. Travis was crushed when he first heard that, thinking that their friendship was based on a lie. He felt that to her, everything that they've done together was just a mission.

She even admitted that in the beginning, it was only that. However, she said that as time went by and the more that she had gotten to know him, it turned into something else. Through all the things that she had to do for The Panthers, he was her only piece of normalcy. It made her want to stay by his side.

When Travis asked about her family, she said that neither of them knew about her. She kept it a secret from everyone. The fewer people knew, the more people she was protecting. Both her mother and brother are being escorted out of L.A. before The Panthers march through the city.

That was another thing that Travis had trouble accepting. The Panthers are trying to start a full-blown civil war! There's no way that they could win a fight with the power that the United States wields. Just thinking about what they will be up against is sending shivers down his spine. California alone has the second largest Naval Base in the country, not to forget about all of the army, air force, and marine bases that are scattered everywhere. They'll be surrounded by all sides if they try this crazy plan. And what's so special about L.A. anyway?

Janaye told him that everything was thought out and planned. The confidence that she has of The Panthers' capabilities scared him a bit. Even when she told them that they have a large enough army to match with the National Guard, it didn't boost any of his faith. He still believes that the odds are extremely against them.

After they talked, he didn't have a lot of time to dwell on his worries. Soon enough, he was thrown out to the wolves as he spent his days with the other soldiers. The training was non- stop. They started with weapon familiarization. The instructors had them go through a vast number of weapons, learning them inside and out of each one. They even had to learn how to dismantle and reassemble the weapons so that they could have a better understanding of what they were going to be using.

After that, it was teamwork exercises and the training room that they used was like a literal war zone. There were points during the exercises that Travis thought he was going to die. A medical unit was always present because of how dangerous the training was. It became a normal thing for Travis to see someone get hauled off from bullet wounds. He's surprised that no one has died yet.

The group of people that he trained with was interesting as well. His unit was comprised of mostly former Crips and Bloods. Even though they're now part of The Panthers, it didn't mean that they lost the past grudges between them. Many fights were started because of that, but all of them were quickly shut down by the instructors. Soon enough, even they learned to tolerate each other.

During that time, he was only able to see Janaye a few times. After their Love and Hip- Hop reunion special was over, they were able to reconcile and went back to interacting with each other like how they used to. It was a whole new breath of fresh air for Travis to have his best friend back finally.

They would talk for hours. Janaye would tease Travis saying how lucky he was to have his room. Usually, all of the soldiers would sleep in the same shared area and only the top officers would have their own space. Travis wondered about that as well but didn't put much thought into it as having his own room has been a blessing, especially after he gets through a rough training session.

He would always complain to Janaye about the training. She would laugh at his grumblings and use words of encouragement to lift his spirits; that is if you can count "stop being a little bitch" as one. It was during those moments together that Travis finally realized that his feelings for her ran much deeper than being friends.

He cherished every second that he spent with Janaye. He loved it when she would laugh, even if it was at his expense. Her smile would always bring his energy back after a long and tiring day. As long as he can see her smile, everything else doesn't matter to him.

Travis didn't believe that he was in love, or it's better to say that he doesn't know enough to understand if he is. It's not an emotion that he has ever felt before for another person, so he doesn't have anything to base off on what he feels. However, he does care about her. He genuinely cares for her to the point that he will take a bullet for her without a second thought. If it's for her safety and happiness, he will do anything.

That was why he was so hurt when they first reunited, and Janaye told him her past. You think that you know someone that close to you and come to find out that you didn't have a single clue. It was a major backhand to the face, and he didn't know how to handle it at the time. Eventually, he was able to move past his feelings of betrayal because the awkwardness that was between them was too much for him.

Besides Janaye, he hasn't seen Ben around often as well. He was only able to catch the man a few times. Travis was confused because when he would meet up with Ben; everyone else around them would act all stiff as soon as they saw the man. They all treated Ben like some general and called him chief. Travis had no idea why they call him that or what that meant. Janaye explained that in The Panthers, there are individuals that are referred to as The Twelve Chiefs. They are the top leaders of the organization and only answer to the man that leads them all, Huey.

Travis would be lying if he said that he wasn't interested in Huey. He still has no idea why he was targeted for their schemes, and no one is giving him any answers. Another person that he was interested in was Kiana, but for different reasons.

He would love nothing more than to pay her back for what she did to him, but Janaye shot that down once she told him that she was a Chief as well and that he wouldn't be able to even touch her. Besides, Janaye informed him that Kiana and the other chiefs had already spread out to the different hideouts throughout the West Coast. Travis was surprised to hear that they have multiple bases and that this one was the main headquarters.

More people started filling in each day as they prepared for mobilization. Today, his unit was told that they would be heading out to Los Angeles in the next three days. After their brief, the reality of the situation hit Travis like a wrecking ball. He had his mind and body occupied with many other things that he forgot one crucial detail; he was going to war. He has no experience as a soldier and even through all the harsh training, going out into the battlefield, terrified Travis. Killing that one guard during his escape was bad enough, but now he's expected to kill more.

It plagued his mind as Travis laid on his bed. He couldn't sleep. He had a sickening feeling in the pit of his stomach and there was no way of getting rid of it. A knock on the door alerted him out of his thoughts.

"Travis, it's me." He heard Janaye call out. He got up and opened the door to see her dressed in nothing but an oversized shirt and booty shorts.

"You sure you can walk around like that?" Travis joked with a sly grin.

"Oh, shut up." She snapped back and pushed him aside, walking in. Travis shook his head as he closed the door and followed her. One thing for sure didn't change, which he was grateful for, her personality was the same. Her fiery attitude in Travis's opinion is one of her best qualities. She never gave in to anyone's bullshit and spoke her mind like a loaded M-16. He watched as she plopped on his bed and he sat down next to her.

They sat in silence for a minute and that made Travis worried. Usually, she would make herself at home and barge right into his room, talking up a storm. Something was bothering her that was very obvious, but he decided to wait until she makes the first move.

"I hear you'll be heading out soon." Janaye said solemnly. Travis rose an eyebrow. So that's what's been eating her.

"Yeah. I take it you won't be joining us?"

"If only, but I have my own assignments to complete."

"So, this is the last time we'll see each other."

"Don't say it like that!" She said sharply, facing him. "We're going to survive this. This isn't the end. Just don't be an idiot."

"Well, that shouldn't be a problem. Since when I have ever been one?"

"I don't know. Sometimes I wonder."

"Wow. The deadly secret agent Janaye Freed is worried about us commoners." He joked but didn't hear her snap back at him. He looked at her and saw her hunched over the bed.

"Of course, I worry about you, you idiot," She said softly. "There's still time. You don't have to do this." Though he couldn't see her face he knew that she was beginning to cry. Travis understood because he was scared as well. The thought of going to war terrifies him, but the thought of anything happening to Janaye was much worse.

"I have all the reason to right here." Travis didn't know what compelled him to do so as he reached his hand over and cupped Janaye's face. He slowly lifted her head so that they were face to face and used this thumb to wipe away a stray tear. He was looking at her like that; he made a solemn vow that this will be the last time that he will see her in such a state.

Janaye didn't know what Travis was doing, but she didn't stop him. His hand was so warm that she could feel the heat warming her body. She soon felt another hand touching the other side of her face. She held her breath as Travis stared down at her. It was as if he could see right through her and down to her soul.

Travis also didn't understand what he was doing, but he couldn't stop. He never realized but can now see just how beautiful her eyes are. Elegant, but at the same time, it stayed true to its primal nature. A predator who bows to no one and yet as gentle as a newborn fawn.

Travis couldn't tell how long they were in that position, but he has never felt this sense of peace. Even with the war looming over the horizon, none of that mattered. Going on autopilot, he slowly pulled Janaye closer to him. If this is truly to be their last moment together, then he had to make sure that there were no regrets in his heart.

He leaned in closer, able to feel the breath coming out of her. He paused for a second, afraid that his advancement was unwanted. Looking into her eyes, he saw nothing but approval and went in closer to lightly press his lips against hers. Rich dark chocolate was what he tasted. He moved his hand from her face to move her closer to him. He savored every flavor that she had to offer.

Janaye responded with wrapping her arms around him. The sensation that she is experiencing was unlike any other. Janaye was never a submissive person. She didn't allow anyone to move her, especially any male. This, however, was different. For the first time in her life, she is permitting a man to take over. It scared her, but at the same time excited her and not because Travis is taking the lead. It's because she's allowing him to and by relinquishing her control, she is letting herself be vulnerable to him.

Janaye felt his hands gently touch her skin. His fingers gliding from her cheek, down to her neck and onto her shoulders. Being in the profession that she's in there were many times when the mission called her to entertain the targets. She always felt disgusted when they touched her, but not now.

She hasn't once shuddered away as Travis' fingers stroked her body like an artist painting a masterpiece. She soon felt herself being lowered. Travis carefully laid her down as if he was handling a precious family heirloom. He moved on top of her, making sure to support himself so that his weight wouldn't bring her any discomfort.

As if anticipating for this moment, it seemed that time itself had stopped as they took off the other's clothing piece by piece. Travis couldn't help but be humbled at the body of perfection that laid before him. He was looking at the entity of a goddess, blessing her presence to a mere mortal.

He could feel the heat of her body penetrating him as he lowered himself inch by inch. She wrapped her arms around his back as their bodies finally touched. He began worshiping her in every possible way from head to toe. Nothing was left untouched. When he came back up, he ran his hands through each curl of her hair as his lips explored the nape of her neck.

Her hands that were around his shoulders began to tighten. He moved from her neck back up so that they were nose to nose. Janaye lifted one of her hands from his shoulder to his face and nodded. That was all that he needed as he held her tightly, melting his body into hers. Her nails dug deeply into his skin, but he didn't feel any pain. This was pure unadulterated ecstasy. The two have now become one being.

In that moment, there was no looming war. The Panthers didn't exist. Nothing else matters. Only a man and a woman together in their own Garden of Eden. They will let tomorrow's troubles welcome them when it comes, but for now, they'll stay here, safe and protected in their small piece of forever.

Chapter

21

Downtown Los Angeles, CA; 3:20 PM

Mayor Lambright leaned over his desk with his hand massaging his temple, trying to deal with the massive headache he has. Why can't anything just go his way? He couldn't even trust his own ears when he heard that those lunatics had the audacity to burn down an entire neighborhood.

And not just any regular one, no, they had to go and attack one of the richest communities in the damn city! His inbox was slaughtered with the outrage of people that lost their homes. While normally, he would have pushed their concerns aside for another date, he couldn't do it this time. The majority of them have supported his candidacy for mayor during the previous election and helped him win.

The only good thing that came out of this whole fiasco is the fact that they have that woman, Jasmine Jones, in their custody. Of course, Alex Williams brought the thunder and lightning into his office, demanding her release. The boy scout tried his best at his junior lawyer act but was no match for Jonathan and the commissioner.

Thankfully, he backed down, but Jonathan wasn't stupid. He knew that Alex was planning something, and sure enough, the following day, City Hall was bombarded by protesters. They were preaching about Jasmine's innocence and that he and the police are abusing their power.

The security tried their best to have them leave the premises since they didn't have a permit, but soon, even that escalated. When things were about to start looking ugly, lo, and behold, Alex Williams swooped in to save the day. He was able to calm the protesters and his security team. Jonathan will give the bastard points for knowing how to sway the people.

It didn't matter what Alex does; they won't relinquish Jasmine. In every major incident regarding The Panthers, she has been there, front and center. It couldn't have been a coincidence, and now that they have her, Jonathan hopes that he will finally be able to gain useful information. They haven't been able to get anything out of her yet, but it's only a matter of time.

Time. Jonathan wished he had more of that right now. After everything that has happened, he didn't believe that it could get any worse, but the universe had decided to screw him over once again. This morning he had received a grave message from Huey. He had immediately called in his top cabinet members, advisors, and all of the heads of the various public services in the city, which included the LAPD.

His office became cramped as everyone arrived, but Jonathan put out their discomfort as a minor issue. After he gets done making his announcement, everything else that has transpired so far will be of little consequence.

"Thank you, everyone, for taking the time to come here on such short notice."

"Mayor Lambright," A director of one of the leading hospitals in L.A spoke up. "What is this about?" Jonathan stood up from his chair, facing all of the occupants in the room.

"I'm sure by now you are all aware of a certain group that has been terrorizing our city. The Panthers." Everyone started whispering amongst themselves when they heard that name. They all have heard of The Panthers, and the rumors that were spreading about them were not flattering.

"What does this have to do with them, Mayor?" Asked the C.E.O of the city's power plant company.

"A few days ago, I was visited late at night by the man who controls them." Everyone was shocked, except for Commissioner Greenfield. The rest couldn't believe that the leader of The Panthers would go and talk to the mayor. All of them wondered what the topic of their conversation was and how does that correlate to why Jonathan had summoned them.

"That night, he gave me a proposal."

"What was it?" One of the County Supervisors asked.

"He demanded that I step down as mayor and surrender Los Angeles to him and The Panthers." The room became deathly silent. No one knew how to react to what they just heard because, honestly, they hoped that Jonathan was playing a prank on them. Their hopes were diminished as Jonathan continued to talk.

"Obviously, that is something that I cannot do. However, they didn't accept my answer very well." They knew what he meant. You had to be blind not to have seen that mountain of smoke and dust that day. The fire department barely came back alive while trying to put the scorching flames out.

"We had hoped to suppress this potential threat at the time before it came to this point, but we were too late." Commissioner Greenfield spoke dreadfully.

"Mayor Lambright, what does he mean by that?" The director of the city's radio communications asked frantically. Jonathan knew that what he would say next will be put into the history of Los Angeles, even the state of California. Whether he lives to see it or not is still up for debate.

"This morning, I have received a notice from that man. They're coming. The Panthers will be marching their way here to downtown within three days." Their reactions were what Jonathan had expected. A mix of utter disbelief and despair. He couldn't blame them; it's not every day that your home is being threatened with invasion. This new reality is something that no one had ever thought would come to pass, not in the U.S.

"What do we do?" Jonathan knew what he had to do, and at the same time, it terrified him. At that moment, he will be committing his last act as the mayor of Los Angeles. He did his best to protect his city, but now this is the only thing that he can do.

"We must evacuate the city, at least all of downtown. That is why I have called all of you here. I will not allow these terrorists to run amuck and defile our home. The LAPD will propel this force and protect Los Angeles. However, we do not know their numbers or capabilities. At this point, it's obvious that they are willing to kill anyone who stands in their way, which is why we must have the citizens take shelter far away from here. I implore all of you to prepare and to assist so that this doesn't create mass hysteria. The people are our top priority!"

Though there was still fear in their eyes, Jonathan could see that they were resolved to do their part to protect the city. The rest of the meeting ended with Jonathan handing out each order to the different heads of public services. Everyone left in haste, except for Commissioner Greenfield. Once the last person had left, Jonathan slid down to his chair, mentally exhausted.

"Is this really the best that we can do?" Commissioner Greenfield questioned himself but was loud enough for Jonathan to hear.

"You and I are the only ones here that truly understand how frightening these people are. They were able to lay waste to an entire neighborhood right under our noses! The city is no longer safe."

"Do you think that we can trust them about having three days?" Commissioner Greenfield wouldn't put it past that The Panthers would promise one thing and then do the complete opposite.

"If nothing else, we can believe in that. They'll be here in that time frame. We have to be ready when they do. Were you able to contact the National Guard?" Jonathan had tried to request outside help from his contacts, but it was like none of them knew what was going on in L.A. It's impossible to think that after everything that transpired here, no one has heard anything. The city should have gotten national attention by now, but it's as if they're isolated from the rest of the country.

"No good. I couldn't patch through."

"What about the Navy? Army? Marines?... Coast Guard?!" All that the commissioner could do was shake his head. It can't be! There's no way that they couldn't have gotten any contact at all. If that's how it is, then Jonathan could only think of one reason why it is so. The Panthers had somehow hacked into their telecommunications and have been monitoring them since the beginning, but it's ludicrous even to think that was possible. Still, that's the only explanation that Jonathan could think of.

"Then we're on our own," Jonathan mumbled dejectedly, then stared up at the commissioner with a newfound resolve. "Once we have successfully evacuated the city, have your men positioned at these pinpoints. We won't let them have their way." Jonathan handed the commissioner a detailed map of downtown with various points around the city. He looked through all of the locations and noticed something peculiar; none of them was where they are currently holding Jasmine.

"What about the woman?"

"Bring her here. No doubt that they'll try to come straight here, and we may have another use for her. Also, have your men find Alex Williams. If we have both of them, then we may survive this. I leave you in charge." The commissioner nodded in confirmation and walked out of the office. Jonathan stood up and went over to a small drawer and took out a bottle of scotch. He poured some in a small glass and took a sip as he overlooked the city in this short tranquility, the calm before the storm.

Location, Unknown; 4:05 AM

Huey took a deep breath of the morning's fresh air. It was something that he hasn't felt in a long time. Today is the day. The markings of the beginning and the end; it all starts now.

The troops were spread out to their given locations, and his chosen disciples were there in command while he took charge of claiming Los Angles. Everything is finally beginning to fall into place, and now all he needs to do is light the torch. The force that he is commanding is all ready for what is to come, and he could not be any prouder of what The Panthers have become. Because now they will show not only this country but the world what it means to rise.

They moved out early in the morning before sunrise. It would take a while for them to reach their destination, but Huey was fine with that. He waited this long; a few hours meant nothing to him. The cold breeze of the new day jolted his senses. The wind rushing through his nose made him feel more alive than ever. The feeling of freedom at this moment, he wouldn't trade for anything.

When they entered the main highway that led straight to downtown, Huey noticed the lack of traffic, or better yet, its nonexistence. It looks like the mayor took the gift that Huey gave him seriously. It works out better for him anyway, the fewer people in the way, the better. As they got closer, each exit was gated off.

"Commander?" The driver questioned in concern.

"Fear not my brother. They are merely welcoming us, and it would be rude to refuse their invitation." With Huey's confirmation, the driver honked his horn loudly, signaling the others to continue forward. They drove down the highway as the sun started to rise to set the stage for their arrival. Soon, they were able to see the majestic sight of downtown as the morning rays of the sun touched the city.

Their journey came to an end as they were greeted with a line of LAPD and SWAT vehicles. Hundreds of cars filled the area behind the line they created. Huey gave the order to stop at a reasonable distance and told the driver to inform the rest not to move until he gave the signal.

Huey got out of the vehicle and walked right in front of it, facing Commissioner Greenfield, who was standing at the head of the police line. Huey took the time to see the assets that they had brought to confront him and The Panthers. He compared it to his force, taking a glance from behind.

The Calvary that Huey brought consisted of black vehicles in all shapes and sizes, with many of them having a machine gun attached and a soldier that is waiting to fill every last one of their adversaries with holes. The majority of them were equipped with front metal shields that had thick spikes sticking out. A true force to behold. Comparing it to this pathetic excuse of a repellant before him, Huey almost felt a bit of sympathy. After his inspection, he turned his attention back to the commissioner.

"It's so good of you to come out all this way just to welcome us," Huey announced loudly. He took a moment to appreciate viewing downtown as the sun was still rising. "A lovely day, isn't it?"

"This is your last chance!" The commissioner shouted to Huey. "We don't have to do this. Innocent blood can be spared today. If you continue this path, you know that there is only one way that this can end!" Huey stared back at him for a moment and then laughed. It wasn't something that Commissioner Greenfield imagined it to be. It was cold and dark. It was a laugh that one would make as if they heard a really funny joke, and if he was being honest with himself, that made Huey look even more menacing.

"No." Huey corrected as he raised his hand in the air. Every officer in the line took out their weapons, and at the same time, The Panthers drew theirs. In the next few seconds, Commissioner Greenfield will thank God that they were able to get everyone out of the city.

"There is only one way that this will end." The moment that Huey closed his hand into a fist, multiple explosions went off throughout the downtown area. The force that it created took the police officers by surprise. Commissioner Greenfield looked over and noticed that where the explosions had set off were around the exact areas that his men were hiding. *Damn it!* He cursed. The Panthers are more capable than he realized.

The collective war cry from The Panthers was deafening. Commissioner Greenfield and his force steeled their resolve, preparing for the worst to come. They didn't know if they will be able to see tomorrow, but one thing is for sure, and that is no matter who wins or loses, whatever happens, today will forever leave a lasting mark on the state of California. The battle for Los Angeles has begun.

Chapter

22

China Town, Los Angeles, CA; 7:45 AM

Travis waited anxiously inside a black truck, alongside Devante at the driver's seat. They're accompanied by three other vehicles, all waiting for the signal. Travis' group, as well as the others that have spread throughout the city, had left The Panthers' headquarters about two days ago before the main force had arrived.

They hid in the areas that they were given to be in charge of and were briefed that those points were where the LAPD was planning on ambushing the main force as they marched through downtown. So, they stayed out of sight as the rest of the city was being evacuated. Travis was thankful for that because he didn't want any more innocent people caught up in this mess.

"Nervous?" Travis turned to Devante. Judging by the look on his face, it seems that Travis wasn't the only one.

"Of course. Anybody would be, only an idiot will deny it."

"Just keep your head straight and try not to get shot." Travis laughed, but he didn't know whether Devante was joking or not.

"I should be telling you that. Since you're the driver and all." Devante snorted as he leaned back. While it didn't make him any less nervous, it did drop the tension a bit. Travis noticed something out of the corner of his eyes and turned to see Devante holding his fist out to him.

"We'll survive this." Devante said firmly. He sounded confident, but Travis could still hear a trace of fear in his voice. He couldn't blame him; he's scared too. However, Travis decided to strengthen his resolve so that he'll be able to see another day.

"Yeah." Travis replied back as he bumped fists with Devante. At that moment, they felt the massive tremor as the explosions went off. The signal has been made!

"Hang on!" Devante shouted as he stomped on the gas pedal, speeding off into the street with the others following them. In all honesty, their mission is not a complicated one. They have only one real objective, which is to keep the enemy in their area at bay. While the LAPD is occupied with them, Huey and the main force can storm into City Hall and capture it.

Their job may be simple, but that didn't make it easy. They were briefed that the opposing side will not hesitate to hunt them down so the second that they engage, it's going to be kill or be killed. Everything was right on schedule, because as soon as they entered the China Town district, they were intercepted by the enemy squad.

Devante increased his speed and made a sharp right into a shopping area. The others that were initially following them went their separate ways. Split the enemy and take them out one by one was their strategy. Devante and Travis were being chased by two of them, and they were rapidly closing the distance.

Travis waited until they were close enough before he opened the sunroof and stood up on the seat with his rifle and began firing at the incoming vehicles. Both of them tried their best to swerve out of the way from Travis' onslaught. One of them lost control of the steering and almost ran into the other one, but they were able to maneuver out of the way, making the one that lost control run into one of the shops.

The remaining car returned fire on Travis and he quickly ducked back inside the truck. Through the chase, Travis could see the various burning shops and buildings that were affected by the explosion and was ever more thankful that no bystanders were here. Up ahead, Travis spotted an area that was heavily covered in smoke.

"Turn there!" Travis directed, pointing in that direction. Devante immediately understood what Travis was thinking and headed straight into it. It was worse than Travis thought because there was nothing but black in their surroundings. Travis hoped that with this idea, the other car wouldn't risk going inside or get lost in their pursuit. Speaking of lost, they have no idea where they were going, the smoke completely blocked their vision.

Devante tried to use the window wipers, but that had no effect. The darkness seemed endless that Travis thought that they would never be able to get out until he was able to see a speck of light. He guided Devante and they were able to escape into the sunlight. Back on the road, Travis rolled down the window and checked behind them to see if they were still being followed. Seeing no one or thing, he sat back in his seat and sighed in relief.

"That was crazy. At least we lost them." Devante remarked. Travis nodded in agreement and was about to take a few seconds to relax until he saw something up ahead. Something was coming out of the corner that they were approaching. He got tensed when he was able to see what it was.

"Watch out!" Travis tried to warn Devante, but it was too late. The car that Travis recognized as the one he thought he got rid of the first time came out and rammed them out of the street and into one of the shops. Devante tried to take back control, but the impact was so hard that before he could attempt to, they had already crashed. Both of them were severely disoriented as the airbags deployed were almost suffocating them.

"Damn." Devante grunted, pushing the airbag out of the way. Once Travis was able to gain his bearings, he did the same and got out of the truck. Taking a look at the state of their truck, Travis patted himself on the back for putting his seat belt on before they crashed. Travis had his rifle in the air as he surveyed the area and saw that the car that ran into them collided into a pole. He took a step closer and could see the dead officers in the car.

That's one down, and hopefully, the other one won't show up anytime soon. He went back to Devante, who was inspecting their truck to see if he could start it. Devante tried numerous times, but the thing just wouldn't start. Since the cop car is entirely busted, they now don't have any mode of transportation. This is not good.

"What not?" Travis asked.

"Our only goal is to occupy this area. As long as we stay here, then we will be doing our job. We need to find some cover." Travis can agree with that. As they are right now, they might as well hold up a big glowing sign saying, 'here I am, come and get me!' They continued going on foot, checking every street corner in case of any traps. So far, they haven't encountered anyone, but it would only be a matter of time. They took cover in a street corner as they heard the sound of a car coming by.

They hid as the car passed by and waited until it was safe to come out. As they walked on the street, Travis could hear a flapping sound in the distance. He looked around but didn't see anything, but the sound was getting louder. He looked up and saw that a helicopter was coming right at them.

"Shit!" Travis yelled as the helicopter that came in turned to the side, revealing someone handling a machine gun that began shooting at them. Travis had no time to think as he dived to the left, trying to avoid the bullets and took shelter in a small shopping area. He waited as the helicopter flew by and noticed that Devante wasn't with him. He peeped to the other side of the street to see that Devante had run off in the other direction. Travis inwardly cursed at their present situation. The plan was to separate the LAPD, not the other way around.

He looked over to where Devante was hiding and saw him giving him hand signals for Travis to move on. Travis didn't want to be alone, but with that helicopter around, it's too dangerous to be out in the open. He jumped as he heard the sound of an engine and turned to see that the car that had passed them came back and had spotted him.

Travis ran further into the shopping area with the car chasing right behind him. He ran as fast as he could, and when he noticed that the car was about to run him over, he dived out of the way, rolling on the ground. He was able to quickly get back up and took a shot at the car's wheel. The wheel busted, causing the car to screech to a stop.

Travis hid behind a stand as four cops came out and started shooting in his direction. He waited for the right moment when there would be a break from the firing. Once the window of opportunity presented itself, he jumped out and retaliated on the officers. He was able to hit one of them, but the others were too fast as they used the car for cover.

Travis continued to fire at the car as he started backing away. When he was on his last bullet, he made a run for it. He could hear then trying to catch up with him and searched frantically for somewhere to hide. He found a seafood stand and hopped over the counter.

His heart pounded as the sound of footsteps passed the stand. Travis eavesdropped on their conversation and thanked God that they chose the split up to search for him. This is perfect! He stayed still as he heard one of them coming closer to him. He glanced up to see the man standing right next to the stand. Travis gripped his rife and jumped over the counter. He used the butt of the rifle and swung it at the officer's head, knocking him down. Travis steadied himself as he aimed at the officer on the ground, ready to take him out.

He stopped, however when he heard the click of a gun. He snapped his head up to see the other cops pointing their guns at him. *Shit!* He screamed internally. They used one of their own as bait, and like a gullible fish, he took the hook. They played him!

"Drop it now!" One of them shouted. Travis reluctantly dropped his weapon on the floor.

"Arms up and back away!" Again, Travis obeyed their commands. He put his hands up and walked away as they helped the one that was on the floor back up.

"Turn around." Travis shut his eyes tightly as he slowly turned around, facing his back towards them. This is it. He knew that he majorly screwed up, and now he's about to pay the ultimate price for it. He had promised Janaye that he wouldn't do anything stupid, and here he is about to die for being an idiot. He waited for the inevitable and flinched when he heard gunfire.

He opened his eyes when he realized that he was still standing. He doesn't feel anything besides his pounding heart. He turned around and jumped at the sight of the dead officers on the ground. He checked himself to make sure that this was real and that we were still alive. Once he was able to convince himself that he wasn't dead, he exhaled a breath that he didn't know he held. That was way too close. He snapped his head at the sound of an engine.

Relief couldn't even begin to describe how Travis felt when he saw Devante coming up to him in a motorcycle.

"Told you to keep your head straight." Travis didn't know if it was the irony in what Devante had said, but he couldn't stop laughing. He wondered how Devante was able to get a motorcycle but pushed that thought aside. That's not important right now. Once Travis had a grip of himself, he walked over to the officers on the ground and searched through them, taking their guns and ammo.

"Come on, let's go!" Devante called out. Travis made his way to him and climbed on the cycle. He held on as they rolled out, passing through shops and buildings that looked remarkably familiar to Travis. He realized that they passed by them when they first entered Chinatown and that they were leaving the area.

"I thought we were supposed to stay here? What about the others?"

"I met up with them. They got everything under control, besides, we got a new mission."

"What is it?"

"Apparently, one of the chiefs took in a prisoner a while back and kept them somewhere not far from here."

"Who?"

"Don't know. From what I've been told, it's some FBI guy, anyway, we lost communications with the guards that were watching him." Travis didn't need any further explanation. They have a possible escapee and they're being sent to verify it. Travis thought of why The Panthers would bother taking in a prisoner? It had to be someone of importance if they are willing to use their resources to keep that person alive.

They drove out of the area and jumped on to the empty highway, but not without an unwanted company. There was a car that was hiding, waiting for anyone that was trying to take the road, and as soon as Devante and Travis passed through the ramp, they were immediately tailed. They didn't notice their stalker at first since when they entered the open road what greeted them was the destruction that Huey had left. Broken cars filled with bullet holes and dead bodies literally flooded the streets. It wasn't until Travis noticed the sound of another vehicle that he realized they were being followed.

They raced through the highway, curving left and right trying to avoid the hazardous obstacles that littered the streets and at the same time the bullets that are soaring in their direction from the other car. Travis turned around and delivered several shots of his own hoping to hit them. However, it had no effect on the bulletproof glass window.

The chase continued as Devante revved up to the max, and Travis focused on the tires hoping to blow them out. The wind pressure due to the acceleration was making it hard for Travis to concentrate.

Travis noticed that each exit that they passed was blocked, adding that their pursuer was catching up with them left them with little options for escape. Over the distance, Travis could hear the faint sounds of choppers and prayed that it wasn't what he thought it was. His fear became real as he saw a helicopter rushing over to where they were. Dealing with the enemy on land was bad enough and now they're about to get flanked by sky enemies; Travis dreaded how screwed they were.

Devante could only continue forward as the chopper came closer, but when it reached them, it flew right passed them. It went straight to the car, instead, and began hammering it with machine-gun bullets. The car didn't stand a chance even with bulletproof glass. They did a complete U-turn and tried to run away, but it was too late as the hood was blown off by the force of the bullets. With the engine exposed, it didn't take long for the car to burst in flames killing the cops inside.

Devante had stopped to witness the helicopter completely decimate their chaser. The helicopter came back around and when Travis saw who was driving it, he was shocked beyond belief.

"Janaye!" He shouted. She waved at him and went over to the next exit and shot down the barrier. Getting the picture, Devante started the cycle and went off the exit. Travis looked back to see that Janaye flew off and wondered if there was anything that she couldn't do.

"I take it, that's your girl?" Devante commented as they got off the ramp and entered into a residential area.

"Yeah."

"That's one hell of a woman." They drove past many streets before they stopped in front of an old broken down house.

"Seriously?" Travis questioned. "Of all the places, they chose something that looks like the setting of The Conjuring? I'm surprised it's still intact."

"Be on guard." Devante cautioned. Travis nodded as they got off and made their way moving past the corroded gate and walked up the steps to the front door. Devante checked the door and found that it wasn't locked. With his gun aimed in front of him, Travis made the first move and moved inside. He searched for anyone, but there wasn't a soul inside except for them. They checked the whole house but didn't find anyone or anything except for dust and broken wood.

Travis walked back to the kitchen and noticed a door in the corner. He alerted Devante and made their way to open the door, but it was locked from the inside. Throwing caution to the wind, Travis fired at the door handle and forced it opened. They crept down the stairs and when they reached the bottom, turning the lights on, they were greeted with the sight of three dead bodies on the ground. Not only that, but there was also an empty chair with broken restraints.

"Shit." He heard Devante whisper to himself. He walked over and inspected the chair and noticed that the restraints were made of tough material. One wouldn't have been able to break from them by themselves, so that meant the person had help. Travis doubted that anyone besides those in The Panthers would know this location. This might complicate things later. Travis turned to Devante, who was making a call and waited till he was done making his report on what they found.

"What's next?" Travis asked as Devante hung up the phone.

"We head to the Staples Center. They need reinforcement." They rushed up the stairs and headed out of the house, going back to the cycle. Heading off to their new destination, Travis would not know it at the time, but later events will force him to be in the middle of the final confrontation between the LAPD and The Panthers. The battle of Los Angeles will soon come to an end.

Chapter

23

Downtown Los Angeles, CA; 3:55 PM

Alex ran through the battlefield streets taking cover in every corner that he could find. This is straight madness! How did the city end up like this?! A few days ago, he had to even hide from the LAPD as they raided his home and the new office he had after what happened to his last one.

He didn't understand why the police were searching for him, and he still doesn't, but he knew that it had to do with Jasmine and The Panthers. What else could it be? Still, he knew that being apprehended by them was not the best option, so he took shelter in an abandoned building.

The following days after that comprised of him watching as the whole city was being evacuated. It puzzled him; why was everyone leaving? Today, after he had felt the shockwaves of the explosions, he had his answer. He couldn't believe it; The Panthers and the LAPD are planning on duking it outright in the middle of downtown.

What was the point of trying to protect the city when they're destroying it fighting The Panthers? And for them, what's the use of taking over L.A. if they're just going to bomb it to sky-high? Nothing made any sense, but Alex couldn't waste time thinking about this. Even though everyone else had left, he knew that Jasmine was still in the city. She was taken in with the charge of being connected with The Panthers. There's no doubt that they are planning on doing something to her, that's why he remained in the area.

While everyone will be busy fighting against each other, he could find her and get both of them out of this insanity. There was just one problem with that; he had no idea where she could be. That damn mayor didn't disclose any information when he went to confront him the day after she was taken in. Alex had searched the nearest holding stations before all of this had begun, luckily since all of the police were off in preparation for The Panthers none of them were there but couldn't find her.

That could only mean that they moved her before The Panthers had arrived, but where? It had to be somewhere that would be adequately guarded and not secluded since he figured that the LAPD wouldn't stretch their resources when they're dealing with a crisis like this. Alex theorized that she had to be somewhere downtown, or near it. A place that is close enough to not decrease their fighting numbers, and there was only one place that Alex thought that fit the criteria. City Hall.

He knew that Mayor Lambright is too proud to just abandon the city, but at the same time, he's not a fighter. If the mayor was taking shelter, then there would be no other place than the heart of downtown. The place would already be heavily guarded, and it's large enough that they can easily hold Jasmine there as well. Kill two birds with one stone.

That solved one problem, but it presented another. Just how the hell is he supposed to get there? Being on foot isn't the most mobile mode of transportation, but he really had no choice. Taking his car was out of the question unless he wants to get shot at by The Panthers and/or the LAPD. He amazed himself that he hasn't gotten spotted yet...or killed. Every block was filled with the opposing forces going after each other's throats. The streets were being littered by either dead bodies or falling debris from buildings taking in all the damage. Alex feared that after today there wouldn't be a Los Angeles anymore.

Navigating through downtown, Alex realized that he had another issue that needed to be addressed. Even if he makes it to City Hall, it's not like he'll be able to walk up to the front door and ask them to return Jasmine nicely. Yeah, he has a particularly good idea of how well that'll go for him.

Making his way, Alex noticed that there were certain areas that were more congested with the fighting than others and theorized that there must be key locations where the majority of them are focusing. All he has to do is avoid those places, and he's been lucky so far, so he should be fine.

"Hey!" *So much for luck.* Alex grimaced sarcastically. He turned around to see two young men riding on a motorcycle. By their lack of LAPD attire, they could only be part of The Panthers. This isn't what Alex needs right now. He tried to run the other way, but the one that was driving was able to predict Alex's motives as he drove to cut him off. With nowhere to go, Alex's only hope is that these two are some of the reasonable members and will let him go once he tells them that he's just a bystander.

"Wait! I'm not involved in any of this!" Alex shouted, raising his hands in the air.

"Calm down," Spoke the rider. "We're not gonna do anything to you. I'm surprised that there's someone crazy enough to be out in the streets like this." Alex sighed in relief, thankful that they're not going to harm him.

"Hey, I recognize you," The other person on the bike said. "You're Alex Williams."

"The one that was running for mayor?" The rider questioned the other young man.

"Yeah. I remember that lady also mentioned him when she came to see me at the Twin Towers." Alex refocused his attention to their conversation when he heard the keywords: 'lady' and 'Twin Towers.' That made him remember when he took Jasmine to that place to talk.

"Travis Miller?" Travis looked over Devante, then to Alex, and nodded his head.

"Yeah."

"Please, you have to help me!" Alex shouted. Before Travis could respond, Devante interjected.

"Sorry. We have to be somewhere, and you need to get out of here." He was about to drive off when Alex jumped in front of them.

"Wait! That lady you just mentioned, her name is Jasmine. She's been taken in by the LAPD. I need to get to her before it's too late."

"That's not our problem." Devante snapped back and turned the cycle around to go the other way.

"She's there because of YOU people!" Alex shouted, making Devante stop. "Because she was accused of being associated with The Panthers, she's now in the middle of all this! Please, I beg you! I just want to keep her safe." Travis was having a hard time watching Alex break down in front of them. It reminded him of how desperate he was to find Janaye.

Even if he didn't fully believe Jasmine at the time, he remembered that she was a nice lady and promised him to look for Janaye and now, just like how he was, she's trapped in a situation that has nothing to do with her. Ironic how the roles have switched. Travis turned to Devante, who sighed in annoyance.

"You've got to be shitting me," Devante complained. "We got our own mission to do. We can't have any sidetracks."

"That's fine," Travis replied. "You can go ahead, and I'll stay with him."

"And lose my head when they find out I left you alone? Nice try," Devante turned back to Alex. "Hey, you know where she is?" Alex was relieved and surprised that they were even willing to listen to his request; maybe he has a chance after all.

"City Hall." Devante facepalmed when he heard the location.

"The one place that we were told not to go to. Of course, she's there." He took another glance at Travis and knew that the idiot would run off with Alex. If he let him go by himself, he'll get in more trouble than disobeying an order. *Why me?* he groaned.

"Fine, but we all can't fit on this." He said, turning the engine off. Travis and Alex were at a loss since neither of them had a clue about obtaining another mode of transportation. Devante rolled his eyes and searched the area and found a decent looking car across the street.

He hopped off and headed over to the vehicle while picking up a rock. He used it to smash the window and reached his hand through to unlock it. Travis and Alex jumped when they heard the window being smashed, followed by the car alarm going off. Once Devante got inside, he went under the driver seat and opened a hatch where the wires were and hotwired it. The alarm was cut off, and Devante sat up in the driver seat, turning on the car.

"Let's go!" He shouted honking. They ran to get inside, with Travis sitting in the passenger seat. Driving off, Devante could tell that Travis was staring at him.

"What?"

"I didn't know you could do that." Devante laughed at his honest answer.

"There's a lot of things you don't know. What do you think I went to jail for?" The ride was shorter than Devante had wanted as they were reaching their destination. The closer they got, the more LAPD and SWAT cars that were in the area. Luckily, they haven't been spotted yet as Devante took the back streets and narrow alleys.

They parked behind a building that was across from City Hall. They crept out and surveyed the path that led to the front entrance, which was swarmed, and if Devante was a betting man, he could bet on all his money that the inside of the building will be just as heavily guarded.

"All right listen up. Obviously, we can't just rush in the front with guns blazing, or we're dead men. We gotta go through another entrance." They followed Devante as he led them to another path, and they were able to make their way to the side of City Hall that was surrounded by trees. It was the perfect cover for them, even if the sun was out. They stealthily moved in closer till they were able to see the door. Devante peeped from behind a tree to see that the entrance didn't have as many guards as the other. In fact, there are only two of them.

"Now what?" Travis whispered.

"This." Devonte responded as he jumped out of hiding and shot the two guards. Knowing that the sound alone would alert the others in a matter of seconds, they rushed inside before they were seen.

"Great plan." Travis sarcastically said as he caught his breath.

"We're inside, aren't we? So, stop complaining." Travis rolled his eyes but put his focus back to the matter at hand. They moved silently inside the building, thinking of where they could find Jasmine. However, inside was like a maze. Countless doors covered the endless streams of halls, and this was only on the first floor. It would take a miracle to find Jasmine. Just then, they heard the sound of a person that was heading their way. They quickly hid as two guards appeared where they once stood.

"Man, why do we have to be put on babysitting duty?" One of them complained loudly.

"Chill. All we got to do is make sure that she doesn't go anywhere, and we get to stay safe inside. Easy day." Knowing that those two were talking about Jasmine, Alex was about to jump out and have them tell him where she was, but Devante stopped him. The look that he was giving Alex was all that needed to be said that he needed to calm down and think. Exposing themselves now will basically be a death sentence. Alex took a deep breath to calm himself. Devante took the lead again as they tailed the two guards that would take them to where Jasmine is.

They followed them until they reached a pair of doors that Alex recognized as the entrance to the huge observation room where the visitors would always go to. They waited as the guards changed shifts, and the ones that were relieved walked away. Once the area was clear, Devante made his way to the door and hid after he knocked. The moment that he saw the guard's face, he made his move by pistol-whipping him to the ground and rushed inside with Alex and Travis behind him.

There were more guards inside than Devante had anticipated and as soon as they were spotted breaking into the room, all of them began firing at them. Devante thought fast and toppled over the nearest table he could find. Luckily the table was metal, so it was able to take the bullets that were hitting the exterior with minimum troubles, but Devante knew that it wouldn't last long. Looking at a mirror above him, Devante could count that there were five of them and could see Jasmine tied up in a chair blindfolded.

"Our cover won't last long!" He warned the other two.

"We need to take them out now!" Travis nodded, and when he had the opportunity, he reopened fire. However, those opening windows were very few, and he wasn't able to hit any of them. Devante wasn't having any luck either.

"This isn't getting us anywhere!" Devante gritted, exasperated. Peering at Alex, he noticed that he was holding something odd in his hands. *What the...?*

"Hey," He addressed Alex. "What is that?" Alex brought his hands over for Devante to get a closer look, and when he further inspected the object, he almost cried in relief. It was a flash bomb. Devante thanked every deity that he could think of for this blessing. He snatched it out of Alex's hand and threw it in the middle of the room. When the guards realized what has been thrown, it was too late as the blinding light took effect.

"Now!" Devante shouted. Both he and Travis ran out of the table's cover and shot each of the disoriented guards. Jasmine being blindfolded could only hear what was going on and could only scream as she heard the gun bullets shooting off. She was almost deaf by the sound of the flash bomb going off, but otherwise, she somehow didn't get hit.

She had no idea what was going on but knew that someone else was inside the room. Is it The Panthers? She couldn't think of anyone else coming to rescue her, well except Alex, but he's not crazy enough to come here by himself. To her surprise and utter joy when she felt her blindfold being taken off, the first sight to greet her was none other than the man she didn't think she would ever see again.

"Alex!"

"Don't worry. I'm getting you out of here." He said as he took off her restraints. Now being free, Jasmine jumped off the chair into Alex's arms, crying on his shoulder.

"Alex, you idiot! Why did you come here?" Though she was reprimanding him, she has never been so happy to see him. Alex wrapped his arms around her, realizing the feeling of having her here with him.

"I had to. As long as I'm alive, I won't let anything happen to you."

"Great we got her, now let's get the hell out of here!" Devante interrupted, cutting their reunion short. Jasmine finally noticed the other two in the room and her eyes widened when she saw Travis. Before she could say something, she and the rest stumbled as the whole room shook violently, followed by the sound of the wall crashing down.

"What was that?!" Alex yelled, holding Jasmine close to him. Travis looked outside the window to see The Panthers' armada outside the main entrance.

"It's Huey. They're here!"

"Finally!" Devante exclaimed in excitement. "This fight is as good as ours."

"I wouldn't put too much faith in that." All of them turned at the new voice in the room to see the figure of Agent Craftwell. He had six guards accompanying him and they surrounded Travis and the others, pointing their weapons at them.

"You!" Alex snarled.

"No need for hostilities Mr. Williams," Agent Craftwell said as he looked at Jasmine and Travis. "Well, it seems fate has decided for all of us to be together."

"What do you want from us?" Jasmine spoke up.

"I have nothing against you, but orders are orders. You and Mr. Williams are still considered valuable assets; however, my patience is wearing very thin. So, you have two choices here: surrender, or die."

Chapter

24

Downtown Los Angeles, CA; 5:20 PM

Janaye knew that she was disobeying orders, but she couldn't have left Travis to be in the middle of that fight without backup. He's not a soldier, and it's her job to make sure that nothing happens to him. Huey had appointed her to be his guardian, so she didn't understand why he hadn't allowed her to be with Travis. That was her motivation when she took the newly remodeled helicopters that Erica had designed. It was equipped with a direct connection with The Ark that allowed her to tap into every security camera in the city to find him. There were seven major points on the GPS that was spread throughout downtown.

She knew that he had to be in one of those areas, but even then, it took her some time to pinpoint his exact location. However, her search wasn't met without an unwelcome visitor. An LAPD helicopter spotted her and immediately gave her a chase. She thanked God that she had all of that training drilled into her because the guy was relentless in pursuing her.

The person that was mounted on the machine gun was shooting like a mad man trying to hit her. She was fortunate enough that she was able to evade most of them. Her machine gun was mounted under her facing the front, which meant she would have to turn around, and that was a definite no. She checked the rest of her arsenal to see what she could use, and all she had were two missiles. At that time, Janaye made a mental note to talk to Erica about equipping these things with more weapons. She came upon a building that had two connecting towers and quickly came up with a plan.

Flying in closer, she launched one of the rockets at one of the towers, making it explode and start to fall on the other. She maneuvered through the falling pieces of the tower. Her pursuer wasn't able to get out of the way as it fell victim to the falling tower, making it crash into the other.

Once that annoyance was out of the way, Janaye continued through her search. She found him in the Chinatown section riding a passenger on a motorcycle with another person. They were entering the highway and following right behind them was a SWAT truck. She knew that they wouldn't be able to take that on, so she headed over there with haste.

When she was over the highway that they were on, she flew in their direction, and when she saw them, she sped right past them straight to the SWAT truck. She was quickly able to take them out and to provide a path for Travis. She intended to follow them and be their cover until he heard a transmission go through.

"Sister Freed," It was Huey, and judging by his tone, he didn't sound pleased. "What in the hell are you doing?" She knew that she would have gotten caught eventually. There's nothing that goes past Huey without the man noticing. Sometimes she cursed The Ark.

"I'm doing my job." She answered.

"I gave you specific orders and being here wasn't one of them."

"I understand that but remember that my main priority was and always will be to watch over Travis." Hearing Huey sigh, she knew that she had won this argument, considering that he was the one that gave her that order in the first place.

"Using my own words against me, huh? Since you're this determined to take the Ark-1, then you might as well come to the main extraction point."

"What about Travis?"

"Leave him for now. He can handle himself; I need you here." A red dot showed itself on her GPS, indicating where the main extraction point was, and she recognized it as The City Hall. She looked at her camera and searched for Travis and found that he was no longer on the motorcycle and was in a car with two others; the one that was riding the motorcycle and Alex Williams. From the direction that they were driving, it seemed that they were also heading to City Hall. But why? Huey expressed that no one except him and the ones accompanying him is even to come near to City Hall.

She didn't want to leave Travis but did reluctantly, having no choice. She flew, heading to City Hall when she passed by Huey and the main force as they were making their way there as well. She made herself useful by clearing the path and taking out all of the LAPD and SWAT vehicles that were in the way. The main force took care of any stragglers that might have slipped by as they marched to the front of City Hall. Janaye hovered over them as they reached their destination. The force split into four groups, surrounding the entire building leaving Huey with the group that is at the front entrance.

"Sister Freed," She heard Huey call to her through the transmission. "Would you be so kind as to knock on the door for us?" She smirked at what he was implying and used the remaining rocket to blast through the main entrance. Huey wasted no time as he rallied everyone with him and stormed inside.

"Remain in the area." Janaye heard his transit. She didn't need him to tell her that. She knew that Travis and his group would be heading here, so, of course, she's not going anywhere. She checked her GPS and camera to see where he could be since he should be close in the area. She started to grow worried when she wasn't able to find him until she saw the same car, he was riding in that was parked behind a building that was across City Hall. Seeing that no one was in the car, she made a sudden conclusion. *That idiot!*

City Hall, Downtown, Los Angles; 5:57 PM

Travis didn't know what to do, and now he regretted taking pity on Alex. He berated himself for accepting to do this suicide mission because now, they're surrounded by the enemy with no way out. If he moves a muscle, there was no doubt that Agent Craftwell will unleash the firing squad on them.

There was another troubling factor that made this situation even direr. When he heard Agent Craftwell saying that Alex and Jasmine were still deemed useful, he had a horrible realization. He and Devante are a moot point and will be disposed of as soon as it's convenient. The only reason why they're still alive is that Alex and Jasmine are close enough to them that they could be hit. Travis shut his eyes, forcing his brain to work on haywire. *Think! There has to be a way out of this!* He prayed that a solution would come quickly, time is running out.

"This offer lasts only for five seconds. I recommend you make a decision quickly." Came the smug voice of Agent Craftwell. Travis opened his eyes and frantically looked all around the room. There had to be something, anything that he could use. In his heightened state due to his panic, he heard a buzzing sound. He could tell that it's coming from outside, and though it was faint, it was loud enough for him to snap out of it.

The buzzing sound got louder and louder that he was able to distinguish it as the sound of propellers. He made a quick glance outside the window to see Janaye hovering right outside and could see the barrel of the machine gun starting to turn. Travis wasn't the only one that saw Janaye as Agent Craftwell stepped back from shock.

"What the-"

"Get down!" Travis shouted, dropping to the ground. Devante fell right behind him with Alex and Jasmine already on the ground. In less of a second later, the room was assaulted with the full force of continuous rapid fire. The shattered glass fell and covered the whole room like diamonds. The officers that were too shocked to make a move stood no chance as all of them were taken out by the attack. Agent Craftwell, the only one to make a reaction, was able to dive out of the way before the destructive onslaught rained down on his men.

After recovering his hearing from Janaye's attack, Travis moved his head up to see that all of the officers were dead on the floor. He got up and saw that everyone else was safe. This was their chance to escape. He made his way to Devante and got him up and got the rest and made their way through another exit.

"What the hell was that?!" Devante exasperated when he was able to catch his breath.

"It was Janaye." Travis answered.

"Well, tell your crazy ass girlfriend to give us a warning next time. That bitch almost killed us!"

"She saved our lives." Travis replied sharply.

"What the hell are you talking about? We would have been fine if we were just surrounded."

"Alex and Jasmine would have been fine," Travis corrected. "We were disposable at best, and they would have killed us either way. She saved all of us."

"Ok, ok, I get it. My bad." Devante backed down at the glare Travis was giving him. Even he knew when to call it quits and pissing off Travis right now isn't the wisest move, especially when they're still in the enemies' territory.

"We need to get out of here." Alex suggested, joining in the conversation.

"No." Travis shot down.

"Why?" Alex questioned, getting frustrated. "There's no further reason for us to stay. The longer we're here the more risk we take losing our lives!"

"All of the officers in that room were dead except that FBI guy. He wasn't in there, which means he got away and will be expecting us to try to get out."

"Then what should we do?" Travis took a second to think where the safest place for them would be and remembered that Huey and the rest of The Panthers' army were in the building. If they could meet up with them, then their chances of survival would increase. He theorized that to capture City Hall; then there is only one place where Huey would go to.

"We have to go to the mayor's office." Travis suggested.

"What?!" Alex shouted in disbelief.

"That's where Huey and the rest are heading to. We'll be safe with them." Devante agreed. Their small group would barely make it out alive by themselves with all the guards that are still lurking around, hell, it's a miracle that they made it this far without dying. It's best to be with the rest of The Panthers. Alex was thinking about just taking Jasmine and getting out, but then soon realized that the only ones who have any means of fighting are Devante and Travis.

Looking back to Jasmine, he knew that she was still shaken up from everything that has happened and found himself with no choice than to go along. Seeing as Alex was the only one who knew where the mayor's office is, he took the lead as they made their way. They passed through corridors and hallways, avoiding the guards who were rushing off to fight the intruding army. Travis was thankful that The Panthers were causing this much of a commotion since it provided the perfect distraction.

They got spotted a few times, but Travis and Devante were able to take out the guards before they tried to call for backup. With Alex navigating, they were able to make it to Mayor Lambright's office. Two guards were at the door. Keeping the non-combatants of their group in hiding, Travis and Devante rushed out and dispatched the guards without much trouble.

Once they were clear of danger, Travis called on Alex and Jasmine. Devante checked to see if there were any hidden traps and was surprised when he found that the door wasn't locked. He pushed the door open, and one by one, they slowly entered. They were greeted by the figure of Mayor Lambright, sitting in his desk, pouring himself a drink.

"Mr. Williams and company," Jonathan greeted. "It's a bit unexpected, but I am glad all of you are here none the less." It was a little unnerving to see him so calm despite everything that was going on. Since they were the first to come, they would have to wait until Huey, and the rest arrive.

"It's over. The Panthers are on their way here, and even you should know what that means."

"I'm no idiot, Mr. Williams," Jonathan chuckled. "I know exactly what is to come." Right after he had spoken, the door swung open. Everyone turned around to see Huey walking in being flanked by six soldiers that surrounded the room and had their guns pointed straight at Jonathan's head.

"Mayor Lambright. I hope that you don't regret the choices that you have made up to now."

"I take it that since you're here that Commissioner Greenfield is no longer with us?"

"He fought valiantly, but in vain."

"I see." Jonathan whispered as he got up. The soldiers tensed, ready to open fire at any given notice, but Huey raised his hand, telling them to be steady.

"The offer still stands." He told Jonathan, giving the man one last chance.

"I seriously doubt any of that matters now. Especially when you don't plan on keeping me alive for very long."

"That depends on how you behave."

"Oh, I'm sure," Jonathan laughed. "Tell me. What do you think that obtaining one city will accomplish?" This time, it was Huey's turn to show amusement, which confused Jonathan and everyone else in the room.

"It seems that you misunderstand all of this," Huey started to explain. "Allow me to give you a little history lesson. After the American Civil War and the slaves were free, the union promised them forty acres of land and a mule for their dedicated years of service."

"I don't see how any of that has to do with-"

"Let me finish," Huey commanded. "After that, the government was supposed to protect those lands for the free Blacks. No surprise that promise was never fulfilled, and ever since then, we were subjected to humiliation, subjugation, discrimination, and unspeakable horrors. That's why we are here. To correct the wrongs that were brought upon us."

"By taking Los Angeles?"

"Again, you misunderstand. Los Angeles, Seattle, Portland, San Francisco, San Diego, Phoenix, and Las Vegas. We will have them all." Mayor Lambright could only stare at Huey in total disbelief before finally finding his voice.

"You're insane!"

"I am only taking what was promised to us. You can keep your mule, but we will take the forty acres. For each African American descendant of the slaves that this country had lied to, we will take them all. We will form new land in which my people can prosper and truly be free."

"You're delusional if you think that the White House hasn't caught on to your little rebellion. You Panthers will be slaughtered like pigs."

"I welcome the challenge." Jonathan could tell how serious Huey was and surprised everyone in the room when he was consumed in a fit of laughter.

"Well, since you already told me this much, my time must be up." Suddenly the entire room began to finally shake as if an earthquake was wreaking havoc.

"What now?!" Devante yelled in panic. While everyone was trying to get a hold of themselves, Huey and Jonathan stood still, in place, staring down at each other.

"Stubborn until the end, aren't you?" Huey said with a hint of annoyance.

"If I were you, I would focus on not being buried alive. I set off enough explosives to collapse everything to the ground. I may not have been able to stop you from wreaking my city, but at least I'll be able to stop you here." At that moment, Huey couldn't help but admit that this will be the first and only time that he will give Mayor Lambright any ounce of respect. The captain is planning on going down with his ship. He will at least give the man that point.

"We'll see," Huey rebuked. "Everyone, leave now!" He ordered. No further words were needed as they all ran out of the room as everything was falling apart. It was a race against time, and unfortunately, they didn't even know how much they have. However, with the building crumbling on itself and pieces of the ceiling were falling, it was easy to tell that they didn't have much left before City Hall completely turned to dust.

Running for their lives Travis could see some the LAPD officers that survived were trying to escape as well. Some of them were crushed by the heavy pieces of debris that toppled on them while others fell to their death by falling through cracked holes on the floor. Some of The Panthers were unfortunate to get caught under danger as well.

Another set of explosions went off that separated Travis and his group from Huey and the rest of The Panthers. There was no other way they could go around and had to find another way out. Thankfully, Alex knew where they were and that the side entrance from where they came from wasn't far. They quickly made their way, passing by anyone that's unfortunate to get caught in the destruction. There is no time to be sentimental, and they had to leave people behind to save themselves.

They finally made it to the exit and wasted no time rushing out the door. Reaching outside, Travis dropped to the ground, having all the adrenaline that was coursing through his veins leave his body. He greedily took a breath of air as he looked on the burning, rumbling building. At last, it's over.

Jasmine held on to Alex tightly, trying to take control of herself. Everything happened so fast that she couldn't process it all. The past few hours were like a horrible nightmare, but with Alex next to her, she knew that now she is safe. She turned her head to the site of City Hall as flames consumed the building.

Any soul unfortunate enough to be still inside would have no chance for survival. It made her more thankful than ever that Alex came to rescue her. There were many times throughout this whole ordeal where she could have easily died, but she somehow made it with her life. As she took comfort being next to him, she noticed the figure out the corner of her eye.

"Do you think I'll just let you get away just like that?!" Came the cry of Agent Craftwell as he aimed gun pointing at them. "I don't care what headquarters say, you're more dangerous alive!" Time seemed to have stopped as no one knew what to do. During their escape out of City Hall, Travis and Devante lost both of their weapons, so now everyone is defenseless. Jasmine could tell that he was aiming at Alex and, without a second thought, she shoved him out of the way as Agent Craftwell pulled the trigger. Alex helplessly watched as Jasmine was shot in the back and fell limply on the ground.

"Jasmine!!!" Alex cried in agony. He ran to her and dropped to the ground picking up her body. He could feel the blood that was rushing out of her back and tried everything he could to stop it. Agent Craftwell aimed his gun again to fire but stopped at the sound of propellers.

Travis turned around to the sound and covered his face as the wind that was rushing at them. It was Janaye once again, and she didn't skip a beat as he fired at Agent Craftwell. Alex desperately clutched to Jasmine's body but panicked when he felt her warmth gradually leaving her body.

"No! No! No! Don't do this, Jasmine! You're going to be ok!" Alex cried. This can't be happening, not after everything that he went through to finally be by her side again.

"Alex," He stopped as he heard Jasmine's whisper. "It's ok."

"Please don't talk," He begged, tears pouring down his face. "Save your strength. You'll be fine, I promise!"

"Thank you, Alex," Jasmine whispered as she slowly raised her hand to touch his face. "I'm so glad that I was able to see you again. Please continue to be the wonderful man that you are. This city still needs you. Our people still need you."

"I need you!" He cried desperately. Jasmine smiled despite the pain that it caused her.

"You'll be fine. I know it." With the last of her strength, she used her hand to pull Alex in closer so that their lips could touch.

"Thank you." It was the last words she whispered to him as her hand went from his cheek and fell lifeless to the ground. Alex could do nothing as he clutched her body and howled in despair. Travis and Devante could only watch as Alex folded into his anguish clutching Jasmine's body. They soon heard the sound of propellers again as Jasmine flew back to them.

"Hurry, get in!" Janaye yelled as she landed the helicopter after chasing off agent Craftwell. She wasn't able to get rid of him and prioritized Travis and the rest of the group's safety. Travis and Devante raced to get inside the helicopter as Alex slowly stood up, carefully carrying Jasmine's body. He made his way inside and sat on the floor, holding Jasmine tight. No one had any words that they could say to him.

"Hang on." Janaye announced as she took off. Flying away, Travis was able to see the destruction that ravaged the city. Crumbling buildings and fire spread, destroying everything in their path. After everything that has happened Travis found himself drained of all his energy. He leaned against the seat and closed his eyes.

The following day, Travis found himself standing right outside the dismembered pile that used to be City Hall. Next to him was Janaye and Alex, who was standing next to Huey. There was nothing that anyone could have done for Jasmine; she died before they even entered the helicopter to try to get her medical attention. When they headed back to the main headquarters, they were welcomed by Lanika, which surprised Travis. It was then that he learned that not only was she part of The Panthers, as one of the chiefs but that Jasmine was, in fact, her sister. She was distraught when they brought Jasmine's body in. She and Alex were completely inconsolable until Huey came and talked to them alone.

Travis looked over to Alex and could see a drastic change has occurred to the man. He now was sporting a hard-jaded look. Whatever that he and Huey had talked about somehow made Alex join them. The rest of The Panthers' army was spread throughout the entire city, organizing all of the citizens that evacuated to the ruins of City Hall. Alex stood next to Huey as they wait for the people to arrive.

"Huey," Alex spoke, getting the man's attention. "Don't forget our deal. I am the only one that gets to kill that bastard."

"Of course," Huey confirmed. "I wouldn't have it any other way. My dear disciple." The people were beginning to file in as they took into the site of what had happened to their home.

Everywhere that they looked at, were The Panthers' soldiers standing watch, which was a little more than intimidating. However, what concerned them the most was when they reached City Hall to see its remains and Huey standing in the front with a huge flag waving behind him. It wasn't the American flag; it was something different. It was a black flag with a giant golden paw in the middle, with three claw marks going through it colored in red, black, and green, outlined in gold. The show of power did not make the people ease in their fear.

"My brothers and sisters," Huey announced to the public. "Today marks the beginning of a new era. No longer will you be subjugated to a land where your existence is disowned. We will create our own land, where every man, woman, and child is treated equally. A land where the color of your skin doesn't dictate who you are. A land where your children can grow and not worry if they'll be able to return home safely. One of prosperity and protection. A land where you will finally be free! Join us, and we will find paradise. We will be able to taste the fruit of the labor and suffering that we had to endure. We will create our own promised land. We. Will. Rise!"

Travis watched the crowd and can see the vast emotions on their faces. Fear, sadness, anger, hatred, disgust, hesitation, determination, excitement, inspiration, and hope. On the face of every African American that Travis could see, there was hope in their eyes.

It was that hope that made a single clap grow to deafening applause. Travis could hear them shouting out 'Panthers' and 'we will rise'. Watching the scene before him, Travis couldn't help but compare Huey to a great Prophet leading his people to freedom. Travis looked into the crowd and the half destroyed city and knew that this was only the beginning. He remembered what Huey had said to the mayor the night before, and it has just dawned to him that it had started.

Seattle, Phoenix, San Francisco, Portland, and San Diego. In the upcoming months, all of these cities will be under siege and captured. The White House and Pentagon would not have any knowledge until it is too late. The Panthers have made their move. Conquering the entire West Coast will spark an event that will forever be a part of the history of the United States. The second American Civil War has begun, or as the rest of the world will know it as...The Panthers' Revolution.

Lightning Source UK Ltd.
Milton Keynes UK
UKHW020431030720
365951UK00012B/617